MW01616010

The
Advocate's
Illusion

Teresa Burrell

Silent Thunder Publishing
San Diego

THE ADVOCATE'S ILLUSION
Copyright 2018 by
Teresa Burrell

All rights reserved.
Cover Art by Madeline Settle
Edited by Marilee Wood

Library of Congress Number: 2018900633
ISBN: 978-1-938680-26-7

Silent Thunder Publishing
San Diego

Dedication

To Ralph and Betty Hekman,
two of the most wonderful people I know.

Your loyalty and your love for one another is amazing.
Your determination is inspiring, your kindness is
comforting, and your strength is encouraging.

Thank you for sharing your life with our family.

Acknowledgements

Thank you to all those who helped with this book:

Mike McCormick
David Servantes
Michael Showalter
Gregory Simard

Special thanks to **Irene Serlis** for all her legal research

My Wonderful Beta readers:

Beth Sisel Agejew
Linda Athridge-Langille
Vickie Barrier
Nancy Barth
Dianne Biscoe
Meli White Cardullo
Gena 'Fortner' Jeselnik
Janie Greene-Livingston
Laura Hightower Gwynn
Crystal Kamada
Jess Kissir-Velasco
Sheila Krueger
Marilyn Voli LaFiura
Lily Qualls Morales
Rodger Peabody
Gabrielle Land Reed
MaryAnn Schaefer
Colleen Scott
Nikki Tomlin
Tanya Wheeler
Ellen White
Denise Zendel

THE ADVOCATE SERIES

THE ADVOCATE
(Book 1)

THE ADVOCATE'S BETRAYAL
(Book 2)

THE ADVOCATE'S CONVICTION
(Book 3)

THE ADVOCATE'S DILEMMA
(Book 4)

THE ADVOCATE'S EX PARTE
(Book 5)

THE ADVOCATE'S FELONY
(Book 6)

THE ADVOCATE'S GEOCACHE
(Book 7)

THE ADVOCATE'S HOMICIDES
(Book 8)

THE ADVOCATE'S ILLUSION
(Book 9)

TUPER MYSTERY SERIES

MASON'S MISSING
(Book 1)

Chapter 1

Sabre Brown stood on the stage next to the magician dressed in black tails, white gloves, and a tall hat, his face painted half white and half kelly green, the trademark of the Great Silent Thunder. The magician's assistant had tied both the magician's and Sabre's hands in front of them.

Sabre had been chosen from the audience after her boyfriend JP had declined to participate in the trick. She stepped inside the box, and the magician followed. The assistant closed the door behind them. A scrambling noise and pounding against the wall came from the box and then silence.

The audience was very still. Nearly a minute passed without any movement on stage. The audience began to murmur. Another minute, still nothing.

"What's taking so long?" JP said to his friend Bob, sitting next to him.

"It's a show," Bob said. "The longer he makes the audience wait, the more the anticipation builds."

Another minute passed, and JP shifted in his seat as if he was going to stand.

"Where are you going?"

"On stage, to see what's going on. This is taking way too long."

"You're going to ruin the trick."

"I'm supposed to care?"

Bob glanced at a huge security guard standing near the exit. He nodded toward him. "You may want to care about *him*?"

JP shot a quick glimpse his way. "If he wants a fight, he better pack a lunch and bring a flashlight."

Just as JP started to stand, the assistant walked to

the opposite end of the stage toward the Great Silent Thunder, who was sitting on the wall by the steps. Surprise emanated from the crowd followed by loud applause.

The magician stood up and looked around. He stretched his hands out in a swooping motion and then scanned the audience. He looked back at the stage and out into the audience again.

"Where is Sabre?" JP asked.

"Will you relax? She's going to pop up any minute now."

The magician swooped his arms out again. The spotlight scanned the room. The assistant moved back toward the box, but before she got there, JP had run up the six steps and onto the stage.

"What are you doing?" she asked.

"Getting my girlfriend."

"Stop. You'll ruin the trick."

"Does it always take this long?"

"No, but we were told to just wait."

"Then you do that," JP said and opened the door of the box.

Lying on the floor was Sabre with her hands still tied together.

Three Weeks Earlier...

Chapter 2

Attorney Sabre Brown received a disturbing phone call. She hung up and called Steve Matzel, the social worker who had worked with her on the Parker case.

"I just got a call from Sarah Parker," Sabre said. "She told me her house is so filthy she can't stand it."

"That case has been closed less than six months," Steve said. "She really had to work at it to get it unlivable in that short a time."

"I know."

"Did she say if her mother was using drugs again?"

"No, but she said her little brother was sick and there was something else I needed to know. She wouldn't say what, so it's probably drugs. She said I'd find out when I got there."

"The mother doesn't have to let you in, you know."

"I know, but she does have to let *you* in. Are you coming with me?"

"Of course. It must be pretty awful if Sarah's calling for help."

"That's what I thought. Remember how she fought foster care?"

"She ran away four times, until we finally detained her with her father, and then *he* blew it, and she ended up back in foster care," Steve said. "I'll meet you there in about twenty minutes."

"I'll be waiting outside when you get there."

~~~

Sabre sat outside the small duplex in National City, waiting for the social worker. She phoned JP to let him know she was going to be late.

"Okay, darlin'," JP said in his slight Texas accent. "Just let me know when you're headed this way."

She sat there thinking about JP, which brought a smile to her face. She pictured him with his handsome face, his black Stetson hat, and his western boots. The two of them had been dating for over six months, and he had been her friend and private investigator for several years before that. She was cautious because she didn't have a good track record with men. Her first love in high school, the team quarterback, was caught on video with a more popular girl. A teenage prankster managed to have the video shown on the screen during a film in a student assembly. It took several minutes before the school staff could get it stopped. Sabre was humiliated, but it seemed to boost the popularity of her beau and the other girl. A few days later, her ex came to school with a black eye. He made up some lame excuse for it, and although her brother Ron never admitted it, she was pretty certain he had something to do with the injury.

There were several more losers in her repertoire, not the least of which was her last guy, who turned out to be a mobster. She had dated some nice guys too, but they all seemed to get too serious too fast, and Sabre would bail. But JP was different. He was smart, handsome, and very protective of her, like the cowboy that he was. Sabre had discovered new interests with him and deepened her appreciation for country music. Even though JP had a bit of a jealous streak, especially when they were on a dance floor, he never smothered her like some men had in the past. He didn't need to go everywhere she did and be with her every minute. She had her interests and he had his, and he was quick to try new experiences with her—at least once, as long as they didn't include eating broccoli.

Sabre often wondered what the future held. She would be thirty-one years old in October, and her mother was hoping for grandchildren. They had all pretty much given up on her brother having any children, but Sabre knew she wasn't ready, and maybe never would be. She liked things the way they were and was glad that JP wasn't pushing for more. Besides, JP was eighteen years older than her, a fact that bothered him way more than her, and he might not be interested in being a parent. They had never discussed it.

Sabre jumped when Matzel tapped on her window. She exited her car.

"Are you ready for this?" he asked.

"Let's do it."

The duplex sat close to the sidewalk with approximately five feet of dirt and weeds leading up to the front door.

"It doesn't look bad out here, except the weeds could use some mowing," Sabre said.

When Matzel couldn't find a doorbell, he knocked. "It could be the neighbors keep up the yard," he said.

"Or maybe the Parkers don't spend enough time out here to get it dirty."

No one answered the door, so he knocked louder this time. They heard a woman yell, "Sarah, get the door."

About thirty seconds later, the door opened and a horrible stench escaped. Sarah, a nine-year-old girl with cinnamon-colored braids and a button nose covered in freckles, stood there. She swallowed uncomfortably and said, "Come in."

"Who is it?" her mother yelled from the sofa.

Sarah turned toward her. "Uh...."

The social worker stepped inside, and Sabre followed. The curtains were all closed, keeping much of the sunlight out of the room, but there was enough light to see that the floor was covered with debris and trash. The smell of urine and sewer permeated the air.

"It's Steve Matzel, Department of Social Services," he said as he stepped toward the sofa.

"What the ...?" Sarah's mother, Ellesse Parker, said.

Matzel interrupted her. "We received a report that your children are in danger, and we're here to investigate."

Ellesse threw a shirt onto the coffee table in an obvious attempt to cover something, but not before Sabre and Steve saw the drug paraphernalia, some of it still exposed. Ellesse straightened the shirt, trying to hide the rest.

"Get out of here," she said. "My case is closed."

Steve ignored her comments. "What's that awful smell?"

"The toilet is backed up again."

"Did you call the landlord?"

"I called him about the rats and the roaches before, but he won't do nothing. He blames me for not keeping my house clean enough."

"How long has the toilet not worked?"

"About a month," Sarah said.

"Shut up, Sarah," the mother yelled. "It's been on and off for about a month, but it's only been completely clogged for a few days."

Sarah lowered her head and remained silent.

Sabre noticed that although Ellesse was still thin, she looked like she had gained some weight, but when her eyes adjusted to the light and Ellesse turned a little to the side, Sabre understood why. "Where's your brother Denny?" Sabre asked Sarah.

"He's in the bedroom."

"Please show me."

"You can't go in there," Ellesse yelled.

"Yes, she can," Steve said. "We need to see if Denny is okay."

Sarah led Sabre to the bedroom, the stench increasing as they neared the bathroom. Sabre was glad the bathroom door was closed. The smell in the bedroom wasn't much better. A small wastebasket stood near the closet overflowing with dirty diapers. The pile of soiled diapers next to it was almost as tall as the wastebasket itself.

"Sarah, is your mom pregnant?" Sabre had to speak louder than she intended in order to be heard over Ellesse, who was still yelling at the social worker.

"Yes, and she's using drugs again. I know that's not good for the baby. And she's saying all kinds of crazy things."

Sabre tiptoed to the unmade bed where Denny was sleeping, afraid of what she might step in, and trying to avoid the trash on the floor. Dirty clothes were strewn about the room. The sheet on the bed was covered with urine and feces stains. Denny's face and hands were dirty, his hair looked like it hadn't been washed or even combed in weeks, and mucus was caked below his nose and on his cheeks. She watched him for a few seconds as he breathed rhythmically in his sleep.

"She can't take care of a new baby," Sarah said with wet eyes. "She can't even take care of us. And Denny's not getting enough to eat. Look at this house. I tried to keep it clean at first, but I couldn't keep up, and then when the toilet overflowed, I didn't know what to do."

"You did the right thing calling me," Sabre said. "We'll let Denny sleep for now. Are you okay?"

"I'm hungry."

"We'll get you something to eat as soon as we leave here."

"Are you taking us to Polinsky?" Sarah said, her lips quivering.

"I'm afraid so," Sabre said. She had gotten very attached to Sarah the last time the case was in the system, and wished she could take these kids home with her, but that wasn't practical. The best she could do was get them to a safe place, and Polinsky Receiving Home was a secure and comfortable temporary placement. She knew Sarah actually preferred it over foster care. "You can't live like this, and your mom needs some help for that baby."

Sarah's head dropped. "I know."

"Why don't you get a few things together that you want to take with you."

Sabre walked back to the living room, holding her breath as she passed the bathroom. When she reached the living room, Matzel was trying to calm Ellesse who had stood up and was yelling in his face. There was a knock on the door.

Matzel answered the door and let in two police officers, a male and a female.

"You called the cops?" Ellesse yelled.

"Yes, you said you weren't going to let me take the children. You know I have to."

Ellesse took two quick steps toward Matzel and started swinging at him. The policeman grabbed her arms and pulled them behind her.

"Be careful," Steve said. "She's pregnant."

"Alright," Ellesse said, a little calmer. Then she started to cry.

Steve and Sabre walked into the kitchen. Sabre gagged when she saw the weeks of dirty dishes and the moldy and rotting food with maggots and flies all over it. Cockroaches scattered as they neared the sink.

"Sorry," she said and turned to go. "I've seen enough."

Chapter 3

The Parker Case

Sabre walked into the cramped attorney lounge at San Diego Superior Court, Juvenile Division, and found her friend, Bob Clark, reading the detention petitions, the forms that are filed when a child is removed from a home for abuse or neglect.

"Are you on detentions?" she asked.

"Yes, are you?"

"No, but I have a returning case—Parker." Sabre shuffled through the box where the petitions and morning reports were kept. "Here it is." She handed Bob a copy. "I have the minors, but they'll need an appointment for the mother, Ellesse Parker. It was Bonnie Jordan's case, but since she's no longer here, I guess that's you."

Bob and Sabre were best friends. They had bonded on their first trial together seven years earlier, and since then, they had become work spouses. Bob was the one who had introduced her to JP. Bob's wife, Marilee, was also Sabre's friend, and although they all occasionally socialized, most of the time Bob and Sabre spent together was work related. Bob was only a couple of years older than Sabre, but his prematurely gray hair made him look closer to JP's age.

Bob glanced over the paperwork. "Looks easy enough. We get her into a clean house and return the kids."

"Read on," Sabre said.

"And, get her into a drug treatment program," Bob said.

"And?"

"And, keep her away from the Kool-Aid." Bob smiled. "Oh, this is good." He continued to read the report. "She said Jim Jones spoke to her from the afterlife. He wants her to follow in his footsteps and watch for the next Halley's Comet."

"Does she know it's not due for another forty or fifty years?"

"She must be a very patient woman, and she'll only be in her eighties. She could have quite a following by then."

"She has her mass suicides all mixed up. Jim Jones was the leader of the Guyana mass suicide. It was Heaven's Gate that was waiting for the comet, not Jonestown."

"Maybe she knows something they didn't. After all, she's waiting for Halley's Comet. Heaven's Gate was looking for the Hale-Bopp Comet. Maybe they had that part wrong."

"You're weird, you know that? You're a perfect match for your client."

Bob laughed out loud as he read.

"What's so funny?" Sabre asked.

"Have you read this?"

"Not all of it."

"Apparently, Jones not only spoke to her, he impregnated her. She listed him as the father of her unborn baby. He assured her it would be a boy, and she was to teach him the wisdom of his ways. Her son would be the great disciple. It says she wants to name her baby after the comet."

"She wants to name the baby Hale-Bopp?"

"No—Halley." He looked at Sabre. "Try to keep up."

Bob had a strange sense of humor. It was one of the things that endeared him to Sabre. He joked about things that often weren't politically correct, but working

Teresa Burrell

in juvenile court could do that to you. Working with abused children and seeing the atrocities every day required a certain attitude to cope with all the suffering they witnessed.

"Let's go see if we can get this done," Sabre said. They left the lounge and walked down the hallway toward Department Five, the courtroom where the case would be heard.

Bob was still smiling as they walked down the corridor. Kourtney Ingram, a young, inexperienced attorney from the Dependency Law Group, greeted them in front of the department's door.

"Hi, Sabre," Kourtney said. "I see you're on the Parker case. I'll be appointed for the father."

"Jim Jones?" Bob asked.

"No, I don't think that's his name. It's for Denny's father." She glanced at her petition.

"Are you sure it isn't for Jim Jones?" Bob asked. "Because it can't be Marshall Applewhite; he had himself voluntarily castrated." Sabre nudged him with her elbow. She was certain Kourtney was too young to remember the incidents that happened in Guyana or with the last coming of the Hale-Bopp Comet.

"Who are Marshall Applewhite and Jim Jones?" Kourtney asked.

"They're both dead guys," Bob said. "Suicides."

Kourtney frowned at Bob and shook her head.

"Jim Jones was the leader of a cult that committed mass suicide in 1986 in Guyana," Sabre explained. "Marshall Applewhite was the leader of Heaven's Gate, another group that killed themselves."

"And what's all the stuff in the report about Halley's Comet?" Kourtney asked Sabre.

Bob answered. "In Guyana, more than nine hundred followers took their lives by drinking a poisoned punch. Then, in 1997 in Rancho Santa Fe, a

18

little north of here, thirty-nine members of Heaven's Gate killed themselves. Heaven's Gate believed there was a spaceship on the tail of the Hale-Bopp Comet, and they could shed their earthly bodies and catch a ride to the next level. They drank lethal cocktails of phenobarbital, applesauce, and vodka, which was a much better idea than Jim Jones' Kool-Aid, which wasn't actually even Kool-Aid, just some generic punch. The cops found the Heaven's Gate group lying in bunk beds, their faces covered with square, purple cloths, all wearing black, Nike Decade running shoes."

Kourtney squirmed.

"I still wonder about those Nikes," Bob said. "Do you suppose they wanted good running shoes in case they had to catch the spaceship?"

Sabre ignored him. "The mother, Ellesse Parker, seems to be a little confused about the father of her unborn baby. I'm sure Bob will sort it all out when he talks to her," Sabre said to Kourtney. "Is Denny's father here?"

"He's in custody, but I'll have him produced for the next hearing. So, I'm ready whenever you two are."

"We need Wagner, so it might be a while. He's the attorney for Sarah's father. And Bob needs to talk to the mother," Sabre said. "And there she is." Sabre nodded toward a woman who was sitting alone on a bench against the wall. "I'll introduce you."

A young woman carrying a baby walked over to where Ellesse was sitting and sat down, then wrinkled her nose, stood up, and moved to the next bench. Even though it was a crowded hallway, no one was within six feet of Ellesse Parker.

Bob glanced at Sabre. "Is it that bad?"

"Just be glad you have no sense of smell."

Chapter 4

The Parker Case

Sabre introduced Bob to his client, then walked away.

"I hate that bitch," Ellesse muttered before Sabre was out of earshot.

"She's not so bad once you get to know her," Bob said. He wanted to tell her she wasn't half the woman Sabre was. Sabre was his best friend, and Bob didn't like anyone putting her down, but he knew most of the parents in these cases blamed the minors' attorneys or the social workers for taking their kids. The rest blamed their own attorneys for not getting them out of the impossible messes they'd gotten themselves into. He knew that if the parents put half as much effort into getting their lives in order as they put into fighting the system, they would have their kids back. But even though his clients often irritated him, it never stopped him from giving them the best defense. This would be no exception.

"I know her well enough to know I don't like her," Ellesse said. "She has no business nosing around my house. I kept that house clean for nearly eight months last time. I let it slip a little bit, and they yank the kids out. It hasn't been easy, you know, with being pregnant and all. And with the father not around, how am I supposed to get help?"

"Let's talk about that," Bob said. "Who is the father of your unborn child?"

"Jim Jones, the evangelist," she said as she looked Bob straight in the eye. He didn't flinch. "I know it sounds crazy, but he came to me one night and made love to me."

"Did he just appear?" Bob asked without any hint of sarcasm.

"Of course not. He followed me home from a bar one night. He said he had been watching me for a while, and I was the chosen one. He was so sexy and sweet. We made love all night long. And in the morning, before he left, he told me I was pregnant, and I would have a boy. He said someday our son would be a great spiritual leader, just like him."

"Did he say anything about a comet?" Bob asked seriously.

"He did." She squinted her eyes and looked at Bob for a couple of seconds. "But how did you know that?"

"I read it in the report."

She nodded her head knowingly. "You know more than that, don't you?"

Bob had a hard time containing himself, but he managed to keep a straight face. "No, I just read what the social worker wrote."

She took a breath. "Jim told me that when Halley's Comet returns to earth, a spaceship will be traveling in its wake. It will pick up me and our son, and his many children, and take them to Heaven. He said our son, Halley, will father ninety-nine children, and they'll all go with us."

"And it was Halley's Comet, not the Hale-Bopp Comet?"

Ellesse looked confused.

"Never mind," Bob said. "Did he tell you he was...uh...dead?"

"He told me he was a spirit who had returned and that together we would have a heavenly experience."

Bob made a coughing sound and covered his mouth to keep from laughing. "And did you?"

"Yes. It was the best night of my life. It was trippy."

"Did you ever see him again after that?"

21

"No. He only had one night on Earth and could only be with one woman. Imagine that—he chose me."

"Yeah, imagine that."

At first, Bob thought she was making it all up, or she was just crazy, but the more he listened to her, the more he realized she believed every word.

"How can you be certain Jim Jones is the father?"

"I just told you. Before he left, he said I was pregnant."

"Other than that. Is it possible someone else impregnated you?"

"It had been months since I slept with anyone before Jim."

"And since then?"

"No one. I'm not sure I ever could. It just wouldn't be the same."

Bob explained Ellesse's constitutional rights to her and discussed what would happen at the hearing, suggesting that she not explain in detail in court about Jim Jones. As they discussed her plea, Richard Wagner walked past and entered Department Five. Kourtney, the attorney for Denny's father, went inside as well.

"I think they may be ready for us," Bob said.

"Good. I want to get out of here."

Bob stuck his head inside the courtroom and saw that the judge was on the bench, but they were not in session. Sabre was talking to the court reporter. "I'm ready on Parker," Bob said to the judge. "It looks like everyone is here."

"Let's do it," Judge Chino said.

Within a few minutes, the parties and their attorneys were all seated at the counsel table, along with Deputy County Counsel Linda Farris.

After the case was called and pleas of denial were entered to the petition, Linda Farris asked the court to inquire about the father of the unborn child.

Bob stood up. "Your Honor, I don't believe that's an issue for this hearing since that child is not under the jurisdiction of this court."

Judge Chino said, "That is correct, counselor, but can you shed any light on this issue anyway?"

"According to my client, the child is a result of a one-night encounter with a man who said his name was Jim Jones."

"It wasn't an *encounter*," Ellesse said. "It was...."

Bob leaned down and whispered in her ear, and she stopped talking.

"Did your client want to add something, Mr. Clark?"

"Not at this time, Your Honor," Bob said. "We would like to address the issue of visitation."

"Go ahead."

"We're asking for unsupervised visits. The mother has never harmed her children and does not pose a risk to them. The real issue is the condition of the house, and since they are no longer living there, that issue no longer exists. She is staying in El Cajon with some friends whom the children knew well. The mother misses her children and would like to spend as much time as possible with them." He sat down.

"The Department is requesting supervised visits for the mother," Deputy County Counsel Farris said. "There were drugs and drug paraphernalia found in the home."

"The mother submitted to a drug test the day her children were removed, and she was negative," Bob said.

"Only because the social worker arrived before she had a chance to use them," Farris said.

"Okay," the judge said. "I'm ordering the mother to continue testing, and as long as she is clean, she can visit her children in their respective homes or at DSS.

She does not need to have someone in the room with her, but she cannot take them out until further order of this court."

"Thank you, Your Honor," Bob said. He leaned over and explained to his client that that was the best they were going to get for now. She frowned.

Mr. Wagner said, "My client, Sarah's father, would like his daughter detained with him. He is a non-offending parent."

"Your Honor, the father, Russell Drake, is presently living in a halfway house," Farris said. "He was recently released from San Diego County Jail and does not have appropriate housing for a child."

"He's making plans to move in with his sister this weekend," Wagner said. "We would like her home evaluated and discretion for the social worker to detain Sarah there with her father."

Sabre stood up. "Your Honor, I'm not comfortable with that. The last time we tried detaining Sarah with her father, he was arrested for possession of drugs."

Drake whispered to Wagner.

"They weren't his drugs, Your Honor."

"Of course not," Judge Chino said in his usual flippant tone.

"No," Sabre said. "He claimed they were his sister's."

"Same sister?" the judge asked.

"He only has one," Sabre said.

"Does the sister have any history of drug use?"

"Not that we're aware of, Your Honor. The father ultimately took a plea on the drug possession charges and vindicated his sister. Sarah has not done well in previous foster home placements, so it would be good if she can be with family. However, I'm not sure Sarah's aunt is strong enough to follow the rules when it comes to her brother."

"The sister's home is to be evaluated," the judge ordered. "Discretion to detain Sarah with the aunt, as long as the father isn't living there, and with the concurrence of minor's attorney. Supervised visitation for the father."

Bob stood up and followed his client out of the courtroom. He was talking to his client when Sabre came out.

"Hey, bitch!" An angry, sandy-brown-haired man in his mid-forties yelled, as he stomped down the hallway toward Sabre.

Chapter 5

The Lynch Case

Sabre watched the man as he approached. She didn't recognize him and hoped he was looking at someone behind her, but she wasn't comfortable turning around to check. He was glaring directly at her. Fear came over her at first, but it was replaced by determination not to be bullied. Bullies were one of her pet peeves. They were the worst kind of coward.

"Are you talking to me?" Sabre asked.

The man was only a few feet from her, with his arm extended and his finger pointing at her. "Yes, I'm talking to you, bitch," he yelled.

Just then Wagner exited the courtroom, and he and Bob simultaneously stepped between the man and Sabre. The buzz in the hallway had stopped. Everyone was staring and listening.

"Calm down," Bob said in a commanding voice.

"I got this, guys," Sabre said, but her voice couldn't be heard over the yelling. Neither Bob nor Wagner moved.

"Step back," Wagner said to the man.

"I want my damn kids back." The man spat out the words with contempt.

Jerry, the bailiff, flew out of Department Five and quickly assessed the situation. He looked at Bob and Wagner and motioned with his hand for them to step back. As they did, he stepped up to the man and stood face to face with him.

"What's going on?" Jerry asked.

The man continued to yell. "My stupid wife was using drugs, and they took my boys from her. I haven't done anything wrong, but *she* won't give me my kids."

He pointed at Sabre when he said "she."

"You need to lower your voice and calm down, or we can go to the back and have this conversation."

"I'm madder than hell," he said.

"I can see that, but this isn't how we're going to do this."

Michael McCormick, the bailiff in Department Four, came out of his courtroom and stood behind the yelling man. Another bailiff came up the hallway and moved the crowd back a little, creating some open space between them and the situation.

"You'd be ticked off, too, if they took your kids for no reason." The man twisted back and forth, balling up his fists. Suddenly, he clasped his hands together so tight his knuckles turned white. He held them in front of his face for a few seconds, almost as if he were praying, but his mouth tightened in a stubborn line.

"Okay, let's take this somewhere else. Turn around."

"Are you arresting me?" the man yelled.

"Not yet, but I will if you don't calm down right now."

Just then, Attorney Wes Hodges walked up. He was 6'4" and weighed about two hundred pounds. He was forty-five years old and worked out in the gym every day. When he was young, he was Mr. Oklahoma, and for a short time he had played for the Miami Dolphins.

"Jerry," Wes said to the bailiff, "this is my client. What's going on?"

"He's out of control. You need to get him out of here, or I will."

Wes looked at his client and firmly, yet softly, said, "Todd, let's go outside where we can talk."

Todd's mouth tightened, and he shuffled his feet as if he weren't sure what to do. Then he turned and walked out with Wes.

"Who was that madman?" Bob asked.

"I've never met him, but I think he's the father on a case I got last week. Mom and Dad are divorced. She got custody of the three boys, and he gets visitation, but he lives in Los Angeles so he can't see them as much as he'd like. Now that his ex is using drugs, he thinks he should have the kids."

"That makes sense. So what's the issue?"

"He has some serious anger issues."

"Really? I hadn't noticed."

"When he found out his kids had been taken to Polinsky, the first thing he did was call and threaten the social worker. I don't blame him for being upset, but had he handled this with a little more concern for his boys, the Department probably would've given him the kids and never filed the case."

"So why is he so mad at you?"

"Because at the detention hearing last week I objected to the boys going home with him until I had the chance to talk to them."

"You had to do that. You couldn't just agree without seeing the children."

"I know, but the father didn't see it that way. He wasn't in court, but Wes argued against me. The judge gave discretion to the social worker with my concurrence."

"And you didn't concur?"

"No. After I spoke to the boys, I thought I needed to investigate further. The boys do not want to go home."

"Of course not. Who would want to live in L.A. if they could live in San Diego?"

Sabre shook her head. "It's a little more than that. None of them have given me many details, but they're definitely afraid of him. I'm hoping with a couple more visits, they'll open up some."

"I take it you're on the court calendar this morning?"

"Yes, the detention hearing was continued so the father could be here. I expect Wes has told him by now that the boys aren't going home this morning, unless Judge Hekman orders it over my objection."

Bob chuckled. "Like that's going to happen. If he acts like a bully in her courtroom, he'll never get those kids."

"I'm sure Wes has told him that, but Hekman already knows about his threats from the social worker's report."

"I'm done with my cases this morning," Bob said, "but I think I'll stick around and watch the fireworks, and then we can go to lunch."

Chapter 6

The Lynch & Fowler Cases

Bob sat in the back of the courtroom as the parties on the Lynch case took their seats at the counsel table. Along the table from right to left were Wes Hodges, his client Todd Lynch, the mother, Heather Lynch, with her attorney Regina Collicott, Sabre, and Deputy County Counsel Tom Hughes. After the case was called, introductions were made for the record, denials were entered on the petition, and Wes asked for a trial date five weeks out.

Todd started to speak. Wes put his hand on his shoulder and glared at him. Todd stopped and Wes turned back to the judge.

"Your Honor," Wes said, "my client would like the children detained with him awaiting the trial. He is a non-offending parent who has no history of drug use. He pays his child support and visits his children regularly, despite the distance between them. Up until eight months ago, when the mother moved to San Diego, the father saw his children almost every day and was heavily involved in all their activities."

Heather Lynch sat there shaking her head in disagreement.

"The Department would object to detention with the father at this time," Tom Hughes responded. "Mr. Lynch has exhibited a lack of control on several occasions. On his first encounter with the social worker, he started shouting at her before she could even explain the circumstances. When she tried to explain the process, he continued to shout at her, then threw his pen against the wall and stomped out of the room. Security walked him out of the building to the parking lot, where he was observed smashing his own car window before he drove off."

"Your Honor, my client was understandably angry that the mother of his children was using drugs and putting them in danger. He wanted to take them home where they would be safe. As for the broken window, he had locked his keys in his car and needed to get inside," Wes said.

"He used a ninja kick to break the window," Hughes said.

Sabre thought she heard Bob chuckle, followed by a quick clearing of his throat to cover up. Judge Hekman scowled at him but didn't say anything.

"And this morning he was yelling at minor's counsel in the hallway," Hughes continued. "We do not believe it is safe to detain these children with the father at this time. And we request supervised visitation."

"Your position, Ms. Brown?" the judge said.

"I concur with County Counsel. The minors are not ready to live with their father, and I agree with supervised visitation."

Todd Lynch was seething, but he didn't say anything.

"Your Honor," the mother's attorney, Regina Collicott, said, "we would ask that the court order a home evaluation on the maternal aunt, Delores Greene, and detention with her upon home approval."

"No," Todd Lynch blurted out before Wes could stop him. "Dee hates me," he said in a half-whisper, that was still audible to the entire courtroom.

Wes leaned in and whispered to his client for a good minute until Todd nodded his head.

"Your Honor, we don't object to the evaluation, but we'd also like the same done for the paternal grandmother."

"Where do these relatives live?" Judge Hekman

asked.

"They both live in L.A. More specifically, the Pasadena area. We have already put in a request with L.A. County. They're pretty backed up, so it may take a while."

"Is there anything else?" Hekman asked.

"Yes, Your Honor," Wes said. "My client is requesting the venue in this case be changed to Los Angeles County."

"File the motion, counselor, and I'll give you a hearing date." The judge glanced at the other attorneys, but no one objected. "All previous orders remain in full force and effect."

The parties stood up and left the courtroom, followed by their respective attorneys. Sabre stepped to the back where Bob was sitting.

"That was pretty boring," Bob said, "except for the ninja kick. Did he really do that?"

"That's what the social worker said, and Lynch doesn't seem to be denying it."

"Are you done?"

"Yep."

Bob stood up, and they started toward the door. Suddenly the judge called out to them.

"Bob, Sabre, can you help us out on a case? We need a couple of attorneys."

"Of course, Your Honor," Sabre said, turning back. Bob followed.

The courtroom door opened, and Attorney Irene Serlis walked in.

"Ms. Brown, you'll be representing the minor. She was initially assigned to the Public Defender's Office, but they had a conflict with one of the parents. Irene Serlis represents the mother. The father had retained counsel for the hearing two days ago, but he apparently quit before we could do the detention hearing. The father said he had since retained Mr. McGlynn to represent him, but when no one showed up for the hearing this morning, the clerk called McGlynn's office, and as it turns out, the attorney had declined to take his case. Mr. Clark, will you represent the father, Seth Fowler?"

"Absolutely," Bob said. He whispered to Sabre, "If McGlynn turned it down, it's gotta be good."

"The case may involve some First Amendment issues," Judge Hekman said.

"Freedom of speech?" Bob asked.

"Religion."

"Even better."

"Does she know you're an atheist?" Irene whispered to Bob.

"Let's just say I don't believe in institutionalized religion."

"Close enough."

"But I do believe in the Constitution and everyone's right to their own religious views."

Michael McCormick, the bailiff, walked up and handed the attorneys the petitions and the reports that were available. "You're gonna love this guy, Bob. He's right up your alley." He smiled and walked away.

"What's the issue?" Bob asked before he looked at the paperwork.

"Let's go outside where we can talk," Irene said.

Bob started to read the petition as he walked out. "It looks like a simple molest, by a friend of the father."

"A molest? Yes. Simple? No."

They walked to the end of the hallway where no one was sitting.

"Oh, my," Sabre exclaimed.

"What? What is it?" Bob asked. "Are they claiming they have a religious right to molest or something?"

"Not exactly," Irene said. "The parents claim the

perpetrator can't be molesting the child because she's his wife."

"She's twelve!" Sabre said, way louder than she intended to. She shook her head in disbelief.

"And her 'husband' is forty-two," Irene said, making air quotes around the word "husband."

"What does her mother think of this?"

"She doesn't want the judicial system involved in her life. So much so that she was willing to go along with her daughter getting married when she discovered they were 'messing around,' as she put it."

"This is disgusting," Sabre said. "And what about the father?"

"He's the one calling the shots," Irene said. "My client was only fourteen when he married her. He was thirty-eight. He can't understand what the problem is."

"I need to talk to my client," Bob said.

"Let's go. I'll introduce you. He's a real peach."

Bob put his arm around Sabre's shoulder. "Looks like we're going to battle on this one."

"I know," Sabre said and watched Bob and Irene walk away. She knew Bob didn't have to like his client or what he stood for to give him his best defense. That was one of the things for which she admired him.

Since her client was not at court, Sabre couldn't know how she felt about the whole thing, but she knew she had to do everything she could to help her. She sat down and read through the report, trying to get as much insight as she could. The more she read, the more she cringed.

Chapter 7

The Fowler Case

Reverend Seth Fowler was a slender man with squinty, close-set, azure-blue eyes and pale skin. He had a thin, straight nose and a beard halfway down his chest. His full head of wavy, wheat-colored hair was slicked back, exhibiting no signs of baldness.

Irene spotted him with his wife right outside the courthouse. She introduced Bob and then walked away to speak to her client, Mrs. Fowler. Bob reached his hand out to shake. Fowler seemed reluctant, but after a moment's hesitation, he moved the manila folder he was holding to his left hand and shook Bob's hand loosely.

"I don't trust the government," Seth said.

"I'm your appointed lawyer, but I do not work for any government agency. I'm independent. I only have to answer to my client and the Professional Code of Ethics. So tell me what's going on. We may be able to beat this thing, but you have to be straight with me."

Seth eyed Bob from top to bottom. "Are you a Christian?"

"My beliefs and values are not important. Yours, however, are. Let's concentrate on those."

"I'm a God-fearing man, and everything I do or did, I did for my family in His name."

"I'm sure you did," Bob said. Then he looked at the petition. "It says here:

On or about May 2, Lester Gibbs molested Mary Margaret by committing the following acts:

"Blah...blah...blah...," Bob said. "We don't need to rehash the specifics."

Bob continued to read the petition.

Teresa Burrell

"Mary Margaret has been sexually abused, and the child is at substantial risk to be further abused, as defined by Section 11165.1 of the Penal Code, by a member of her household, and the parent or guardian has failed to adequately protect the child from sexual abuse when the parent or guardian knew, or reasonably should have known, that the child was in danger of sexual abuse. Further, the parent or guardian allowed Mr. Gibbs to move into their household and sleep in the same room as Mary Margaret."

"Do you understand the petition?" Bob asked.

"Yeah, I understand it, but none of that matters because they're married. I wouldn't have allowed him in her bed if they weren't married. There's nothing wrong, in God's eyes, for two married people to sleep together."

"Do you have a marriage certificate?"

Seth retrieved a paper from his folder and handed it to Bob.

"This is from your church?"

"It's a copy of a page from the family Bible and sanctioned by the church."

"And you gave permission for your child to be married?"

"Yes, I did."

"Did you get a marriage license from the State of California?" Bob was certain he knew the answer to that question.

"No, we did not, and we won't." Seth's voice grew louder as he began to preach. "The state cannot tell me, or any other citizen, that they can or cannot marry. That is a God-given right. No Christian needs to get a license from the state to marry. According to Black's Law Dictionary, 'a license is a permission, accorded by a competent authority, conferring the right to do some

36

act, which without such authorization would be illegal, or would be a trespass or a tort.' A license confers a right to do something, but it's not the state's place to grant such permission. According to the Bible, Deuteronomy 22:16, Exodus 22:17, and First Corinthians 7:38, it is a father's right to give permission. The right to marry is not a right granted by the state since a higher power already granted that right—God's law according to Genesis 2:18-24. God instituted marriage, and only God can decide who marries and who doesn't. We have prayed at length for and with Brother Lester Gibbs, and God answered our prayers. Lester is a good, God-fearing man who will do well by our daughter."

Bob looked at the photocopy he held in his hand. "And you performed the ceremony, Reverend?"

"Yes, I did."

"And you have performed other ceremonies?"

"Many."

"Did you require a license from the state for those marriages?"

"No, I did not. Quite the opposite. I refuse to perform any ceremony where the couple has a state license. I will not be an agent for the state and their unbiblical, immoral body of laws. The state has tried to usurp the family and God's place in marriage, and I refuse to be a part of that in form or substance."

"I understand," Bob said.

"So you agree with me?"

"It doesn't matter whether or not I agree. My agreeing with you will not help you. My job is to represent you and I'm eager to do that. I see a constitutional issue here that might work for you."

The reverend sized Bob up again with his eyes. "I don't believe you've been saved, and maybe someday I can help you with that, but you strike me as a man who'll fight for his client."

Bob let that slide. "Now let me tell you how this is going to work. I know you don't think the state should be interfering in your family or your life, but we're here now and we have to use whatever legal means we can to get out of this situation. So, we'll enter a denial to the petition today and set it for trial. At that trial, the State has to prove the petition is true. We'll defend your right of religion and your parental position. In the meantime, I'll do some research, and I'll file a motion on First Amendment grounds. Chances are it'll be heard the same day as the trial."

"And my daughter?"

"I will argue that she be allowed to go home, but I doubt if this judge will send her home awaiting the trial. I know she will not, as long as Gibbs remains in your home. Even if he is out, she would have to trust that you wouldn't let him around your daughter until this is sorted out. Even that is a long shot. So you decide how you want to proceed, and I'll make the appropriate arguments."

"Fair enough."

"And your wife—do you know what her position is on this matter?" Bob asked.

"She'll do whatever I tell her to do."

I bet she will, Bob thought, but decided to make light of it. "Not my wife," he said. "She never does what I tell her to do."

"That's because you don't have God's help."

"Yeah, I'm sure that's it." Bob stepped toward the courtroom door. "I'll see you inside. Please wait outside the courtroom. I'm going to try to get this moving so you can get out of here."

When the attorneys and parties were all ready for the Fowler hearing, Bob approached his client.

"What did you decide about Mr. Gibbs moving out

of your home pending trial?" Bob asked.

"The truth is that Brother Gibbs does not live with us. He only stayed that one night. He has a place of his own. Is there any chance the judge will send Mary Margaret home since he's not living with us?" Fowler said.

"Truthfully, it's very unlikely, but if you don't allow him access to your home, it will show the court you're putting your child first. That could help later on."

"No. I can't be hypocritical. They are married in the eyes of God, and I won't bend at the whim of the state."

"Suit yourself. I'll still make an argument for the record."

The detention hearing was just what Bob expected. A trial date was set, and Judge Hekman agreed to hear motions on the First Amendment issues either on the day of the trial, or earlier, if the motions were filed timely. Deputy County Counsel requested that the minor remain in a foster home. Bob requested the minor's name on the petition be changed to Mary Margaret Gibbs, instead of Fowler, but the court refused.

Bob stood. "Your Honor, my client would like to see the minor returned to her husband so they can live in the holy bonds of matrimony, as God would want."

"That's not going to happen, Mr. Clark," the judge said.

"Then we would request that the minor be allowed to attend services in her church on Sunday mornings and Sunday and Wednesday evenings pending the trial," Bob said. "It is our position that the minor has a constitutional right to attend the church of her choice without interference from the State."

"Ms. Brown?" the judge said, looking at Sabre.

Sabre stood alongside Bob. "Your Honor, I don't know if my client wants to attend the services, but I will gladly speak to Mary Margaret to see what her position is on the matter."

"With all due respect," Bob said, "my client's position is that her husband should be making that choice, but since the court does not recognize his authority, then we ask that the court at least recognize the will of her parents. It is the position of their church that the minor remains under the direct supervision of her parents until she is married. Since the court is not giving credence to the marriage ceremony at this time, then we maintain the child is still a minor, and those decisions should be made by her parents."

"I hear you, Counselor."

Sabre started to speak, but the judge held up her hand to stop her.

"The minor will remain detained in foster care pending the trial," the judge ordered. "The social worker will make every effort to get the child to her church for at least one of the services each week if the minor's attorney agrees that the minor wants to attend. The minor is to have supervised visitation with her parents, and no contact of any kind, at church or otherwise, with Mr. Lester Gibbs. All other orders remain in full force and effect. This hearing is adjourned." She stood up and left the courtroom.

The father stood up to leave. On his way out the door, he raised both arms in the air and thundered, "What therefore God hath joined together, let not man put asunder."

Chapter 8

The Fowler Case

Sabre and Bob sat at Pho's, their favorite lunch hangout. Bob ordered a #124, as he always did.

"I thought JP was going to join us," Bob said.

"No, he can't make it," Sabre said. "How do you like your client on the Fowler case?"

"He's an extremist, for sure, but I have to give people credit when they believe in something so much that there is no doubt in their mind. Decisions come easy because it's all black and white. It must be nice. There aren't many things in life I'm that sure of, and most of those are science-based. But I'll fight tooth and nail for their constitutional right to believe in whatever they choose, even if it is in direct conflict with my beliefs."

"I know you will." She saw the determination in his face. "And I'm ready for the fight."

"But can you believe all the times we referred to the perps on molest cases as 'Lester, the molester'? We finally have a molester who is actually named Lester."

Sabre chuckled.

"Have you met Mary Margaret yet?" Bob asked.

"No, but I'm going to see her this afternoon. I'll let you know her position on attending church."

"Thanks." Bob took a drink of water. "You know Irene and I will be filing a demurrer on this case?"

"Really?"

"You bet. We're not contesting the facts. The demurrer would basically say, 'So what?' Because if they're married there is no illegal act."

"That's true. I guess I shouldn't be surprised, and I

wouldn't expect you to do anything less, but don't forget now with the new law, we have to have a 'meet and confer' before the judge will hear the demurrer."

"Irene is already working on it."

"Of course she is." Sabre smiled.

"What about the Parker case? You've been on it a while. Do you think the mother will clean up her act?"

"She will, but it probably won't last. You need to get her into a drug program right away. I don't think she's been using that long this time, so she may be able to get back on track. I don't know about this 'new crazy' she's going through—she's pregnant from a ghost. Do you think that's the drugs talking?"

"No, after my conversation with Ellesse this morning, I think she got duped by some low-life in a bar. She just has such low self-esteem that it's easier to believe the Jim Jones story. From the way she tells the story, I think she may have even been drugged by him."

"I wondered about that. I'm going to have JP look into it. Do you mind if he talks to your client? Only on that issue, of course."

"Sure, that's fine. Have him call me. I'll set it up and we'll go together."

~~~

Sabre left the restaurant and drove to Polinsky Children's Center to see Mary Margaret. One of the workers brought her to an interview room. Sabre was surprised when the little girl came into the room. She was less than five feet tall, had sandy blonde hair, a boyishly-straight body, and the soft, angelic face of a child her age. Sabre had expected a more developed teenager, not a twelve-year-old who could easily pass for ten. She felt a knot in the pit of her stomach when she thought about what this girl had already endured. She looked at the little girl and wondered if she had even started her menstrual cycle yet. She guessed not.

"Are you Mary Margaret Fowler?" Sabre asked.

Mary Margaret stared at the floor. "Yes," she said.

"Come sit with me." Mary Margaret followed Sabre to the sofa, and they sat down. Sabre left a little room between them so Mary Margaret wouldn't feel like her space was invaded, but not too much, as she wanted to keep their talk intimate. She explained to the little girl about her role as her attorney, and the need for her to be honest about everything so she could help her. She was never certain how much her minor clients understood, but she often reiterated the rules to remind them, especially about the confidentiality. Most of the children she encountered trusted very little adults told them because they had been disappointed so many times. She expected this time it was going to be even harder than usual to gain this solemn little girl's confidence.

"How's it going here at Polinsky?"

"It's not bad. I don't mind it."

"Did the social worker talk to you about going to a foster home?"

"Yes, she said I was going tomorrow to live with a nice couple." She glanced up at Sabre for a second.

"Are you okay with that?" Sabre asked.

She shrugged. "I guess."

"The Venables are a lovely couple. I think you'll like them. Mrs. Venable is a really good baker. She makes lots of cookies and brownies and things." Sabre smiled, but got nothing in return. "Mary Margaret, are you sad?"

Again, without looking up, she said, "I miss my brothers and my friend, Penny."

"You'll get to see your brothers soon. Where does

Penny live? Is it near you?"

"Only a block away, and she goes to my church."

"Does she go to your school?"

"My brothers and I are home-schooled. Penny goes to regular school."

"Who does the teaching?"

"Papa does, but Mama helps."

"Is Papa your father?"

"Yes, that's what we call him."

Sabre hadn't seen anything in the report about home schooling, but it didn't surprise her. Seth Fowler, Mary Margaret's father, seemed to have a pretty strong rein on his family.

"It must be nice being home-schooled. You get a lot more help with your studies."

"Yeah, but sometimes I'd like to go to school and make new friends, or at least see Penny."

"It's nice that you have a friend you can share your secrets with."

"Yeah, we tell each other everything."

"Did you tell her that you got married?"

Mary Margaret looked up and directly at Sabre for the first time. "I did," she said softly.

"Did you want to get married?"

"Papa said I had to."

"What did your mother say?"

"She said I had to do what Papa said, but to just pretend like the wedding was make-believe and that I was a princess marrying my prince. She said that's what she did when she married Papa."

"Is that what you did?"

"No, I didn't feel like a princess, and Brother Gibbs was no prince. He was more like an old toad."

Sabre started to smile but caught herself when she saw the serious look on Mary Margaret's face.

"When did Mr. Gibbs move into your house?"

"He didn't exactly move in. He stayed there for a few nights after the wedding because I ran away from him. He took me to his house and I left and went home. Papa said I had to go back, but Mama convinced him to let us stay there."

"Where did Mr. Gibbs sleep?"

"In my room with me."

"Did he hurt you?" Sabre hated having to ask these questions, but she had to know.

"Not really. I told him not to touch me, but he did anyway. He said it was okay because we were married, but that's all he did. I think he was afraid I would scream. The next day CPS came and took me away."

"Was that the first time he touched you?"

Mary Margaret bit her lip. "I'm not a bad girl."

"I know that. You are not a bad girl. You haven't done anything wrong."

"I don't want to talk about this anymore."

"Okay, let's talk about something else. Tell me about your brothers. You have two, right?"

"Yes, they're pretty cool, for boys."

"How old are they?"

"They're ten and eight. They share a room. I wish I had a sister sometimes, but it's also nice having my own room."

"Do your brothers bug you sometimes?"

"Sometimes, but they're fun too. They have a fort in the backyard that Papa built for them. He made me a dollhouse when I was young, but I've outgrown it. I like the fort better, but it's for boys only. My brothers only let me go in it when none of their friends are around."

"That's cool."

There was a moment of silence, then Sabre said, "Your parents were asking about your going to your church. We can arrange for you to go sometimes if

45

you'd like."

"Do I have to? I don't want to see *him*."

"Who is *him*?" Sabre assumed she was talking about Gibbs, but she wanted to be sure.

"Brother Gibbs. I don't want to see him."

"As long as you are in foster care, you do not have to see Brother Gibbs. We'll make sure of that. If you don't have to see him, would you want to go to your church?"

She nodded.

"The judge ordered the social worker to get you to your church at least once a week, but only if you wanted to go. So it's up to you."

"Could I go on Wednesdays?"

"Probably, but why did you choose Wednesday and not Sunday?"

"Because that's more Bible study, and Brother Gibbs won't be there. And I'd get to see Penny and my brothers." For the first time, the little girl seemed to brighten up a bit.

"I'll talk to Mr. and Mrs. Venable to see if they can arrange to get you there on Wednesdays. If not, I think the social worker can work something out."

Mary Margaret looked up. "Thank you. You're a nice lady."

Sabre fought back her tears.

Chapter 9

JP opened the door to Sabre's office and was greeted by Elaine, the receptionist.

"Good afternoon, Cowboy," Elaine said.

JP nodded his head in acknowledgment and said, "Good evenin', ma'am. Is she with anyone?"

"No, go on in."

JP stood in the open doorway for a few seconds watching Sabre as she worked. *She's so beautiful*, he thought.

She looked up from her desk and smiled at him. "I was just thinking about calling you."

"I must have felt the vibe."

He approached her, and she stood up and eased herself into his open arms. He kissed her gently, but she stayed for more, holding him tightly.

"Now that's what I call a welcome," JP said.

"It's been a rough day, and you always make it so much better."

"What happened?"

"I had three cases in court this morning that left a sour taste in my mouth. I have a child whose mother is pregnant and believes she was impregnated by the ghost of Jim Jones, the evangelist; an irate father who yelled at me in court and called me names; and a twelve-year-old child who may be married to her forty-two-year-old molester."

JP's face reddened at the last issue. He had a hard time restraining himself when it came to child molesters.

"I know how you hate to work these type of cases, but I need your help."

"I just think the best way to the heart of a man like that is a knife through the chest."

"Okay, that might be going a little too far."

"I know, darlin'." He smiled at her. "I'll do whatever you need me to."

She gave him the petition and the report, along with a brief description of the case. "I need you to talk to anyone at the church who will give you information. See if a wedding actually took place, for starters. Find out if Mary Margaret, that's the minor, told anyone what was going on." She hesitated.

"What is it?"

"I need you to talk to Lester Gibbs, the groom, if you will."

"Really?"

"He's not a party to this action. At least, not yet. I expect someone will be filing a motion to give him standing, but I don't think it will fly with Judge Hekman."

"No, I mean is his name really *Lester*?"

"I'm afraid so." Sabre smiled. "Mary Margaret has a friend named Penny that she says she confided in, but I'll talk to her. I think it would be easier on the little girl if a woman talked to her."

"I'll get started. Anything else?"

"Yeah." She handed JP the petition and report on the Lynch case. "Please find out anything you can about Todd Lynch. He's a very angry man, and before I let his boys go home with him, I need to make sure they'll be safe."

"How angry?"

"Angry enough to call me and everyone else names."

"Did he threaten you?" JP asked fervently.

"Not really. He was just letting off a little steam. Nothing to worry about. The bailiffs were watching out for me."

JP shook his head. Sabre wished she hadn't said anything. JP was generally very calm and laidback, but when he was riled, he didn't hold back.

"See what you can find out about him, talk to friends and neighbors, co-workers, whoever you can. By the way, he lives in L.A. Actually, it's Pasadena, so it's going to be a bit of a drive. Dig deep. Oh, and while you're there, make sure you see the grandmother. Todd would like the boys placed with her, so we need to check out her and the house."

Sabre handed him another file. "This is the 'ghost father' case. You'll probably have to hit a few bars. See if you can find 'Jim Jones.' I'm guessing this woman isn't his first or his last."

"That case ought to be a lot more fun than the other two. Which do you want first?"

"Lynch was set for trial today, so we have a little time on that one. Although his attorney will be filing a motion soon to change venue, so it might be best if we were armed for that." Sabre thought for a second. "Fowler, the child bride case, needs to be dealt with as soon as possible. The Parker case, with the elusive Jim Jones, is not that urgent. He really isn't even a party to this case yet. Once that baby is born, it would be good to know who the father is, but until then there's not a lot we can do. On the other hand, if there is some crazy guy going around luring women into bed and maybe drugging them, we need to get on that too."

"Okay, I got it. You need them all yesterday. I'll move faster than a sailor on a four-hour pass."

JP kissed her and left.

Chapter 10

The Fowler Case

JP sat at his computer with Louie, his beagle pup, at his feet. He had already set up files for each case with the pertinent information and started to run his own criminal checks. He had previously obtained a lot of the information from the Department of Social Services, but sometimes he found things they didn't. Often, he ran checks on players DSS had not and gained invaluable insight on the case.

It was too late to drive to Pasadena to investigate Lynch and too early to hit the bars looking for Jim Jones. Besides, he needed to get more information from Ellesse Parker on Jones before his search would be fruitful. He called his friend Bob, Ellesse's attorney, and asked if he could talk to her about Jim Jones.

"I'll see what I can set up and get back to you," Bob said, and hung up.

JP decided to start with the Fowler case. He wanted to talk to forty-two-year-old Lester Gibbs before he had a chance to lawyer up. His stomach churned when he saw where Lester worked—a group home for troubled teenage girls.

JP got directions from his cell phone for Merlot Group Home, which appeared to be named after the street it was on rather than the wine. He pushed Lester out of his mind for a bit and thought about Sabre as he drove. He was glad to be working some new cases with her again because it gave them more time together. Lately, she had been too busy to even have dinner together. *That wasn't fair,* he thought. He had been just as busy, even out of town for a while, on other cases. He had gotten pretty involved in a high-profile murder case for Attorney Jerry Leahy and had to cancel a weekend in San Francisco he and Sabre had planned. That was the beginning of the lull. When he finished that, Sabre took on a long trial that kept her busy every night. These new cases Sabre had recently started didn't look like they were going to give her much time either, but at least they were working them together.

JP was startled out of his daydream by his ringing phone.

"We can meet with Ellesse tonight, if that works for you," Bob said.

"Sure, what time?"

"Pick me up at my house around 7:30. That'll give me time to eat. She's staying with some friends in El Cajon, so it's not far from here."

JP checked the clock on his dashboard. He had plenty of time. He drove on, still thinking about spending time with Sabre. He didn't think she was interested in anyone else, but he didn't want to get complacent about their relationship either. He often got bored very early in relationships, but that wasn't happening with Sabre. He was crazy about her and wanted her to know it. He decided to come up with something to make up for canceling their weekend getaway.

JP turned onto Merlot Street. It was a residential neighborhood just like most group homes were in. The neighbors often fought to keep these homes out because they felt like they lowered property values and increased the crime rate. That was probably true of some of them, especially if they housed hardcore delinquents. But JP's experience was that it was more about management and resources. Many of these group homes were private businesses, and even though they received funding from the state, they didn't always spend the money wisely. When profit was the bottom line, they often scrimped on resources. Others were well managed and provided great service. He had never had a client here before, so he was unfamiliar with this home. He was already not impressed with their hiring an employee like Lester Gibbs. JP hadn't met him yet, but he had formed an opinion about him based on his so-called marriage to a twelve-year-old. JP cringed, took a deep breath, and exited his car.

He walked to the front door. The two-story house was not marked with a sign, but he double-checked the address and it was correct. He knocked on the door. A girl who appeared to be around fifteen answered. Her blonde, shoulder-length hair had three or four inches of brunette roots. JP wondered if it was the style she chose, or if it had been previously bleached and was now growing out.

"Yeah?" she said.

"Is this Merlot Group Home?"

"Yeah. Are you a social worker?"

"No, I'm not."

"Who you here to see?"

"Lester Gibbs."

"He ain't here."

JP thought he saw a look of disgust on her face. "Do you have a problem with Lester?"

"Naw, he's alright." This time there was no expression. JP thought he probably projected his own feelings on the situation. "Want to see anyone else?" she asked.

"Whoever is in charge."

"Well, that ain't me."

I figured that much out, JP thought, but before he could say anything else, the girl yelled, "Veronica, someone here to see you."

The young girl walked away, leaving him standing

in front of the open door. Within a minute, a thirty-something woman, about five-foot-ten, in good physical shape, appeared.

"May I help you?" she said.

"I'm JP Torn. I'm a private investigator on a juvenile dependency case. I'm actually here to see Lester Gibbs, but I understand he's not here. Right?"

"That's right. He's off today."

"Do you have a minute?"

"Sure, come on in."

JP followed Veronica through the living room, past two younger girls who sat watching television, and into a small office.

"How well do you know Lester?" JP asked.

"I only know him from working here. He was here when I came to work. That was just under a year ago. Why?"

"He's the friend of a family we're working with in juvenile court. I was hoping he could give me some insight. I've never met him. Is he good to work with?"

"Yeah, he's alright, I guess."

"Do the girls get along with him?"

"He has a lot of control over the girls."

"What do you mean?"

"I'm not sure how to explain it. They don't seem to like him really, but they always do what he tells them to. When he gives an order, it gets done. Maybe it's just that he's been here longer and has experience, or that he's a man, but it seems easier for him."

"Have any of the girls ever complained about him?"

Veronica rolled her eyes. "They complain about all of us. They're not really good at accepting responsibility for themselves. So, if they don't like something, it's our fault."

JP thought he had learned as much about Lester

as he could from Veronica. He asked for the name and phone number of the director of the home and left. The two girls were still in the living room. They both looked up as JP passed through. One of the girls had burn scars on one hand and arm. Her sleeve covered part of it, but JP surmised they went all the way up because he could see some scarring on her neck as well.

"Hello," JP said and kept walking.

The girl with the scars ignored him. The other responded.

He wondered what their stories were. Most of the girls in these homes didn't get a very good start in life, and they were angry at the world for the hand they were dealt. He couldn't blame them, but he didn't see that he could do much for them either. He admired Sabre for the empathy she had for her "kids," but more importantly for the time and effort she put into helping them when she could. Whenever they had one of these cases, Sabre's heart seemed to open a little more. All JP wanted to do was kick some ass.

Chapter 11

The Parker Case

Bob and JP were invited into the house where Ellesse was staying. This house didn't appear to be much better than the one Ellesse had left, except there was running water and working plumbing. Two adults besides Ellesse, three girls under the age of six, and a one-year-old boy occupied the two-bedroom home. Clothes, toys, and junk were strewn throughout. The sofa was covered with bedding where Ellesse sat watching a horror movie. A man sat in an armchair a few feet away drinking a beer, his eyes aimed at the blaring TV. The children were chasing each other around, yelling, and rolling on the filthy, worn carpet.

Ellesse moved over, making room for Bob and JP to sit on the sofa. The man yelled at the kids to go to their room without taking his eyes off the screen. They didn't seem to hear him as they continued to play.

Ellesse didn't introduce anyone.

"Why don't we go outside and talk?" Bob suggested.

Ellesse led them through the kitchen, through a small, messy bedroom, and out a side door that led to a fenced backyard. A short, thin woman crushed her cigarette butt against the side of the stucco house and then dropped it in a coffee can on the ground. A few butts that had apparently missed lay on the ground around the can.

"I'll be out here for a bit talking to my lawyer," Ellesse said.

The woman shrugged and said, "Okay." Then she went inside.

Ellesse led them to an old bench under a pepper

tree. She and Bob sat down. JP remained standing.

Bob nodded toward JP. "This is JP. He's a private detective, and he'd like to ask you some questions about Jim Jones."

She looked at him with a furrowed brow. "I've already told you everything I know."

"Humor me," Bob said. "It's important."

"Where did you meet Jim Jones?" JP asked before she could object again.

"In a bar."

"Do you know the name of it?"

"The Watering Hole."

He made a note in his notepad. "On Clairemont Mesa?"

"Yeah, you know it?"

"Not well," JP said. "Did you talk to him at the bar?"

"Yeah. He kept looking at me at first. He looked around a lot. I think he was trying to pick just the right woman. He explained all that to me later. Sometimes," she hesitated, "he would disappear."

"You would see him fade away?" Bob had to ask.

"No," Ellesse said, "I would see him sitting or standing somewhere, and then I'd look again and he'd be gone. Suddenly, he'd reappear somewhere else in the bar. When I first sat down at the bar, he was at the end to my right. Later he was sitting at the bar to the left of me. Once he was leaning against the wall near the door to the bathroom. He kept popping up."

"At some point, he approached you?"

"Yes." She sighed as if she was having a pleasant memory.

"Then what happened?"

"He said his name was Jim. When I told him my name, he said that was perfect, that my name meant 'shining light,' and that he had picked the right one. I asked him what he meant by that, and he said it would all be clear soon. He was very mysterious and charming. Then he bought me a drink."

"Just one?"

"Yes. I started feeling kind of woozy. I don't think I realized how many drinks I had already had. Jim noticed and offered to walk me to my car."

"Did he?"

"I told him I was on foot and I'd be fine, but he insisted I not walk alone. He was worried about me. He said it wasn't safe for a beautiful woman to be out there by herself so late at night."

Bob rolled his eyes. JP could see Bob wanted to make some sarcastic remark, but he didn't.

"So he walked you home?"

"Yes. At first, I wasn't going to invite him inside, but he had been so sweet to me." She paused. "I don't remember what happened right after that. I guess I had too much to drink. A few hours later, I woke up in his arms. We made love again, and then we talked for a long time. He explained more about who he was and what his purpose was on Earth. It all seemed so clear at the time."

"And now?" Bob interjected.

"I don't want to lose my baby. He has important work to do, and he'll be famous someday."

"You mean to the system?" Bob asked.

"Jim told me that he was on Earth once before and he impregnated a woman, but then she stopped believing, and she miscarried. He told me to never stop believing."

"Can you tell me what Jim looked like?" JP asked.

"He was really handsome." She paused. "I didn't think so at first, but he seemed to change and look more handsome all the time."

Everyone looks better after a few drinks, JP thought. "Can you give me a description—height, weight, eye color, stuff like that?"

"He was probably 5' 10, dark hair that fell across his forehead, but he had a little point in the front, right in the middle, when his hair was pushed back." She pointed to the middle of her forehead at her hairline.

"Eye color?"

"He was wearing sunglasses so I didn't see his eyes at first."

"He wore sunglasses in the bar?"

"Yeah, at first, I thought that was strange, but he explained that the light hurt his eyes."

"Did you ever see his eyes?"

"Yeah, he took the sunglasses off later. He had brown eyes."

"What shape was his face? Round, square, oval?" JP asked.

"It was more square than round, and he had a high forehead."

"Do you think you could help a sketch artist draw a picture of him?" JP wasn't certain if Sabre wanted to go that far or not, but he would ask.

"I have a picture of him," she said. "He didn't know I took it. I was going to tell him, but then I figured it would just disappear anyway. I've heard that happens when you take a photo of a ghost, but when it didn't disappear, I realized he wasn't really a ghost. He was more like a spirit."

"What's the difference?" Bob asked.

"With a spirit, the photo doesn't disappear. With a ghost, it does."

"I mean, what's the difference between a ghost and a spirit?"

"Jim was sent here on a mission. Ghosts are here because they have unfinished business, something they're unhappy about."

"I'm glad we got that cleared up," Bob said.

"Can we see the photo?" JP asked.

"Sure." She took her cell phone out of her pocket and brought up a photo.

JP looked at it first, then Bob. It wasn't a very good shot, but if it was enlarged, it might help.

"Do you mind if I send this to my phone so we can get a better look later?"

She shrugged. Bob texted the photo to his phone. A few seconds later, his phone pinged. "Got it," he said.

"It won't do you any good," Ellesse said.

"Why is that?" JP asked.

"I told you, he's gone. He went back to heaven."

Bob and JP thanked her for her time and walked to their car without going back through the house. They got in and drove away.

"She sure got snowed," Bob said.

"I think he drugged her at first," JP said. "It ticks me off that there's some fool out there taking advantage of vulnerable women. I plan to find him, whether Sabre wants me to do it for this case or not."

"I don't know if Ellesse is a little whacky, or if she wants to believe it because she just can't accept that she was duped."

"And he still has a hold on her with that threat of believing or losing the baby."

"Do you think she believes all that?" Bob asked.

"I don't know, but either way, she's about half a bubble off plumb."

Chapter 12

Sabre looked at the time. It was after eight, and she was still at her office. She hadn't worked there that late since the incident with her stalker. She had promised both JP and Bob that she wouldn't, but the time got away from her. She packed up her briefcase and headed for the back door. She suddenly felt uneasy. All her old fears had returned. She stood there for a minute in the hallway by the back door. Then she realized how silly it all was. She opened the door to the brightly-lit parking lot. JP had replaced the small light on the wall with a floodlight right after the incident. She looked around, then walked to her car, and drove away.

Her phone rang.

"Hi, Bro," Sabre said when she saw it was her brother, Ron, calling.

"Have you eaten?" he asked.

"No, and I would invite you over, but I don't really have anything in the house to eat. Do you want to meet me at Pieology on Balboa?"

"Sure, see you there in a few."

Sabre hung up and called JP.

"Hey, kid," he said. "Where are you?"

"I just left the office."

Before she could say anything else, he asked, "Were you there by yourself?"

"Yes, the time just slipped away. Don't fuss. I'm fine." Sabre appreciated his concern, but still felt a little annoyed by his overprotectiveness. She was perfectly capable of taking care of herself. She had to be. She couldn't live her life in fear, and that incident had happened long ago.

"I don't like you there by yourself that late."

"I know," Sabre said and changed the subject. "Where are you?"

"Bob and I just left Ellesse and we're headed to a bar to follow up on Jim Jones."

"A bar?"

He told her what he had learned from Ellesse.

"See what you can find out, but keep in mind, he's not a party to this case yet."

"I can't stand the thought of that predator out there. He may think it's just a clever way to get laid, but if he's drugging them, it's really tantamount to rape. I'd like to pursue it."

"Do what you need to do," Sabre said. "I'm going to meet Ron at Pieology." She was hoping he would be able to join them, but she didn't say anything since he already had plans. "I'll talk to you tomorrow."

~~~

Ron was waiting outside of the restaurant when Sabre arrived. He was never one to go inside a building any sooner than he had to, unless it was to get away from the elements.

"Hi, Sis," the handsome blond man said when Sabre walked up. He gave her a quick hug.

They walked inside and got in the short line to order. Pieology had become one of their new favorite restaurants. It was a thin-crust pizza place that was set up like a Subway. You ordered the individual crust, wheat or white, and then went down the aisle picking whatever toppings you wanted. It started with the sauces and cheeses, then the vegetables, meats, and whatever else you might like. Everyone got the kind of pizza they wanted.

Sabre went first, and when she got to the cash register, she paid for both pizzas.

"You don't have to do that," Ron said.

"I know."

Sabre was concerned about Ron. He hadn't had a steady job since he returned to San Diego nearly a year ago, and she knew that was starting to get to him. He had worked a little for Sabre, and JP had given him some surveillance work on a couple of cases, but he didn't have that much for him to do. Ron was in his thirties and struggling to find his way in life. He loved the outdoors and had held a couple of good jobs with Parks and Recreation, but no one was hiring right now. He had applied everywhere he could think of, even out of state, but nothing yet. He was living with their mother, which was nice for both of them at first, but Sabre knew that was starting to get old.

Ron took the number the clerk gave them, and they sat down and waited for the pizzas to be delivered to their table.

"How's Mom?" Sabre asked.

"I don't see her that much. She's involved in so many things, volunteering for different organizations, playing bridge three times a week, and..." He hesitated.

"And what?"

"I think she might have a boy...male...friend."

"A boyfriend?"

"Yeah, it just seems weird calling someone that old a 'boy'."

"How old is he?"

"I don't know. I haven't met him, but I'm pretty sure she's interested in someone. She's acting different. She's been kind of giddy. And she takes more time getting ready for things."

"Mom always looks nice when she goes out, even to the grocery store. She wouldn't be caught dead at Target without her lipstick on."

"I know. It's not that. She'll change her clothes a couple of times, and she sings when she's doing things around the house, like she did when we were kids."

Sabre noticed trepidation in her brother's voice. "Ron, does this bother you? Because Dad has been gone a long time. I think it would be great if Mom found someone."

"No, it's not that." Ron's voice perked up. "I would love to see her with someone. It's just that I feel like I might be cramping her style."

Sabre laughed. The clerk brought the pizzas to their table. Sabre was still laughing when she left.

"It's not funny," Ron said. "At least not *that* funny."

"Really, Ron, it's not like she wants to bring him home and...." Sabre paused and looked up, her eyes wide. "Or maybe she does. She's not that old."

"I was thinking more along the lines of serving him dinner without her son looking over their shoulders. But there's that too."

Ron started laughing, and the conversation degenerated even more as they ate their dinner.

"That's our mother you're talking about," Ron finally said.

"And she would appreciate the humor."

"But I'm serious about not wanting to get in her way, especially if she has a chance at happiness."

"If you really think it's a problem, you could come live with me for a while. It's smaller than our old house, but I do have a guest room."

"What about JP?"

"He doesn't stay in the guest room." She smirked.

"No, you goofball, but then I'll be cramping your style."

"Not much style to cramp. Lately, we haven't seen much of each other."

Ron looked concerned. "Are you two fighting?"

"No, nothing like that," Sabre said. "We've both just been so busy and on different schedules. He was out of town a lot on that high-profile case and when he got back, I was up to my ears in alligators with mine."

"Don't screw this up, Sabre. He's a good guy."

Sabre knew what he meant. She had a hard time with commitment, but this wasn't that. At least, she didn't think it was. "What about your love life?"

No response.

They finished eating. As they walked out, Sabre didn't let him off the hook. "You didn't answer my question."

He talked as he walked her to her car. "I've had a few first dates. Nothing has led to a second. Mom set me up twice, but they both bombed. The first was ready to get married before we got through dessert. The second one had a girlfriend, which I figured out the minute we met, but Mom had no clue. We actually had a lot of fun. She's become a pretty good friend."

"Mom means well. Besides, you haven't done that well on your own."

"Seriously? Let's see, I've had three loves in my life: the first had mental issues, the second was married to a crazy man, and the third was a psychopathic killer." He threw his arm around Sabre, pulled her close to him and rubbed his knuckles on her head like he did when they were kids. "Apparently, I like crazies. Why do you think I'm so fond of you?"

"Sister abuse," Sabre said, laughing and pulling away. She got in her car and rolled down the window.

"Thanks for dinner," Ron said.

"My pleasure," Sabre said. "Give it some thought, Bro. My home will always be open to you. I'd love to have my big brother so close."

"I'll think about it."

Chapter 13

The Parker Case

Bob and JP sat at the bar in The Watering Hole watching for anyone who looked like Jim Jones. When JP ordered a Miller Genuine Draft, Bob said, "When did you start drinking that?"

"A few months back. A friend of mine had it at his house, and I kinda liked it. Want one?"

"Sure, I'll give it a try."

JP glanced around as they waited for the beer. There weren't more than a dozen people in the room. "It might be too early for this guy, even if he were to come back here."

"I think it was closer to midnight when Ellesse left with him," Bob said.

When the bartender brought the beers, JP pulled up the photo of Jim Jones that Bob had sent to him on his phone.

"Do you know this guy?" JP asked.

"Are you a cop?" the young bartender asked.

"No," JP said. "I think he's about to be a father, and I thought he might want to know."

The bartender gave him an odd look, but glanced at the photo. "It's hard to say, but it doesn't ring any bells. I don't usually work this late. I'm mostly on the day shift. I'm just waiting for Nigel to get here. He's the night bartender, but he's running late tonight."

"Any idea when he'll arrive?"

"Any time now," he said, and left to take another order.

JP and Bob visited as they perused the room. A slightly gray-haired man in his fifties stepped into the bar from the back. All of a sudden, the small crowd roared, "Nigel." JP looked around and saw they were all lifting their glasses to the bartender. He felt like he was in an episode of Cheers, and Norm had walked in the door.

Nigel waved both hands in the air. "Let the party begin," he said, and stepped behind the bar.

"I'm guessing that's Nigel," Bob said.

"Ya think?"

They waited until Nigel worked his way down the bar. Bob ordered vodka, but JP nursed his beer. When Nigel returned with Bob's drink, JP showed him the photo and gave him the same explanation he gave the other bartender, leading with the fact that he was not a cop.

Nigel studied the photo carefully. "Not a very good photo. It could be a lot of guys who come in here. He does look a little familiar, but unless he spends a lot of time up here at the bar, I'd probably not recognize him. Hold on, I'll ask Kathy." He walked down to the other end of the bar where the waitress was getting her orders. A few minutes later, a woman around forty, carrying a tray of drinks, walked up to JP.

"Let me get these drinks out before my tips get any lower. I'll be back."

JP watched the door as a few more customers came in, but no one looked like Jones.

Kathy returned within minutes, and JP showed her the photo.

"He looks familiar, but it may just be the sunglasses."

"Do you have a lot of people who come into the bar wearing sunglasses?"

"No, most of them remove them as soon as they walk in, but not this guy. He left them on the whole time."

"How long ago was that?" JP asked.

"He's a semi-regular. I've seen him maybe a half a dozen times, always with the sunglasses. He comes in trolling every couple of months."

"Does he usually leave with someone?"

"More than you can imagine," Kathy said. "You said he may have fathered a child. Was it consensual?"

This woman was no dummy, and there was no reason to lie to her. "We're not sure. Why do you ask?"

"Because he's creepy. I don't know why anyone would leave with him, but they do. Most of the time, they're pretty drunk. I'm not sure the women are in a state of mind to give consent by the time they leave, but what do I know?"

"Have you seen him lately?" JP asked.

Suddenly someone yelled, "Hey, we need some drinks over here."

"I have to go," she said. "It's been quite a while since I saw him last. At least a month." She started to walk away.

"Wait," JP said. He handed her his card and a twenty-dollar bill. "Thanks for your time. Please call me if you see him again."

She smiled. "Sure will."

JP turned to Bob. "I think we're done here, but if Jones comes in every few months, he probably doesn't live too far from here. Want to try another bar?"

"Sure, if you're buying."

"You used to live around here. What's the next closest place?"

"Peter D's. It's a karaoke bar; at least it used to be. Maybe we'll discover Jones sings like an angel."

"You're sick."

Peter D's was right up the street so within minutes they were in the bar. Bob was disappointed to find there was no karaoke blaring and the bar was pretty quiet. JP showed the photo to the bartender and the waitress, but neither was able to identify the man in the picture. The waitress did remember a guy coming in there with sunglasses and leaving them on.

"How long ago?" JP asked.

"A couple of months maybe. It was shortly after I started working here. I didn't think too much of it. I figured he had some eye surgery done or something, but then he came back about three weeks ago."

"Was he alone?"

"Yeah, both times."

"Did he leave with anyone?" JP asked.

"I don't remember the first time, but last time he did. It wasn't that late, but she was pretty wasted when they left."

"Had you served her a lot of alcohol?"

"Only a beer or two," she said defensively. "The boss is good about cutting people off who have had too much."

"I'm not suggesting you did anything wrong. I'm wondering about her state of mind."

"Like I said, she didn't order much from me, but it was karaoke night and it was busy, so I wasn't the only one serving. And she could've gotten it from the bar as well."

Bob and JP hit two more bars, both within three miles of the first one. No one recognized the man in the photo, but one bartender remembered a guy with sunglasses. He thought he'd been in there a few times, but he wasn't sure.

They continued east on Clairemont Mesa Boulevard until they reached JP's Pub in Tierrasanta.

"Look, they named a bar after you, JP," Bob said, his words a little thick. "Have you ever been here?"

"Nope."

"Me neither."

Bob ordered a drink. JP hadn't had anything since

the second bar, and he didn't finish that one. After they got the usual "I'm not a cop" business out of the way, he showed the photo. No one recognized him, but the waitress said, "He's a lousy tipper, I can tell you that."

"So you do remember him?" JP asked.

"No, but I would if he tipped good."

JP thanked her, tipped her well, and left his card.

"It's getting late, and the farther east we go, the less luck we have. I'll try the area just north and south of Clairemont Mesa another night."

On the way home, Bob asked, "How are things with Sabre?"

"Why? Did she say something?"

"Why are you so defensive? You haven't screwed this up, have you?"

"No," JP said.

"You'd better not, because she's my little buddy."

"It's just that we haven't had a lot of time together lately."

"Well, fix it."

Chapter 14

The Lynch Case

JP got up early on Saturday morning, and after spending a little time researching Todd Lynch and mapping out his stops, he drove to Pasadena. Before he left, he made sure Louie had enough food and water for the long day. He hated to leave the dog behind, but he was going to the city and wasn't sure what he would encounter. At the very least, Louie would be stuck in the car too long.

Lynch was a salesman for Xerox and made decent money. Other than his aggressiveness in the courthouse toward Sabre, and his ex-wife complaining about his unstable behavior, JP knew little about him. According to the social study by the Department, he had no criminal record, no earlier marriages or children by previous relationships, and no family other than his mother, who also lived in Pasadena, and an estranged older brother who'd had no contact with either Todd or his mother for over five years. The last Todd knew, Ian Lynch lived on the streets somewhere in Orange County.

JP had made a couple of appointments with people Todd had listed as "friends." Usually, people only gave names of those they expected to speak highly of them, but JP had discovered that sometimes it didn't work out that way. He found that was especially true of those with inflated egos who thought everyone saw them in the same light as they saw themselves. Lynch struck him as one of those guys, so maybe he would get lucky and get some valid information.

JP was a little early for his first appointment, so he stopped at an Arco gas station and bought himself a cup of coffee. He arrived at the house at 9:28, close enough. He was welcomed into the home of Bill and Sandy Winston, who were both very cordial.

"How do you know Todd?" JP asked, although he already knew.

"I've worked with him for about six years, and we socialize as well," Bill said. "He's a good worker, one of the top salesmen in our department."

JP turned to Sandy. "So you know Todd as well?"

"Yes," Sandy said.

"And do you know his ex-wife, Heather?"

"Yes, we used to spend a lot of time together," Sandy said. "We have two boys about the same ages, and we used to do a lot of family stuff with them, until Heather stole the kids and left."

"Is that what Todd told you?"

"Oh, we know what happened," Sandy continued. "She got into drugs. Sometimes, she wouldn't show up when we had things planned, but Todd would bring the boys and come anyway."

"Do you know why she didn't show up?"

"He always told us she wasn't feeling well, but later he told us the truth—that she was already using drugs. It's a shame."

"I know Todd is a good friend, but I need to ask you this. Does he have a temper?"

Bill and Sandy exchanged glances, then Bill spoke. "Not so much."

"Have you ever seen him get angry?"

"I saw him blow up once at a guy at work, but he had it coming. Todd didn't hit him or anything, just shouted at him. Before you ask, I don't remember what it was about, but I remember that at the time, I felt it was justified."

"What about you, Sandy?"

She squirmed a little. "I've never seen him totally

lose it. Maybe raise his voice at the kids or at Heather. That's about it."

"Have you ever seen him spank the boys?"

"No. He's a good father. He's very strict and they don't ever defy him. They could get away with a lot more with their mom, but not Todd. They listen to him."

JP left there not really knowing anything more than before. He wanted to find some dirt on this guy because of his verbal attack on Sabre, but he didn't want that to cloud his judgment. He decided to cut Todd some slack and try to be more objective. It would make for better investigation.

Next stop was Todd's mother, Grandma Lynch, a large woman in her early seventies. She wasn't quite as friendly as the previous stop. She did not invite him inside, and her first question was "Does Todd know you're here?"

"I'm not sure, ma'am. I work for the attorney who represents his children. I'm here on their behalf."

"Why do the kids have an attorney? That's just silly. I suppose Todd will have to pay for that too."

"The children have an attorney to make sure their rights are protected and that they are safe."

"What rights do they have? They're kids. Their father will take care of them and keep them safe."

It was useless to try to explain any further. "I understand Todd wants the children placed here with you. Is that what you want?"

"Of course, if that's what Todd wants, then I'm good with that." Her large stature and her gruff voice didn't make her seem very "grandmotherly."

"Do *you* want the boys here, ma'am?"

"I don't understand why they aren't with their father. That's where they should be."

"And if they can't be with their father right now, do you want them to stay with you?"

"Well, of course. They won't be any trouble. Todd will make sure they stay in line. He always does."

He didn't bother to explain that Todd wouldn't be able to live there without agreement from the court. He decided to leave that up to the social worker, assuming it became a viable option, which he didn't think was likely.

"Is he strict with the boys?"

"No more than any other decent parent. He's a good father, and he's a good son."

"Does he ever hit the children?"

"He spanks them sometimes, I suppose. I don't know. They listen to him. He doesn't have to do much. They show him respect. That no-good wife of his was the problem."

They were still standing at the front door, and JP was anxious to get this over with, but he had a few more questions.

"Does Todd have any other family in southern California?"

"Just his brother, but he wouldn't take the kids. He don't even come to see his own mother."

"Why is that, ma'am?"

"Because he's too much like his good-for-nothing father. That's why." She stared at JP for a few seconds. "But I don't think that's any of your business, young man."

"You're probably right," JP said. "Thank you for your time."

Chapter 15

The Lynch Case

Before JP left Pasadena, he decided to talk to some of Todd's neighbors. He would have to canvass the neighborhood because he didn't have any names. That was always tricky, because he couldn't divulge much about the case or why he was there. He had to be especially careful this time because he knew if Todd got wind of his actions, he would surely make an issue of it.

JP drove past Todd's house. He didn't see a car in the driveway, but it was likely in the garage if he was home. He parked across the street and walked to the house directly across from Todd's. They had the best view of the Lynch house. He rang the doorbell.

A woman around fifty-five answered the door, holding her purse and keys.

"Are you Heather Lynch?" JP asked.

"No, you have the wrong house. Her house is directly across the street." She pointed to the Lynch house.

"That's odd. I was there a couple of days ago, and the gentleman there told me I had the wrong house. I thought maybe there was a typo in the address."

"No, you had the right house, but I don't think she lives there anymore."

"Dang!" JP said. "I work for a trust and estates attorney, and we need to find her for an inheritance. You wouldn't happen to know where she moved to, would you?"

"No, but I'm sure her husband does."

"Where can I find him?"

She pointed across the street again. "He still lives

there. They're going through a divorce."

JP nodded his head. "That would explain why he didn't want to talk to me. He acted like he didn't even know her."

"I don't think the divorce has been too amicable. She took the three boys and left him. It's been a lot quieter over there since then."

"I suppose three boys can be kind of loud."

"It wasn't that. I hardly ever heard the boys when Todd was around. They were too afraid of him to be disruptive. Todd yelled a lot, sometimes at the boys, but mostly at Heather."

"Do you know Todd very well?"

"Not really. He seems friendly enough when we come into contact, but he likes to keep to himself."

"What about Heather?"

"I knew her better. We weren't best friends or anything, but we've been in each other's houses a few times, mostly just neighborly stuff."

"Did Todd and Heather have any physical altercations that you're aware of?" He tried to just sound curious since this was way off the issue of the inheritance. She didn't seem to notice.

"I never saw any, but the curtains were always closed when Todd was home, and he's way too smart to take a fight outside where others could see. If I were her, I would've left a long time ago." She paused. "You don't suppose she knew she was getting an inheritance and thought she could make it on her own, do you?"

"I doubt that she knew about it. And if she did, I would expect she would've made sure we knew where she was."

"Good point."

JP gave her his card. "If you see her or the boys, could you please give me a call? Or if anything unusual happens at that house, I'd like to know."

"You don't think he'd hurt her, do you?"

"Let's just say I have some concerns. But I've taken enough of your time and it appears as if you were on your way out."

"It's fine. I was just running to the grocery store."

"Thank you, ma'am." He started to step away and then turned in Colombo fashion. "If you don't mind, I'd appreciate it if you didn't say anything to Todd about my visit."

"No, of course not. There's no reason for me to."

JP walked to his car and sat there acting like he was on the phone until the woman drove away. Then he visited the homes on either side of the Lynch house. No one answered the door on the left. The couple on the right were retired and had lived in the neighborhood for forty-plus years. They told JP the Lynch family had lived there for about four years and told him a story similar to what he had already heard. Todd yelled a lot and the kids seemed intimidated by him. They were much more relaxed around their mother. Neither of them had seen any physical altercations between Todd and Heather.

He walked to a couple more houses in each direction, but didn't obtain any more information, either because they didn't know the Lynches, or because no one was home. The house on the corner at the end of the street, he soon discovered, was occupied by a couple, Andrew and Marilyn LaFiura, and their two children, a boy and a girl. Only Mrs. LaFiura was home, but she knew the Lynch family better than some of the others. Instead of posing as the investigator for the trust and estates attorney, JP decided to try the divorce angle. It made it easier to ask more questions about the children. It was risky, though, because if she favored one party over the other, especially the father, JP was unlikely to get much information. As it turned out, she did not think much of Todd.

"The middle boy, Drew, was best friends with my son Andrew, who was named after his father." Marilyn gave a slight laugh. "We call our son Drew as well, but whenever the other Drew was around, we called our son Andrew. Actually, their Drew was named Drew, not Andrew, so it was only fair to call him by his name and use the more formal one with my son."

"So you saw a lot of Drew Lynch?"

"Yes, he came here all the time and Andrew went to his house. Of course, I met the parents before I let Andrew go over there. I always do that. They seemed normal enough, and the boys have been growing up together. They moved here shortly after we did, so I've known them for, I don't know, four or five years. Let me think. Andrew was three, or was he four? No, he was three. He recently turned eight. But they moved here in the summer. I remember because it was pretty hot. Yeah, I've known them about four years."

JP thought she'd never stop talking, but he didn't try to stop her. Even though she was mostly talking nonsense, she might say something that was helpful. JP was about to ask another question when she started talking again.

"I feel bad for Drew. You know they're going through a divorce, right?" She waved her hand in the air dismissively. "Of course you do. That's why you're here, right?" She didn't wait for an answer. "Heather left him six months or so ago. The divorce may even be final by now. My, how the time flies."

When she finally stopped talking, JP asked, "You feel bad for Drew because of the divorce?"

"Yes, and no. He didn't want to leave this neighborhood, but he's better off with his mother. After a while, I only let Andrew go to that house when the father wasn't home. They could play here any time, as far as I was concerned, but when Drew's father was home, he expected the boys to be home too. I guess that's good in some ways. You know, family bonding and all, but Andrew says they didn't really spend the time together. So I'm not sure what his problem was. Andrew says the father is real mean. Andrew is afraid of him." She quickly added, "So is Drew."

"What did Mr. Lynch do to them?"

"He never did anything to Andrew. I wouldn't have put up with that. I would've had him in court so fast, his head would spin. No one touches my children."

"Did he do something to Drew?"

"Not that Andrew ever said, but he must have done something because he scared those boys. Andrew says he yelled all the time."

Chapter 16

The Lynch Case

Sabre was on the road, making home visits to her minor clients, something she did almost every Saturday. She carried a case load of nearly 450 active cases. Most of those were in the review stages, so they didn't require as much attention, but she still needed to visit the minors to make sure everything was okay. She had just finished her third visit when she received a phone call from her brother.

"Can you come to dinner tonight at Mom's?" Ron asked.

"I don't know. Why? What's up?"

"I want to ask her about the boyfriend."

"So do it already. You don't need me."

"You're better at this than I am. Besides, it's been a while since you saw Mom. You should visit her more often."

"Enough with the guilt trip," she paused. "I guess I can. JP's in Pasadena on a case and I haven't heard from him yet, but I expect he'll be home late."

"I'll tell Mom. She'll make us something good."

"You haven't talked to her yet?"

"No, but I will."

"How do you know she isn't going out?"

"She's not. I'll just tell her there'll be one more for dinner."

"Ron, you're impossible. If she doesn't feel like cooking, tell her I'll take us out to dinner."

Sabre hung up and drove to the foster home of the youngest Lynch boy, Evan. She hated that the boys weren't all placed in the same home, but at least the two older ones were together, and it appeared that their home might have an opening soon. It was the best she could hope for. It wasn't easy finding a placement for three or more at the same time. Foster homes were scarce, and finding two openings in the same house was a victory in itself.

Five-year-old Evan Lynch was a cute little towhead with a good disposition, but at the moment he looked sad. He sat on the floor in the room he shared with another foster child, playing with Legos. He had built a tower about a foot high.

"Great job. You're good at that." She touched it. "And it's nice and sturdy. Do you have Legos at home?"

"Yeah. I had a lot at my dad's house. He said he'd get me more if I came home with him."

Sabre tried not to react to the father's bribery attempt. It was, however, a good segue into her next question. She chose her words carefully so she didn't give him false hope. She had learned over the years that if you asked kids what they "wanted," they assumed you could get it for them. So instead she asked, "Did you like living with your dad?"

He shrugged. "I miss my mom. When can I go home?"

"I don't know yet. We're trying to sort it all out. Your mom needs some help right now."

"Is she sick?"

"She needs some treatment, but she's getting help." Then Sabre added, "Did you have a visit with her yesterday?"

"Yeah. She came here and played with me. I cried when she left, but she wouldn't take me with her. I promised I'd be good."

Sabre's heart ached for the little boy and her anger mounted against the parents. She didn't know which one she was angrier at, the overbearing father or the druggie mother. She wished parents would put their children first before their own needs and desires. *Why do they have children if they're not willing to take care of them?*

"Things will get better." That's all she could think of to say. Then she remembered she had set up a visit with his brothers. "How would you like to see Nolan and Drew?"

His eyes lit up, and his lips turned up at the corners in a hesitant smile. He nodded.

"I've made arrangements for you to go to the park with them tomorrow."

A full smile crossed his face as he went back to his Legos.

~~~

When Sabre saw the other Lynch boys, she wished even more that an opening would come up soon so they could all be together. She spoke to the boys separately, starting with Nolan, the nine-year-old. He was average height for his age and had blond hair, but not as light as Evan's. He was more sullen than the other two boys, and seemed to share some of his father's temper, but for the most part he was well-behaved. The foster mother told her Nolan got into a fight with another boy in the home when he first came, but things had settled down and they pretty much kept away from each other.

"Are you doing okay here in this foster home?"

"It's been alright. The foster parents aren't mean or anything. They're kind of nice actually. Bobby's kind of a pain."

"Who is Bobby?"

"He's another foster kid. He's ten, and he's been here for eight months. He thinks he's the boss around here because he's been here the longest. But he says he's going home next week. I can't wait."

"That's what I heard. We're trying to get Evan placed here if Bobby leaves. What do you think of that?"

Nolan looked pleased. "That would be good. Evan can be a pain sometimes. He would always butt in when I had friends over, but now I kinda miss having him around."

"Are you and Drew getting along okay?"

"Yeah, he's no problem most of the time. Besides, he's smarter than me, and he helps me with my homework."

"I understand you saw your father a couple of days ago. How did that go?"

"Alright. He asked us if we wanted to come to Pasadena and live with him."

"What did you say?"

He hesitated. "I said I'd rather stay with Mom, and he got real mad. His face turned red, and he did this." Nolan clasped his hands together and held them tight in front of him. Sabre wondered what that was about, but before she could ask, Nolan said, "Drew didn't say anything right away. Then Dad looked at him and asked him again. Drew almost started crying, but then he said he wanted to live with Dad."

"What did your dad do then?"

"He asked me again, like he was giving me a chance to change my mind."

"Did you?"

"I told him I wanted to go home with him, but I don't really. But you can't tell anybody, because Dad will be real mad. Drew doesn't want to live with him either. He told me later he was too afraid to say no."

"But you both told the social worker yesterday that you wanted to live with your father."

"I know, 'cause Dad said to tell her."

"Why don't you want to live with him?"

"He's too scary."

"Does he hit you?"

"Not really."

"What do you mean, 'not really'?" Sabre asked.

"Sometimes he gives us a swat, but it doesn't hurt that much."

"How does he punish you when you do something wrong?"

"We don't do anything wrong around Dad. We just have to do what he says, and everything is okay."

Sabre wanted to ask why he obeyed without question, but she was afraid it would sound like she was encouraging them to not listen to their father. Normal kids questioned their parents; why didn't these boys? She wondered what it was exactly that made these children act the way they did, and why they didn't want to live with their father. All anyone had ever reported was that he yelled a lot, but the boys seemed so afraid of him. She hoped JP came up with something that would be helpful one way or the other.

When she spoke to Drew, he gave her the same scenario, and couldn't really express why he didn't want to live with his father, but he was sure he didn't.

Sabre called JP on her way to her last minor visit.

"Hey, kid. I was about to call you. I'm just leaving Pasadena. Can I take you to dinner tonight? Something romantic would be nice."

"I'm sorry, JP. I just made plans with my brother. I didn't expect you back until late."

"It went quicker than I expected."

"We're meeting at my mom's. I'd drag you along, but Ron seems to think Mom has a boyfriend, and we're going to ask her about it. She may not want to tell us as much if you're there."

"No problem." He didn't want to show his disappointment, not about joining a family dinner, but that he and Sabre wouldn't have some time alone. "I feel like I have one wheel down and my axle is draggin' anyway. I'll just go home and catch up on a little well-deserved rest."

Chapter 17

Sabre rang the doorbell, and then started to use her key to open her mother's door. Ron was there before she could get it open.

"Hi, Mom," Sabre said, as she approached her mother to give her a hug. Her mother, Beverly, looked like something out of a 1950's television sitcom, like June Cleaver without the pearls. She always dressed, combed her hair, and put on her lipstick before she made breakfast, and freshened up before dinner. She maintained that if you looked good first thing in the morning, you would feel better all day long. "Besides," she would say, "you never know who might drop in on you."

Neither Ron nor Sabre had picked up that habit, but in her adult life, Sabre did follow in her mother's footsteps when it came to making her bed when she first arose and never leaving dirty dishes in the kitchen sink. Her mother convinced her that she would feel so much better if her room didn't look messy every time she entered it. And if she fixed her bed first thing, she would have a feeling of accomplishment right off, making the rest of her day more productive. Sabre struggled with it during her teen years, and often had to spend hours on Saturday cleaning her room instead of going out and having fun. Ron, on the other hand, was always a bit of a neat freak.

"Thanks for coming, Sabey," her mother said.

A familiar aroma filled the air, and Sabre sucked it in. "Mom, you made pot roast."

"I know it's your favorite, so when Ron told me you were coming, I ran to the store and got the roast and carrots. I already had potatoes."

Beverly patted her daughter's arm. "I'm sure you're too busy to make it for yourself."

"Too busy?" Ron said with a guffaw. "She'd have to know how to make it first. Sabre thinks her kitchen is for the sole purpose of making tea, and she uses an electric pot for that because she burned up too many teakettles." He looked at Sabre. "Have you ever used that new stove of yours?"

Ron had been teasing her since she was born, and she had learned to not let it get to her. "Yeah, I used it once when I entertained the Pope. He never came back for a second meal. I wonder why."

"I'm sure you're a good cook, Sabey. I tried to teach you when you were young."

"I know you did, Mom, but if you remember right, I usually got out of it. Ron was the one who learned to cook. Besides, I do just fine cooking for myself. It's not as bad as Ron makes it sound."

"I'm sure it's not, dear." Their mother sighed. "Ahh, it's good to have you both here with me."

As Sabre set the table, she felt a little guilty for not making the effort to spend more time with her mother. Their relationship had been a little strained ever since her teen years, and when her father died, it got worse. Sabre was busy, and her mother was very involved in her community, making lack of time a convenient excuse to not get together. A few years ago, Sabre made a greater effort and things had gotten better. Now that Ron was home again, she had kind of slacked off. Sabre was grateful to Ron for picking up the slack. It made it easier, but still, she needed to try a little harder.

Ron went to the kitchen with his mother, and they returned with the pot roast, vegetables, and hot, homemade rolls.

"It all smells so good, Mom."

"Ron made the rolls," she said proudly.

As they sat at the table eating, Ron caught Sabre's eye and nodded his head toward his mother. She knew he wanted her to bring up the subject of the boyfriend.

"So, Mom, what's new with you?"

"Nothing really."

"How are you spending your days?"

"The usual, playing bridge and helping out at the women's shelter. They've started a high-end thrift store, and the profit all goes back into the shelter. I'm volunteering there one day a week."

"And how's your bridge game?" Sabre asked. Ron was pretty sure it was bridge that had brought the man into her life, so she pursued it further.

"It's been good. Shirley and I have been in a few tournaments, in which we did quite well."

"Do you have any other bridge partners?"

"Just Millie. She fills in when Shirley can't make it."

"Are you meeting any new people at your bridge games?"

Beverly looked curiously at Sabre and asked, "Are you that uncomfortable?"

"What?" Sabre said. "No."

"Why are you trying to make small talk? I thought we had moved past all that. I'm sure our table conversations will move along just fine without the artificial questioning."

"I'm sorry, Mom. It's not that."

Ron cut in. "Sabre wants to know if you have a boyfriend."

Sabre glared at Ron. "*I* want to know? You were the one who said you thought Mom was seeing someone and you didn't want to cramp her style."

Ron and Sabre shot accusations back and forth until their mother interrupted them. "Yes, I'm seeing someone. Is that okay with you two?"

Silence filled the room for a few seconds, then Ron said, "Of course, Mom."

"Yes, Mom, if you want to start dating, you should. You've been alone long enough," Sabre said. "Is he from your bridge game?"

"No."

"Where did you meet him?" Ron asked.

Beverly hesitated.

"Mom, where did you meet him?" Sabre said.

"The internet."

"The internet?" Sabre shrieked. Then, as she turned to Ron, her hands flew out, palms up in a gesture of disbelief. "Mom is seeing some guy she met on the internet, and you didn't even know it was going on? He could be a rapist or a con man or who knows. What's the matter with you?"

"What's your point?" Ron asked. "Even if she met him at a bridge game, he could still be a rapist or a con man."

"Calm down," her mother said. "I met him on Match.com. A lot of people my age are doing it. We've met for coffee a couple of times. He seems perfectly normal, except for that skull and prison number he has tattooed on his forehead." Sabre's mouth dropped open. Ron stared at his mother. "But I think he got that last year in the juvenile facility. He's old enough now for real prison, but he doesn't plan to go back any time soon. I think we may be in love."

Sabre and Ron burst out laughing, and their mother joined them. Sabre wasn't sure what was more surprising, that her mother had a male interest, or that she made a joke about it. She was always so serious, especially after their father died. It was nice to see her laughing and joking again.

"Tell us about him, Mom."

She described him physically and told them about

the two times they had met. "He is sixty-five years old and owns his own real estate company. He's a widower with three grown children. His son is a lawyer. His oldest daughter is a school teacher, and his youngest daughter is in college. Oh, and he has a nephew who is a priest. Other than that, there isn't much to tell. We're just getting to know each other. But I'm having fun."

"Have there been others?" Sabre asked.

"I've had lots of winks, or hits, or whatever you call them, but after a few email exchanges, I knew they weren't for me. Harley is the only one I've actually met."

"He sounds harmless, but all that could be a cover."

"Sabre, his nephew is a priest."

"Yeah, but his son is a lawyer, so that's kind of a wash, isn't it?" Ron said.

"You're so funny." Sabre sneered at him. "So, it's either the truth, or he's good at what he does. The priest thing would be a nice touch, if he's a con man. Did he tell you that before or after he knew you were Catholic?"

Beverly thought for a second. "After, but—"

"What's his name? I'm going to have JP do a background check on him."

"Is that really necessary? He's a very nice man."

"Just let her check it out, Mom," Ron said. "It can't hurt. If he's for real, he'll never know she looked into his background. If it's a scam, he'll be sorry he picked you to run it on."

Beverly acquiesced. "But don't take too long. I'm seeing him next Friday."

Chapter 18

The Fowler Case

The Square With God Church, where Reverend Fowler was pastor, was small but nearly full at the Sunday morning service. JP sat on the side end of a pew, three rows from the back, trying to look inconspicuous. Uncomfortable in his suit and without his hat, he thought about how long it had been since he attended a church service other than a wedding or a funeral. It wasn't that he didn't believe in God, he truly did, and he had attended church every Sunday all throughout his childhood. Once he left home and joined the Marines, he stopped going. He stopped doing a lot of things he *had* to do when he lived at home.

JP watched the people and tried to pick out those who might talk to him. He expected he would only get one chance at this. He was sure he wouldn't be welcome once Fowler found out who he was, and that he was asking questions. He felt a little bit guilty sitting in a house of God while he plotted his investigation, but he couldn't think of another way to find out who attended the church, and he needed to talk to them. He reached for the church missal in the cubbyhole on the back of the pew in front of him. When he pulled it out, he discovered a church bulletin. *Of course*, he thought. *Why didn't I think of that?* He hadn't even checked for a website. He chastised himself for not looking for one, but he normally didn't equate church with the internet. He might have been able to avoid this whole trip. He sat back and listened to the sermon.

JP left the church as soon as the service ended so he would be outside when the others came out. He thought it might give him a chance to meet a few parishioners. He stood back a little and watched, then stepped forward as a young woman whom he guessed to be about twenty approached.

"Good morning," JP said.

"Good morning." She stared for a second. "Are you new to our church?"

"Yes, it's my first time. I don't really know anyone here. I'm John Phillips." He used his first and middle name, which he often did when he didn't want to give his full name.

"I'm Lucy Jennings. It's nice to meet you."

A heavy set man and a short, thin woman approached. "You ready, Lucy?" the man said.

"Yes, I was just talking to John. He's new to our church." She turned back to JP. "This is my mom and dad."

JP reached out his hand. "Nice to meet you."

The man reciprocated. "Welcome to our church. I'm Victor and this is Linda. We'd like to visit a while, but I'm afraid we're in a hurry. Maybe next Sunday."

"No problem," JP said.

"Come on, Lucy," Victor said.

Most of the people had exited the church. Some were standing around talking and others were leaving. JP looked around, trying to figure out which one was Lester Gibbs. Just as he thought he had spotted him, Pastor Fowler came out. JP turned and slipped away, but before he reached the parking lot, the Jennings family passed him in a white Toyota. He memorized the license plate, and then jotted it down when he got to his car.

~~~

Back at his office, JP called his deputy sheriff friend, Ernie Madrigal, and asked him to run the plate. Then he glanced through the church bulletin looking for names of members. He started a list of people to investigate later. He found a website for the church, which consisted of two pages. The home page had a photo and a short bio of Seth Fowler, the church location, and the times for the services. The other page was a blog page that appeared to have a number of contributors. A few posts had a byline of Seth Fowler, but mostly they seemed to be written by younger members. They wrote about coming events such as baptisms, weddings, and fundraisers. Often there were posts after the events, depicting their success. JP perused the posts, looking for the wedding of Lester Gibbs and Mary Margaret Fowler, but there was no entry.

JP jotted down the name of each person who had written a post. The only one he recognized, besides Seth Fowler, was Linda Jennings, Lucy's mother, but he had a list of about fifteen names with which to work. After looking around the blog, JP discovered there was an editorial staff that consisted of Seth Fowler, Linda Jennings, and Miles Cunningham. The name Cunningham sounded familiar to him, so he looked through the social worker's report for witnesses or people the Fowlers had mentioned. The only person Seth and Candace Fowler had talked about, outside the immediate family, was Lester Gibbs, but Mary Margaret talked about her best friend, Penny Cunningham.

JP got up and fixed himself a sandwich before he started the boring task of searching for information about the people on his list. He started with Google, which would lead him to the person's social media connections, if they had any. If they had a business, that usually showed up. If the name was unusual, it was a lot easier. The job was laborious and time-consuming, and he hated sitting that long at the computer.

A few hours later, JP had a workable list with enough information to at least begin some interviews. Over half of his original list had no social media connections or Google entries of any kind, which he found unusual. His final list contained an elementary school principal; a nurse at a convalescent home who was on Google because she made the news when she saved several patients during a flood; a young woman who was a student at Mesa Community College and very active on Facebook and Twitter; and the owner of a dry-cleaning business. JP had enough information to find these people, hopefully, learn something about Fowler and/or Gibbs, or lead him to someone who could give him some insight. He decided to start with the student who was on social media. She seemed the easiest because she posted so much personal information. *These kids have no idea how vulnerable they make themselves,* he thought.

JP knew from her recent posts that she was going to be studying at The Forum Coffee House for the next couple of hours. It was the perfect place for an accidental meeting. He called Sabre on the drive over.

"Hey, kid. I'm on my way to a coffee shop to see one of the Square With God Church members." He explained about his list, and how he found her. "I also came across the name 'Miles Cunningham.' Do you know if he is related to Mary Margaret's friend, Penny?"

"Yes, he is. Her father and her brother are both named Miles. I have an appointment tomorrow evening to see Penny. Do you want to come with me? Maybe you can talk to Miles."

"That works. Any chance we can get together this evening?"

"Oh, I would love to, but I have a nasty hearing

tomorrow I really need to work on. How about dinner after our interview tomorrow?"

"That would be fine," JP said. He pulled into The Forum parking lot and went inside. The shop hadn't been open very long, but the owners had done a good job of making it inviting. It was a rectangular room with black pillars covered with comments written in white. One wall, the length of the room, was covered with more interesting "coffee quotes." He saw a sign on the side of the bar that read "Life Happens, Coffee Helps." There was plenty of seating, spaced well, and free Wi-Fi, which attracted students.

Sharon Droppo was easy to spot from her photos on Facebook. She sat by herself at a table toward the back of the room. JP bought a cup of coffee and strode back to a table as close as he could get to her and took a seat. Since it was Sunday, he was surprised by the number of students in the shop studying. He looked around at all the patrons with laptops, and it made him feel a little naked.

After a few minutes, he caught Sharon's eye. "I see you're studying, and I don't mean to be rude, but don't you attend the Square With God Church?"

She looked at him with a blank face. "Yes, but I don't remember seeing you at any services."

"I'm new to the church. I only know a few people so far. I met Lucy Jennings and her parents this morning after the service. I'm trying to make some new friends, people with good, moral beliefs."

"Lucy is a good friend of mine. Her parents are real nice too. They'd be good people for you to get to know. They're both very active in the church. Mr. Jennings is in construction, and he has helped fix a lot of things around there. Mrs. Jennings is very active on our church blog. She writes a lot of posts, edits the others, and is very diligent about not letting any inappropriate comments get posted."

JP gave her a puzzling look. "What do you mean, inappropriate? Like bad language or something?"

She sighed. "Some of us who write the blog are a little more forward-thinking than others, and the pastor doesn't like to see that sort of thing posted. Mrs. Jennings is the gatekeeper."

"So you're one of the writers?"

"Yes."

"And I take it by your comments that you've been censored before?"

"Censored is a harsh word. She's just doing her job." She gave a little laugh. "Who else have you met?"

"I know Pastor Fowler and his family. I know Lester Gibbs." JP watched her face when he said his name. There was an obvious twitch of her mouth and neck, so he pushed it. "I don't know how to put this, because it makes me a little uncomfortable." He paused. "Is it true that the pastor's daughter just got married to Mr. Gibbs? She seems so young."

"It's true."

"Was she betrothed at birth or something?"

"I don't think so."

"I really like the tenets of this church," JP said, "but that seems kind of odd to me."

"A lot of the members were concerned about it, but they figure the pastor was guided by the Lord, and he had good reason for giving his blessing."

"You said 'they;' does that mean you don't agree?"

"It's not my place to question it. But please don't judge the church by that one thing. No one else has gotten married in the church that young." She hesitated. "Except the pastor and his wife. She was pretty young, I guess."

Chapter 19

The Fowler Case

JP looked at his list. Since it was Sunday, the school principal wasn't in, and the dry cleaner was closed. He didn't know where to find the Jennings family. He would see Cunningham tomorrow with Sabre. That left the nurse at the convalescent home and Lester. He decided to start with the nurse, if he could catch her at work.

The familiar smell of the aged, mixed with medicine, urine, and rubbing alcohol, permeated the air as JP stepped into the home. He had been in nursing homes that didn't smell like that, but they housed the wealthy. There was something degrading about the places where so many of the elderly had to spend the last days of their lives. It bothered him as he walked to the desk and asked for Susan Olson.

The young woman at the desk said, "I'll check to see if she's here and available. Who should I say is asking for her?"

"JP Torn."

"Please have a seat. I'll check." She left and returned about five minutes later.

"She's with a patient right now, but she'll be out as soon as she's finished."

While JP waited, he picked up a Time magazine from the end table. The cover had a photo of Muhammad Ali when he was in his prime. It was a commemorative edition depicting the life of an icon, dated June, 2016. He read the article and then flipped through some of the other magazines. They were all at least a year old, and most of the news in Newsweek was no longer news. All that remained were entertainment magazines, in which he had no interest.

Approximately a half-hour later, a thirty-something woman in purple scrubs appeared.

"You must be JP Torn," she said. "Sorry to keep you waiting. I had a patient who needed more than I anticipated."

"No problem. Thanks for seeing me."

"What can I do for you?"

JP noticed the clerk eyeing them. It was probably the most interesting, or at least the most unusual thing, she had witnessed this evening. "Is there somewhere we can talk that's a little more private?"

"What's this about?"

"I'm a private investigator—"

Before JP could say any more, she said, "There's a conference room we can use." She led him down the hall.

The conference room looked more like a lounge with a sofa and a couple of armchairs. JP wondered what was in her past that made her not want the clerk to hear.

They sat down, and JP continued. "I work for an attorney and I have a few questions."

"About me?"

"No, about someone you know. It's a confidential case, so I can't say too much, but it has to do with Lester Gibbs and Mary Margaret Fowler."

She let out an obvious sigh of relief, then composed herself.

"What about them?"

"You know them both, right?"

"Yes, they go to my church. But I don't know either of them that well. You'd probably do better asking someone else."

"Perhaps, later, you can give me the names of those who might be more knowledgeable, but for now, if you could just tell me what you know, I'd appreciate it."

"Like what?"

"Did you know they got married?"

"I heard that."

"But you didn't know beforehand they were planning to marry?"

"No, and neither did he, apparently."

"What do you mean?"

"He asked me out a week or so before the wedding."

"Did you go out with him?"

She wrinkled her face and shuddered. "No, I've always found him a little creepy. Now, I think he's despicable."

"So you don't approve of the marriage?"

"She's twelve," she said, as if that said it all, and as far as JP was concerned, it did.

"Do other church members feel the same way?"

"Most of them won't say anything about it or about Pastor Fowler giving his consent, but I don't think anyone supports it. I'm sure he knew that too, because the wedding was done quickly and quietly."

"Do you know anyone who witnessed the wedding?"

"I haven't heard who was there. It was announced after the fact—the next Sunday during services."

"There was no other discussion about it from the pulpit?"

"No. I was in the rotation to write the blog for the church website. I wrote an 'opinion' piece, but it was never posted. I wasn't really surprised, but I couldn't write something celebrating their marriage."

"Did you report it to CPS?"

"No." She looked down at her feet. "But I should have." She glanced back up at JP. "Is that what this is about? Did someone report them?"

"I can't really discuss that, and I would appreciate it if you wouldn't say anything to other church members until we've had a chance to investigate."

"I won't."

"By the way," JP said, "do you know if there is anyone else I could talk to who might have known about the wedding before it happened?"

"No, unless Mary Margaret told them. I have to wonder if she even knew before it happened."

"What about Lucy Jennings or her parents?"

She opened her mouth in surprise. "Do you know them?"

"I met them at church this morning. I went there to see what it was like, and to see if I could get some information. I don't remember seeing you there."

"I didn't attend. I haven't been back since the wedding announcement." She raised her voice. "Don't get me wrong; it's a good church with a lot of good people. I believe in the tenets of the church. And I know that according to the Bible, girls were married very young, but things were different then. I still don't think it's right today, and I have some soul searching to do."

"Do you know where I can find the Jennings?"

"Of course. Lucy works at the Starbucks in Fashion Valley, but they're always so busy, I doubt you'd be able to talk to her at work. Mr. Jennings works for some big construction company, not sure which one. Mrs. Jennings doesn't work outside the home, but she does a lot of volunteer work for the church. She's on the editing staff for the blog." She hesitated.

"Is she the one who stopped your blog entry?"

"Yes, and the one Sharon Droppo wrote after mine. I don't think Mrs. Jennings agreed with the marriage, but she'd never say anything against the pastor, so I can't be sure. I think she didn't approve of our posts because she didn't want any church scandal. She's very protective of the church."

Chapter 20

The Fowler Case

JP sat outside the principal's office, a scene he had played only a few times in his youth. More often than not, it was his brother, Gene, who would be there. JP ruminated on the many times he had seen his brother sitting outside the office. On more than one, occasion it was because Gene got in a fight protecting JP. *How things had changed.*

A man with gray hair, mustache, and beard approached. "I'm Donald McGill," he said, extending his hand.

Looking up at him, he seemed so big and intimidating. JP's childhood feelings welled up. Once he stood up and shook his hand, the principal shrank to his five-foot-nine inches.

"Nice to meet you," JP said.

McGill led him to his office. Once inside, he said, "I understand you're a private investigator. Does this have something to do with one of my students?"

JP took a seat where the principal had gestured. "No. It's about a couple of members of the Square With God Church. I understand you attend that church as well."

"I do," he said guardedly.

"I work for an attorney who is representing Mary Margaret Fowler."

McGill sighed.

JP was sure the principal understood that CPS was involved, but he couldn't explain any more. "Did you report it?"

"I'm ashamed to say I did not." He rubbed his forehead. "I should have. As a principal, I'm a mandated reporter. I know that applies, even though it wasn't related to my job. I'm just glad someone did."

"Do you have any idea who might have?"

He shook his head. "Most people don't want to get involved, defy the pastor, or bring any scandal to the church. It's hard enough these days with all the political and religious division in our country."

"But you don't approve of the marriage?"

"She's just a child."

"Did you know about the wedding before it took place?"

"Of course not. I most certainly would have reported it if I thought I could stop it."

"Do you know if anyone besides the family knew it was going to take place?"

"I don't think so. Most of the congregation seemed surprised by the announcement. A murmur went through the church when Pastor Fowler told us, but only for a few seconds because it was met with the pastor's disapproval. He didn't say anything, but his facial expression was very clear."

"Was there any indication that Mary Margaret and Lester were..." JP paused, searching for the correct word. None of them seemed appropriate. "...an *item*?"

"No. I don't recall ever seeing them together. Mary Margaret is a very sweet, reserved girl. Lester is a good friend of the Fowlers, and he spends a lot of time with them, so I'm sure Mary Margaret knows him better than we have witnessed at church. They were sitting together the Sunday when the announcement was made, but I can't imagine her wanting to be married to Lester Gibbs."

"So, you saw them together that Sunday?"

"Yes, but it was very awkward. A couple of people congratulated them, but most didn't seem to know what to do. Normally, the members hang around and chat with each other for a bit, but that day they seemed to be avoiding the couple and kind of hurried away. Most people were gone before Pastor Fowler came out."

"You hung around?"

"I had the same plan, but my wife was in the restroom, so I was waiting for her. I can tell you this much: Mary Margaret was not smiling and appeared uncomfortable when Lester put his arm around her." He rubbed his forehead again, and then his beard in a nervous gesture. "I didn't report it because I assumed it was a legal marriage, but I'm guessing now that it was not, because you're here asking me these questions."

JP felt like a priest hearing the principal's confession. The principal obviously felt guilty for not reporting it. "I can't really go into any details about the case, except to tell you that we're doing what we can to figure it all out. If you learn anything new, please let me know." JP laid his card on the desk and left.

JP still had a few hours before his meeting with Sabre at the Cunningham's house. He stopped at Starbucks to see Lucy Jennings. It was midafternoon on a Monday, and the customers were few. She smiled when he walked in.

"Hello," Lucy said. "You're the new guy at church, right?"

"Yes, we met yesterday."

"What can I get you?"

"Actually, I had a couple of questions. Do you have a minute?"

"Sure," she said. "Mark, please take over. I'll only be a few minutes." She came out from behind the counter and led JP outside to one of the tables in the mall's food court.

"What can I do for you?"

Since everyone else he had talked to seemed open to his questions, he decided to come clean about who he was. "Lucy, I'm an investigator for an attorney who is representing Mary Margaret Fowler."

The pleasant look left her face and she sat up straighter, but she didn't comment.

"I need some information about the marriage of Lester and Mary Margaret."

"I don't know anything about that."

"But you do know they had a wedding ceremony, right?"

"Yes."

"You didn't attend the wedding?"

"No."

"Do you have an opinion about it?" JP was hoping he could get her to say something more than yes or no.

"It's not my place to have an opinion about it."

"Says who?"

"My mother." She bit at her lower lip. "They were married in the eyes of God. I hope they'll be happy." She stood up. "I have to get back to work."

JP left the mall and drove to see Lester Gibbs. He knew from the social worker's report that Lester had moved back to his mother's house in Tierrasanta. He wasn't sure Lester would talk to him, but it was worth a try.

Lester's mother, a trim, fit woman, answered the door dressed in workout clothes and explained that she had just returned from the gym.

"My name is JP Torn. I work for an attorney who is representing Mary Margaret Fowler."

She didn't seem concerned, only interested. "I'm Audrey Wirth. Come on in. Lester will be home any minute." They stepped into the living room, and she introduced him to her husband. He said hello, and then continued watching his television show.

"Come into the kitchen. I was just having a protein shake. I'll fix you one if you'd like."

"No, but thanks."

Audrey picked up a glass of green liquid and sat down at the counter. "Have a seat. Can I help you with anything before my son gets home?"

"Maybe you can. How well do you know Mary Margaret?"

"I've never met her. We don't attend the same church Lester does."

"Have you met her father, the pastor?"

She shook her head. "No, I've never met anyone from his church."

"I take it you weren't at the wedding?"

"I wasn't invited."

"Do you approve of his marriage?" JP asked.

Before she could answer, Lester walked in. He was a large man with a full head of wavy hair and leftover pockmarks from his teenage years. "She doesn't need to approve," he said. "I'm old enough to make my own choices."

"You certainly are," JP said. He hoped he didn't sound as sarcastic as his thoughts.

"Who are you, anyway?" Lester asked.

"My name is JP. I work for Attorney Sabre Brown who is representing Mary Margaret."

"So what do you want?"

"Child Protective Services is concerned about your relationship with Mary Margaret. I want to hear your side of it."

"Then you should be asking me, not my mother."

"You're right. I was actually just killing time until you got here."

"I think this is my cue to leave," Lester's mother said.

"It was nice to meet you, ma'am," JP said and then turned to Lester. "I apologize if I overstepped. I really want to hear what you have to say." JP hoped he could convince him that he was really interested in his side of the story, even though he didn't really believe there were two sides to it.

"What is there to say? We're two people in love who chose to get married."

"Do you think Mary Margaret was old enough to make that choice?"

"She's very mature for her age. Besides, her parents are in agreement. Why should the government care? They have no business getting involved in our personal lives."

"Mary Margaret's attorney just wants to make sure she is protected."

"She's my wife," he said sternly. "I'll be the one to protect her."

"I'm sure you will. I can tell you love her very much." JP decided to play the gender card. "You know how women are. They want to protect their own. Ms. Brown will talk to Mary Margaret and make sure she feels the same way about you."

Lester flung his arm in the air. "I know how this works. They'll put words in her mouth and keep at her until she says exactly what they want to hear. She wanted to marry me. She practically begged me."

"Why don't you tell me exactly what happened? If you can make me understand, then maybe I can convince my boss." Lester gave him a skeptical look. "Start with how long you two have been dating." JP almost choked on the word.

"We haven't spent a lot of time alone. Mostly we do things with her parents, like barbeques and movie nights, stuff like that. I spend a lot of time at the pastor's house."

"But you have had *some* time alone?"

"Yes, sometimes her parents would leave, and we'd be home alone. Or sometimes I would take her with me when I went to Home Depot or something."

"When did she tell you she wanted to get married?"

"She told me more than once."

"How long ago was the first time?"

"A couple of months ago."

"Women. Go figure," JP said. "Did she come right out and ask you to marry her?"

"Not in so many words. We were kissing, and it got kind of hot and heavy. I'm a man, you know, I have urges—urges God gave me. I wanted to do more, but she said we couldn't because we weren't married. I knew right then what she wanted, and I told her I would marry her."

JP felt his face getting hot with rage and his fist clench. He looked down, hoping Lester wouldn't see it. He told himself to relax and breathe. "Did that satisfy her? The promise to marry?"

"Not really. She still kept getting me excited and then trying to stop me."

"I know how hard it is to stop when women get us going. They think they can just say no, and we can switch it off. You're a better man than I am if you were able to do that."

"Right? It's not easy. Every time I would touch her, she would say it was a sin and we can't do things outside of marriage. I told her I would take care of that."

"Is that when you asked her to marry you?"

"I didn't actually ask her. Mary Margaret didn't need all that romantic stuff. She just wanted to marry me. She said her mother would never allow it, that we'd have to wait until she was older. But I told her I would take care of it. I know how to get things done. I knew her father would agree with me."

"Why is that?"

"Pastor Fowler understands these things. He has

urges too."

"What do you mean?" JP asked.

Lester raised an eyebrow. "You know what I mean. Just like you said. Men get out of control sometimes."

"Has the pastor been 'out of control' before?"

Lester must have thought he said too much because he suddenly stopped talking about the pastor. "You need to convince that attorney of yours that we are happily married in the eyes of the church. We just need to get back together, and the government needs to stay out of our business."

"I'll see what I can do."

Chapter 21

The Fowler Case

"How was your visit with Lester?" Sabre asked as she and JP drove to the Cunningham's.

JP shook his head. "That man is so low he has to step up to go under."

Sabre smiled. "It went that well, huh?"

"I did all I could to keep from punching that sick son of a . . . No, it wouldn't be fair to call him that. His mother was actually very nice. She seemed so normal, but who knows?"

"Did you learn anything?"

JP shared the conversation he had with Lester about the marriage. "He also said that Pastor Fowler has 'urges'. I'm not sure what he meant, but I think it's worth checking into."

"Fowler did agree to the marriage. What kind of a father would do that?"

"One who has urges, maybe."

"Do you think Lester knew something about Fowler that he was able to use to convince Fowler to let him marry his daughter?"

"The thought crossed my mind," JP said. "Lester told me Mary Margaret said her mother would never allow them to get married. She didn't say her father or her parents wouldn't allow it. She said her 'mother' wouldn't."

"So she had some reason to think her father wouldn't protect her. That could be for a lot of reasons. She doesn't seem very close to him, and he's very strict. See what you can find out and I'll see what Mary Margaret is willing to share with me."

They arrived at the Cunningham's for their

respective appointments. After introductions, JP went to Miles's office, and Sabre met with Penny in her room.

"Penny, I understand that you and Mary Margaret are friends, is that right?"

"We're BFFs, best friends forever."

"How long have you been friends?"

"Since kindergarten. We met at church when Pastor Fowler took over. They had just moved here from somewhere. I don't remember where. We were in kindergarten together, but then her father home-schooled her after that. We stayed friends. She only lived a block away, so we would see each other most every day after school, until she went to foster care."

Sabre was glad Penny already knew something about the case. It made it easier to ask questions without violating Mary Margaret's confidentiality. "What do you know about Mary Margaret being in foster care?"

"My parents told me why she wasn't at church or living at home."

"What did they tell you?"

"They said CPS removed her from her home because she was too young to consent to marriage. I already knew they were married because it was announced at church."

"Did Mary Margaret tell you about the wedding before it took place?"

"No. She didn't believe she would have to marry that creep."

"I take it you don't like Lester."

Penny stuck her finger in her open mouth, making a gesture of disgust. "He's a horrible, old man."

"You said Mary Margaret didn't think she'd have to marry him. Did she tell you that?"

"Yes."

"When? Before or after the wedding?"

"Sunday night at church, after it was announced that morning. I hadn't seen her alone until then. She doesn't have a cell phone, so I couldn't call her, but I talked to her at church that night."

"Tell me exactly what she told you, if you can remember."

"I asked her if she really got married, and she started to cry and ran to the bathroom. I followed her inside, and she told me her parents made her do it."

"She didn't want to get married?"

"No." She shuddered. "She hated it, but her father said she had to. She said Lester told her father that they were in love."

"Did she say anything else?"

"We didn't get to talk very long because someone came in the bathroom and then we had to get back to Bible studies. I went to her house the next day, but her father said she wasn't there. I didn't know whether *she* didn't want to see me, or her father didn't want me to see *her*. I haven't talked to her since."

"She wants to see you," Sabre said.

"You talked to her?"

"Yes, and we're trying to get her to church on Wednesday if we can. She really misses you."

"I miss her too." Tears welled up in Penny's eyes. "Is she going to have to stay married to him?"

Sabre noticed Penny seldom called Lester by name. It was always "he" or "him." She wondered if it was a kind of Harry Potter "Voldemort" thing, where you don't say the evil one's name. "We don't know yet, but I'm working on doing what is best for Mary Margaret."

Sabre looked at Penny for a second. "Did you call CPS about this?"

"What is CPS?"

"Child Protective Services. Someone called and reported it. I wondered if it was you."

She shook her head. "No, but I would've if I had known what to do. How can I help?"

"Just be her friend. She needs that right now."

~~~

Miles Cunningham stood up when JP walked in. He was about the same height as JP and had dark hair, blue eyes, and a pleasant smile. "Make yourself comfortable," he said, pointing to a chair.

"Thank you for agreeing to meet with me."

"I'm glad to help in any way, but I'm not sure how I can."

"You are on the editing committee for the Square With God Church blog, right?"

"Yes, along with Linda Jennings and the pastor."

"I understand that a couple of blogs were written about the Gibbs marriage after it was announced, but they didn't get posted. Were you aware of that?"

"Yes. I fought it at first, but Linda convinced me that it wouldn't be good for the church. She and Pastor Seth would have overridden me anyway. And when I read the submissions over again, I realized it wasn't a good idea. They were too negative and probably would have brought a lot of bad publicity to the church. I didn't want that. It's a good church with a lot of very caring, kind-hearted people. I didn't want to see the bad decisions and choices made by a few ruin it for everyone."

"What about Mary Margaret?"

"I considered her, but the blog posts wouldn't have helped her. I tried to find another way to help."

"Did you call CPS?"

"No, frankly, I didn't think of it as a child protection

issue. That seems so lame now, because I realize that's exactly what it is."

"Did you know anything about the wedding before it took place?"

"No. I don't think anyone did. The whole congregation was shocked, and most of them were appalled by it. The big question is how a father could marry off his twelve-year-old daughter? Looking back on that, it makes me seem even more foolish, considering the pastor's wife is so young. I don't know her exact age, but she couldn't have been more than fourteen or fifteen when they married."

"Fourteen," JP said.

Miles shook his head. "Well, I'm taking some steps now to see that this doesn't happen again."

"How is that?"

"It's a good church with good people, but I think we need a new leader."

Chapter 22

Sabre and JP ate dinner at C Level restaurant on Harbor Drive. The dining room was surrounded by glass windows that gave an expansive view of the bay and the lights downtown.

"This sure is a beautiful view," Sabre said.

"Yes, it is," JP said, looking at Sabre.

She smiled. "I've missed you. We really need to work on our schedules."

"I agree."

"Speaking of relationships, my mother is in one."

"Good for her."

Sabre scrunched her mouth. "I hope so."

"What's the problem?"

"She met this guy online and I'm a little concerned he might not be who or what he says he is."

"Have you met him?"

"No, but my mother isn't that worldly, and I don't want to see her get hurt."

"Do you want me to run a background check on him?"

"Would you?"

"Of course." He reached across the table and took her hand. "Anything for you, darlin'."

"She's seeing him on Friday, so anything you can learn before then would be good."

"I'll be faster than green grass through a goose."

"Nice visual." She smiled. "By the way, I put feelers out at court this morning to see if anyone else has a case similar to Parker. Who knows how many little 'Jim Jones' there are running around San Diego."

"Or whatever other dead guy he has decided to impersonate. Elvis, maybe? Although, I don't think he's

114

clever enough to come up with anything too ingenious." He paused. "Who would fall for that pickup line?"

"At least one we know of. Some people are so lonely, they'll believe anything to be with someone who makes them feel good, even if it's for a short time. Look at Ellesse. She still reminisces about that night to make herself feel good."

"I guess," JP said. "I take it no one you talked to at court knew about any little evangelists running around."

"No, but the word will spread. I know it's a long shot because he seems to stay with them only one night. What are the chances he impregnated another woman, CPS got involved, and the case was filed?"

"Slim, but If there is one, you'll find it."

~~~

They finished their meal and drove to Sabre's condo. Once inside, JP took her in his arms and kissed her.

"Do you want to stay tonight?"

"I thought you'd never ask."

She kicked off her shoes and dashed upstairs with JP right behind her. As they reached the top of the stairs, JP's phone rang. He looked at the caller ID.

"Who is it?" Sabre asked.

"I don't know. It's a local number."

"Well, answer it already, so we can get busy."

"Hello," JP said. Pause. "He's there right now?" Pause. "You're sure it's him?" Pause. "I'll be right there."

He looked at Sabre as he hung up. Her shoulders dropped, and the look of glee had left her face. "Who was it?" she asked.

"The waitress at the Watering Hole. She thinks Jim Jones is in the bar."

"Back from the dead again, huh?"

"Apparently." He pulled her close for a kiss. "I don't want to leave."

"I know, but we may not get another chance," she said.

"Do you want me to come back if it's not too late?" JP asked.

"I think I'll just crash."

~~~

As JP drove to the Watering Hole he wondered why he had answered that danged phone. Nearly fifteen minutes had passed by the time he reached the bar. He went inside and looked around. He didn't see anyone wearing sunglasses as Kathy had described.

He spotted Kathy and approached her once she finished waiting on her table.

"Oh, hi," she said. "He already left."

"With someone?"

"No, he hung around for a while, then he approached that woman sitting over there." She nodded toward a table near the bar. "She must have given him the brush-off because he left shortly after that. I didn't get a chance to call you right away when he came in. I started to, but it got busy and I got side-tracked. He was here about forty minutes."

"Thanks. I appreciate the call. We'll get him next time."

JP walked over to the girl Kathy had pointed out previously. He sat down at her table and said, "Hi, my name is JP and I'm not trying to hit on you."

"That's the best come-on line I've ever heard."

"I really mean it."

"That's a real shame then," she said.

"I'm a private investigator, and I'm looking for someone."

"Apparently, it's not me you're looking for."

"I understand a man approached you a few minutes ago, is that correct?"

"Yes, his line wasn't nearly as good as yours."

"Did he tell you his name?"

"No, we never got that far. I told him to buzz off when he started telling me how beautiful I am."

"I appreciate your time, ma'am."

JP thanked her, left, and drove to Peter D's hoping Jones was making the circuit since he didn't pick up anyone at the Watering Hole. The bartender said he hadn't seen him. JP waited until Nancy, the waitress, wasn't busy and he approached her.

"Nancy, do you remember me? I was in here a couple of nights ago looking for this man." He showed her the photo again.

"Yeah, the guy with the sunglasses."

"Have you seen him tonight?"

She shook her head. "No, he hasn't been in here."

JP handed her another card. "Please call me if he comes in."

She eyed JP for a sec. "Sure will."

JP tried a couple more bars, but to no avail. He gave up and went home.

Chapter 23

The Parker Case

Sabre heard someone call her name as she walked down the hallway at Juvenile Court toward Department Four. She turned to see Attorney Mike Powers.

"Good morning, Mikey."

"Morning," he said, and continued walking with her. "I hear you're looking for a ghost father."

"Yes, do you have one?"

"Maybe. Does this ghost drug his women?"

"We're not sure, but we think so. What have you got?"

"I have a mother on a case who was doing well for a couple of months, and then she started using again. She swears someone drugged her at a bar and that got her started again."

"Did she sleep with him?"

"She did, but he freaked her out because before he left, he told her she was pregnant and the child would rule the world, or some such nonsense."

"Was she?" Sabre asked. "Pregnant?"

"No, but he did tell her that he was from the spirit world or something," Mike said. "It was four or five months ago, and she seemed kind of ashamed of the whole thing, so I didn't get a lot of details."

"I want to find this guy," Sabre said. "If he's drugging them, he's raping them."

"I agree."

They stopped in front of Department Four. "Do you think my investigator could talk to her? JP is very discreet, and it would only be about this issue. You can go with him if you want."

"I'll call her and see if she's willing to talk to him."

"Thanks," Sabre said, and went inside the courtroom.

~~~

Louie lay at JP's feet while JP tapped away on his keyboard, looking for anything he could find on Harley Lindgren, Sabre's mother's new love interest. So far, he had discovered that Harley was an American citizen; his mother was born in Sweden; he was sixty-eight years old; and he owned his own real estate company. He had two daughters and one son, none of whom had followed in their father's entrepreneurial footsteps. The oldest daughter, Joanne, was a teacher in the Poway School District. His son, Eddie, was an attorney for a large San Diego law firm. Chloe, the other daughter, he wasn't sure of, except that she appeared to be living in northern California. He decided to follow that up later.

JP ran Harley's criminal record, but found nothing, not even a speeding ticket. He continued his search through social media sites, looking for anything untoward. The only social media accounts he found for Harley were LinkedIn and Facebook. LinkedIn was all professional contacts. Nothing unusual. He only had twenty-eight Facebook friends, even though he had been on the site for more than six years. They consisted of his children, and what appeared to be close friends and relatives. He found nothing suspicious.

JP continued to research Mr. Lindgren on the internet. His business seemed stable. He couldn't find any lawsuits, past or pending. Then he found it. Louie jumped up from his comfortable spot on the floor when JP blurted, "Oh no. This can't be good."

~~~

Sabre was waiting with Bob to do a case when she saw a text from JP.

--JP: *Are you eating at Pho's today?*

--Sabre: *Yes.*

--JP: *Can I join you?*

--Sabre: *I'd like that. I should be there by noon or shortly thereafter.*

--JP: *Good.*

"JP is joining us for lunch," Sabre said.

"Good. This is my last case. How about you?"

"I have one more, but it should be quick. It's a review in this department."

Sabre and Bob finished their joint case and Bob left to wait outside for her. Sabre completed her review hearing and walked out with Regina Collicott. Sabre told her about the Parker case.

Regina laughed. "Just when I thought I'd heard it all."

"I take it you don't have a ghost father case?"

Regina thought for a moment. "I do have a new case in which the mother doesn't know who the father is."

Sabre gave her a sideways glance. "Ah... half my clients don't know who the father is. Your point?"

"I know, mine either, but this one claims it's either her ex-boyfriend or some guy she met in a bar. Some particular guy, like there was only one. She said she hoped it wasn't him because he was pretty strange."

"Did she get his name?"

"No, she said she didn't know his name. She said she was pretty drunk."

"Did she say he drugged her?"

"No, she didn't say anything like that. It's probably

not even him, but we have a trial this afternoon. If you want, we can talk to her and make sure."

"We may as well."

Sabre and Bob drove to Pho's, the Vietnamese restaurant at which they ate almost every day. They walked inside past the fish tank with the large goldfish. Sabre never tired of seeing them. Someday she hoped to have a large aquarium with lots of colorful saltwater fish. She spotted JP sitting at a table against the wall with her brother Ron.

JP stood up when she approached and gave her a peck on the cheek.

"What are you doing here?" Sabre asked Ron.

"I love you, too, Sis," Ron said.

"You know what I mean. Is something up?"

"I invited him," JP said.

"What's wrong?" Sabre asked.

"Nothing. Well, sort of nothing," JP said. "Sit down and I'll tell you what I found out about your mother's new beau."

"Is it juicy?" Bob asked, as he took the seat next to Ron.

JP told them about the criminal check and all the personal information he had discovered.

"What else?" Sabre asked suspiciously.

"Did he tell your mother he was married before?"

"Yes," Ron said, "and he has three children from that marriage. She knows that."

"And she knows how the first wife died?"

"Yes, she had cancer."

"Does your mother know about the other two marriages?"

Ron's eyes widened. "I don't know. She didn't tell me that she did."

"He's been married three times?" Sabre asked. "Is he divorced?"

"No."

Before JP could explain, Sabre asked, "Is he still married, or are they all dead?"

The waiter came up just then and took their orders. After he left, JP continued, "The second one was killed in a train accident and the third just disappeared."

Silence ensued for about ten seconds. Finally, Bob said, "Did any of them have money?"

"I don't think so," JP said.

"Why would you ask that?" Sabre said.

"Because if he's marrying these women and killing them off, money is the most likely motivator."

"You said he had no criminal record, so he wasn't ever arrested for anything regarding these women, right?" Sabre asked.

"Right. The first marriage lasted eighteen years, and his wife died at home with Hospice there. There didn't appear to be any criminal investigation. The second wife of three years was meeting Harley at Jake's in Del Mar. She crossed the street and they think she caught her foot and was hit by the train. She's not the first person to be killed there. It was listed as an accidental death."

"And the third?" Ron asked.

"The third is different. They were only married a few months. Supposedly, she went to visit her sister in Tustin and never came back. Harley became a suspect in that case, as the spouse always is, but there was never an arrest or anything formally filed."

"And she was never found?" Ron said.

"Not that I could find."

Sabre sat quietly, looking at but not touching the food the waiter had delivered.

"It could be the guy has had some really bad luck," Bob said and started to eat his usual #124. "How long between wives?"

"He was single for seven years after his first wife died. His second was a good friend of both him and his wife. Her husband worked for Harley for about fifteen years until he ran off with another woman. It wasn't until two years later that Harley married her. After she was hit by the train, Harley was alone for three years before he married his third wife."

Neither Sabre nor Ron ate their food as they listened to JP. When he paused, Sabre asked, "Do you know how he met the third wife?"

"I'm not sure," JP said. "Her name was Vanna Norstrom, and I have a hunch they met at some Swedish organization that he was involved with at the time. I haven't confirmed that yet."

"Do you know if there have been any other relationships since Vanna?"

"It's hard to tell without talking to friends and relatives, which I didn't think you wanted me to do. But it has been eleven years since Vanna disappeared. I expect there have been some."

"With that kind of luck, he may have just given up," Bob said. "I would have."

No one else spoke for a few minutes. Ron and JP began to eat while Sabre picked at her food. She finally broke the silence. "Find out everything you can about Vanna Norstrom."

"We have a bit of a break on this," JP said. "An old friend of mine, Vincent DuBois, was the detective on the case, and he has agreed to meet with me this afternoon. Hopefully, we can get some insight."

"DuBois?" Bob asked. "Isn't that the guy who always calls you McCloud?"

"McCloud?" Ron said. "Like the old TV show with Dennis Weaver, the cop from Taos, New Mexico, who is transplanted to New York City?"

"That's the one," Bob said.

"That makes sense." Ron looked at JP. "So, McCloud, do you think you can get to the bottom of this?"

"If you're tryin' to decide between continuing to call me McCloud or cuddling a hornet, you best go with the hornet," JP said in his usual soft tone.

Bob and Ron both laughed and said almost in unison, "Okay, McCloud."

Sabre smiled, but she couldn't quite get into the mood. "It would sure ease my mind if you could find Vanna...alive."

"And preferably before Friday," Ron said.

"What's happening Friday?" Bob asked.

"Our mother's next date with the black widower," Ron said.

Chapter 24

The Parker Case

Sabre waited upstairs in the hallway for Regina and her client. She stood by the short wall where she could look down on the lobby and watch the people. She was always amazed by this view. It fascinated her to watch as the attorneys, defendants and their families, and other court personnel carried on. For some it was just work, for others it was their entire life caught up in a system most had never expected to be in.

Nearly fifteen minutes passed before Regina arrived.

"Sorry, I got tied up," Regina said. "This is Laura Ramage."

"I'm Sabre Brown." She pointed to some chairs a few feet away. "Let's have a seat." They all sat down and Sabre turned to Laura.

"Did Regina explain why I wanted to talk to you?"

"Yes, but I don't think I can help. I don't really know much about that guy."

"I know, and I'm sorry I have to bother you with this, but any little thing might help."

Laura shrugged. "Whatever."

"You met him in a bar, correct?"

She nodded.

"Do you know the name of the bar?"

"Peter D's in Clairemont."

Sabre perked up. "Were you drunk?"

Laura frowned and clicked her mouth. "Tsk."

"I apologize," Sabre said. "I'm not passing judgment. I just want to know your state of mind at the time."

"I was bummed because my boyfriend and I had just broken up. I wasn't drunk when I met the guy, but I seemed to get there pretty fast. When I think about it, I hadn't drunk that much. But I barely remember getting home."

"Do you remember anything specific he said to you?"

"He kept calling me his 'shining light.' He was real charming at first, but then he started talking about God and outer space or something. It all made me very uncomfortable. That's when I asked him to leave."

"Did he go when you told him to?"

"He wanted to stay until morning, but I told him no. That's when he said I was pregnant, which I found very odd."

"But you did get pregnant, right?" Sabre asked.

Regina spoke up. "We just got the paternity tests back and her boyfriend is the father of the baby. She was probably already pregnant when she met this guy."

"Did he ever tell you his name?" Sabre asked Laura.

"He did, but I can't remember it. I think it was a pretty common name."

"Could it have been Jim Jones?"

"Maybe." Laura shrugged. "I don't remember. This was almost a year ago, and it wasn't the best night of my life. I've tried to forget about the creep."

Just then Regina's name was called over the PA system.

"We have to go," Regina said, and stood up.

"Thanks, Laura," Sabre said, and nodded to Regina.

~~~

JP sat across the desk from Vincent DuBois, his old friend.

"What's the story, McCloud?" DuBois asked. "I haven't seen you in years and suddenly we meet three times in the past month."

"As I said on the phone, I'm working on something that led me to the Vanna Norstrom case."

"Yeah, you said that earlier. What's the connection?"

"It's personal. My girlfriend Sabre's mother is dating her husband."

"Harley Lindgren?"

"Yes. I just want to make sure she's safe."

"I understand." He opened the file sitting on his desk. "It's been more than eleven years and there hasn't been any action on the case for a very long time. We investigated Harley when Vanna disappeared, but it didn't lead us anywhere. The sister reported her missing when she didn't show up at her house, but that was two days after Vanna left. When we went to Harley's house the first time, he didn't even know she was missing. He said she was 'in a mood' and had said she was going to her sister's and left."

"And he didn't call her or anything?"

"No, he said he was letting her calm down."

"Had they had a fight?" JP asked.

"Not according to Lindgren. He said she just started screaming at him and said she was leaving. He said she never did anything like that before they were married, but from day one of the marriage she acted bizarre. He had only known her for about six months before they married, and they had never lived together, so he didn't know her as well as he thought."

"Did you believe him?"

"Lindgren said all the right things. He didn't act suspicious or appear like he was trying too hard, but he didn't have an alibi for the evening she left. He was the last one to see her, as far as we know. He worked the next couple of days, which he would have likely done one way or the other. We never found any physical evidence of any kind that was suspect. That was all we had, not enough to arrest him. A few days later, Lindgren came to me and said there was a hundred-grand missing from his safe."

"Whoa, that's a lot of green to have lying around, even in a safe."

"For you or me, but he was a big-time real estate mogul. At the time, he owned about six rentals and had another eight hundred thousand in stocks. I guess that was his pocket change."

"But he didn't tell you about the money until later?"

DuBois looked at the file. "Two days after she was reported missing."

"Do you think it was a cover to make it look like she ran away? Maybe he was feeling too much heat."

"That was my first reaction. When we questioned him, he claimed he didn't know it was gone. He hadn't looked in his safe. I suppose that's possible. If I had a hundred thousand dollars in cash, I'd look at it every day." He chuckled. "But I guess if I had his money I wouldn't be opening my safe that often."

"What did your gut tell you?"

"He was either telling the truth, or was really good at lying. He seemed genuinely surprised and concerned about her well-being. Vanna had some mental history, and even though her sister played it down, everyone else said she was a whack job. Lindgren didn't appear to know about her history. That doesn't explain what happened to her, and we had nothing to go on. We know she bought a train ticket from San Diego to Santa Ana, but we don't know if she ever got on the train. She just disappeared, but if she stole the hundred-grand, she would've had the money to run away. That may very well be what she did."

"Is the case closed?" JP asked.

"It's still open, but I doubt if it will ever be solved. A few years ago, I had her DNA run through a national database, but nothing came up. Other than that, no one has worked it in years. I talked to the sister a couple of times the first year, but she didn't seem that concerned after a while."

"Do you think her sister knew where she was?"

"I asked her, but she said she didn't. I think she had just given up on her."

"Can I see the file?" JP asked.

"Why not? I don't want to see anything happen to Sabre's mother if there is something there." DuBois handed him the file. "I better not give you copies, but you can take notes if you want."

JP looked through the file and jotted down a few notes including the name and address of Vanna's sister.

"I appreciate this, DuBois," JP said as he stood to leave.

"I got your back," he said, and walked him to the door. "I expect to see you at my retirement party in a few months, McCloud."

"I wouldn't miss it."

Chapter 25

The Lynch Case

JP's research on the Lynch case led him to Ian Lynch, a CPA in Costa Mesa. Although Ian's photo on LinkedIn looked nothing like Todd, he fit the age of Todd's brother and had attended Pasadena Community College before he went to California State University, Fullerton, where he received a degree in accounting. JP compared the photo on the Internet with a photo from the high school where Todd and Ian had graduated, and he was pretty certain he had the right guy. He called and made an appointment to see Ian about his taxes.

Then he made the hour-and-a-half drive to Orange County to see Ian Lynch. His appointment wasn't until later in the day, which gave him time to stop and see Vanna Norstrom's sister while he was there.

Helga Norstrom lived alone in a large, two-story house in a gated community. JP followed another car in when the gate opened, and then he found her address. He had not called ahead, so he risked her not being home. He figured the element of surprise was worth the risk. When he knocked on the door, a dishwater-blonde woman about 5' 10" answered the door. JP had studied photos of Vanna and noticed the family resemblance. They were both big women with azure-blue eyes and blonde hair, though Helga's hair was darker than the towheaded Vanna's.

"What are you selling?" she asked.

"I'm not sellin', just askin'. Are you Helga Norstrom?"

"Yes."

"I have a few questions about your sister Vanna.

Can we talk a minute?"

The smartly-dressed woman stepped out and closed the door behind her. JP wondered where she was headed in her tailored suit. According to his research, she was unemployed and living on a trust from her parents, so she wasn't likely going to work. He suspected she probably did some charity work or something to fill her time.

"Did you find Vanna?" she asked hesitantly. "Is she okay?"

"No, we didn't find her."

"Then why are you here? Did they reopen the case?"

"It never actually closed. Something has come up that made us take another look at her husband." JP knew she thought he was law enforcement even though he hadn't actually said so. He was skating on thin ice, but if he told her he was a PI, he would have too much explaining to do, and maybe not get the answers he needed. "How well did you know Harley Lindgren?"

"I never met him."

"Not even at their wedding?"

"No, they went to Vegas and got married. I wasn't invited. No one was."

"Did you find that odd?"

"No, my sister did things like that."

"Was she married in Vegas before?"

"No, I mean she didn't always think things through. She just acted on the spur of the moment. I was always afraid something would happen to her because she took too many chances. She hardly knew that man before she married him."

"Do you think he was involved in her disappearance?"

"Probably, but I can't be certain. She called me

and said she was coming on the train and asked me to pick her up. I waited for her at the train station, but she didn't show. When I called her cell, she didn't answer." She said it all in a monotone voice as if she had said it a hundred times. JP expected she probably had during the course of the investigation.

"Did you call her husband?"

"I didn't have a number for him. At first, I just thought she changed her mind and decided not to come. I kept calling Vanna and when she didn't answer after two days, I called the police."

"And you never heard from her after that?"

"No." Helga shuffled her feet. "Look, I have an appointment. I really need to go."

"Of course, thank you for your time."

~~~

JP drove to Costa Mesa for his "free consultation" with the accountant. He was a little early and he was getting hungry, so he stopped at an In-N-Out Burger and had a double-double with fries. He had hoped he could meet up with Sabre for dinner, but his appointment wasn't until five o'clock and the traffic would be horrible until at least seven. It could be pushing nine before he got home, so instead he agreed to meet Powers and his client Amber Baker, another woman who might have had sex with the ghost.

Due to the traffic, JP didn't arrive at Lynch's office until a few minutes to five. The receptionist was about to leave, but she escorted JP to the back office where Ian Lynch sat. The office was surrounded by windows with wide-open views of the parking lot and the street.

"This is your five o'clock, JP Torn," the receptionist said and walked out.

"Have a seat," the thin man said.

JP was a little surprised by his physique. Todd wasn't tall, but he was muscular and had broad shoulders. Ian looked more like an anemic runner.

"Thank you," JP said as he sat down. He glanced around the office at a multitude of artifacts that looked like they could have come from Africa. "Are these from your travels?"

"Only a few of them. I'm very interested in African art and I have a couple of clients who bring them to me whenever they travel." He eyed JP curiously. "Did you bring any of your tax information with you?"

JP decided to level with him. "Actually, I'm a private investigator on a juvenile case in San Diego." He laid his business card down in front of Ian. "I work for an attorney, Sabre Brown, who is representing some children in a dependency case."

"What does that have to do with me? I don't have any children."

"Is Todd Lynch your brother?"

He sighed. "Oh, no. Has he hurt the boys?"

"So, he *is* your brother?"

"Yes, but we haven't spoken in almost five years. What has he done?"

"He hasn't done anything that we're sure of. He and his wife have divorced and she had the children. They were in her custody when they were removed," JP said. "Why did you ask if he had hurt them?"

"Because it was only a matter of time. He's a mean man. He was a mean kid, and he's a mean man."

"Did he hurt the boys before?"

"I never saw him hurt them or I would've reported it. The last time I was there I saw some bruising on Nolan. When I questioned Nolan, he started to tell me, but then his father walked in and clasped his hands in front of him and he stopped talking."

"He grabbed Nolan's hands?"

"No, his own hands. Like this." Ian demonstrated by intertwining his fingers and holding his hands in front of his chest. "My mother would do that when we were young. If we didn't respond to it immediately, we got a whipping with a belt. I expect he whipped those boys a few times until they learned to respond to the hands. Nolan was only about four years old, but he knew what it meant."

"Did you see anything that might have constituted abuse after that?"

"No, I was never allowed back in his home. The only reason I went at all was to see the boys. I had no interest in seeing Todd. He did some pretty cruel things to me when we were young. I was older than him, but he was always bigger and stronger."

"What kind of things did he do?"

"He would put critters in my bed when I was real little and watch me scream. Lizards, snakes, that sort of thing. He never did anything that left marks. It was mostly emotional abuse. Once he strangled my cat and he threatened to tell our mother that I did it. She always seemed to take his side over mine, so I didn't dare tell."

"What about your father?"

"My dad tried to protect me, but my mother wouldn't listen to him either. I think he was afraid of her too."

"Todd told us you were homeless. Why do you suppose he would do that?"

"Of course, he did. Years ago, I was homeless for about two months. Todd always seems to lead with that. When I was seventeen, I told my dad I was leaving right after high school graduation. He decided to go with me. We rented a little apartment near Pasadena Community College and I started school." He gulped. "We were only there a few months when Dad had a heart attack and died. I couch-surfed when the rent ran out. A friend of mine finally got his parents to let me stay with them until I finished at PCC. Todd likes to tell everyone I'm homeless. He never will admit that I've been successful. He hated it when I did better than he did in school. It didn't matter that he excelled in sports. He had to be known as the 'smart one,' so he did his best to make me look dumb or like a loser whenever he could."

"Todd wants your mother's home evaluated for placement, but the boys don't really want to go there. Is she a good grandma?"

"I hate to say it, but my mother is a horrible woman who has only gotten worse with age. She doesn't like children, even Todd's. I'm surprised she'd be willing to take them, unless she thinks she can just hand them over to Todd."

"What about you? Would you be willing to take them?"

Ian sat silently for a few seconds. JP didn't know whether he was trying to decide, or trying to find a tactful way to say "no." He swallowed and then said, "I can't. I know a little bit about how these things work and there is no way I could control Todd. He'd make all of our lives miserable. Besides, the children don't know me. As I said, Nolan was only four the last time I saw him, Drew was three, and the baby, what's his name?"

"Evan," JP said.

"Yes—Evan. He was a newborn. I used to send them gifts for Christmas and birthdays, but I talked to Heather once about three years ago and she said Todd would throw them in the trash without even opening them. The kids never even knew they came, so I stopped sending them." Ian looked pensive, and then shook his head. "No, I couldn't do it. As much as I'd like to help those boys, I wouldn't be the best placement for them. I'm sorry."

Chapter 26

The Parker Case

JP sat in Mike Powers' office with Mike's client Amber Baker, the woman who possibly had an encounter with "Jim Jones."

"Tell JP everything you remember about that night at the bar," Mike said.

"I went to the bar to have a drink," Amber said. "I was feeling kind of low because my aunt had died, and I wanted some drugs. I thought a drink was a better answer. I should've gone to a meeting, but the bar was close and it seemed like a good idea at the time."

"What bar was it?" JP asked.

"The Blarney Stone. It's on Balboa. I live right across the street from it, so it was very convenient. I would've just gone to Vons and bought a bottle, but I didn't want to be alone. My kids were in a foster home and I was feeling sorry for myself. You know how it is, right?"

JP nodded. "What happened in the bar?"

"I wasn't in there very long, maybe two beers later, when this guy comes up and sits down next to me. He said hello and started making small talk. He said he had had a rough day and that I brightened it up. I was like a shining light, he said. He bought me another beer, which I drank. Then I went to the bathroom and when I got back, he had another one waiting for me. I think he put something in that beer because I got real loopy. That would only have been four beers, and I don't get drunk on four beers. You know what I mean?"

JP wondered how many it took, but he didn't ask. "Can you tell me what he looked like?"

"He had brown hair. It seemed to be combed over

a little like he was hiding a receding hairline, but later when I saw it, he wasn't really balding, so I guess that was just for looks. His hair came to a little peak on his forehead." She reached up to her forehead and drew an imaginary V-shaped line with her index finger and thumb. "It came like this. There's a name for it. What's it called?"

"A widow's peak."

"Yeah, that's it."

"Anything else about his looks?"

"Like, he wasn't great looking or anything, but he wasn't bad either. Oh," her voice escalated, "and he was wearing wire-rimmed sunglasses. I asked him if he had been to the eye doctor or something, but he said no. He said his eyes were particularly sensitive, but mostly he just liked wearing them."

"Did he tell you his name?"

"He said it was Jim. Jim Jones, I think."

"Then what happened?"

"I don't remember too much, but he must have walked me home because the next thing I knew we were in bed together and he was talking about crazy stuff."

"Like what?"

"He kept asking me if I recognized him, but I didn't. I thought maybe I had met him before, but he said that wasn't it. He said he was famous, but he was from another world—the spirit world."

"Did he say anything about a comet?"

"Yes," she said excitedly. "I thought I was hallucinating. Sometimes when I use drugs, I have crazy visions and hear weird things. So when I thought about it later, I just thought it was the drugs talking. But then I remembered I hadn't used any drugs, so I figured this guy had spiked my drink or something, because I didn't really think he was talking about comets and stuff. So maybe he didn't spike my drink. Maybe he was just talking crazy crap." She paused. "Yes, he did. I know he did, because I was high. It wasn't just the alcohol. I know the difference. But you think that part was real—about the comets? I mean, not that the comet part was real, but that he really said it. You know what I mean?"

"Yes, I know what you mean, and he likely said it," JP said. "He's done it before."

"Why would he say I was pregnant? I wasn't pregnant, you know. I had my period a few days later. I was pretty freaked out until I started. But that was really strange. The last thing I wanted was to get pregnant again, especially by some weirdo, you know."

JP asked a few more questions, but they didn't reveal anything new. He thanked her and she left.

"This 'Jim Jones' is a piece of work," Powers said. "How many women have you found that match his M.O.?"

"So far, at least three: our client, Regina Collicott's client, and your client, Amber."

"All juvenile court cases?"

"So far, but in all fairness, that's the only place we know to look. We know he's still on the prowl because he approached someone recently in another bar in Clairemont."

"Are they always in Clairemont?"

"So far, but then that's also where I've concentrated my efforts. I don't have time to hit every bar in San Diego County."

"That's a lot of bars," Mike said.

"And a lot of beer."

"Yeah, the beer—I wish I could help, but I don't have the time either. Besides, the doctor said I had to cut back on my alcohol intake." He slapped one hand against his cheek. "But if I had to drink while I worked, that wouldn't be my fault now, would it? I think I better help with this investigation."

"Right, and try to convince your wife that you're working." JP laughed. "But that gives me an idea, Mike. Thank you." He stood up and stepped toward the door. "Later."

JP called Ron on his way to his car. "Are you busy?"

"No, why?" Ron said.

"I have a job for you."

"Good, I could use the work. What do I need to do?"

"Meet me in twenty minutes at The Blarney Stone on Balboa. We're going to do a little 'on the job' training."

"At the bar?"

"At the bar."

"My kind of work."

Chapter 27

The Parker Case

Ron was standing outside The Blarney Stone when JP arrived. They greeted each other and walked into the bar.

JP told Ron about the Parker case and how they were trying to find Jim Jones, or obtain information from anyone who had contact with him. "Watch and listen. I'd normally tell you to take notes but it might intimidate our sources."

"Got it."

JP looked around, saw that there was only one bartender, assessed the bar's setup, and led Ron to a couple of barstools. When the bartender approached, JP ordered a beer. "Just water, please," Ron said.

"Always try to sit where the bartender will be hanging out," JP said.

"How do you know where that is?"

"If they have a sink where they wash glasses and he's the only bartender, he'll be there a lot. If not, watch for a few minutes and see where he goes after he serves someone. Most of them have a spot. Don't ever sit near the cash register. It's too noisy and they won't want to be bothered while they're handling money."

When the bartender delivered their drinks, JP engaged him and gave him a twenty-dollar bill to pay for his drink. He returned shortly with the change. "Thank you," JP said. "I could use a little information."

"About what?"

"I'm a private eye, and we're looking for a rapist. We have reason to believe he found one of his victims in here a few months back."

The bartender shook his head. "What do you need?"

JP showed him the photo on his phone that Ellesse had given him. "Does this guy look familiar?"

"Maybe."

"He would probably be wearing sunglasses."

"There is a guy who has been in here a few times that doesn't take his sunglasses off." He glanced around the bar. "As you can see, it's pretty dark in here already. I figured he must have something wrong with his eyes, or some disfigurement or something. Does he?"

"Not that we're aware of," JP said. "When was he in here last?"

"I don't know. A few weeks ago, maybe. I've only seen him two or three times, all in the last six months."

"He wasn't in here before then?"

"I don't know. That's when I started working nights. I don't recall ever seeing him in here during the day."

JP gave him his card and a generous tip, and asked him to call if he came back. The bartender assured him he would.

Before they left, JP talked to the waiter, but he couldn't provide any new information.

"I need you to hit about three bars tonight in El Cajon. Tomorrow night, hit three bars in Lakeside, National City, Escondido, downtown, maybe Pacific Beach. I don't expect you to do them all in one night. Whatever it takes. You need to try to do this on weeknights because the weekends are too busy, especially downtown. If we can determine what area he is frequenting, it may help us find him. Also, the more feelers we have out, the greater the chance that someone will call when he goes after his next victim."

"You got it," Ron said.

"I'm guessing you don't have any business cards,

right?" JP asked.

"I haven't had any need for them, but I can get some made up if you want me to."

"For now, use mine. Just tell them to call me if they learn anything. Write your name on the back before you give it out."

"Okay."

"And here's a hundred bucks for the drinks and tips."

"I don't need your money, JP. I have a little."

"Take it. It's a business expense."

Ron hesitantly took the money and put it in his pocket.

JP continued. "If you're a cop, you don't need to order a drink, your badge will suffice, but if you're anyone else seeking information from a bartender, you better order something. It doesn't have to be alcohol, but order something besides water. If you order alcohol, don't drink it if you're hitting a lot of bars." JP didn't think he had to explain that, but he wasn't sure and the last thing he wanted was for Sabre's brother to get picked up on a DUI while he was working for him.

"Don't worry. I don't drink and drive."

"And tip well. If there is a tip jar or something like that, make sure they see that you are tipping. It's always best to give it to them directly, if you can. Make as much personal contact as you can. You want them to think of you when they have new information."

~~~

Ron was a little uneasy at his first bar in El Cajon, partly because this was unfamiliar territory for him. He had been to a lot of bars in San Diego in his day, but few in East County. Most of his bar-hopping had been done either downtown or at the beach, and this bar was a lot more crowded than The Blarney Stone. All the seats at the bar were filled, so he found a table and took a seat. Within a few minutes, a waitress in a short, flared skirt and a low-cut blouse that showed just a peek of cleavage approached his table.

Ron smiled and said, "Good evening. How has your night been so far?"

She looked at him for a second and then said, "Not bad. Thanks for asking. What can I get you, Sugar?"

"A Pepsi, please."

"Will Coke do?"

"Sure."

A few minutes later she returned with his drink, set it on the table, and surprised Ron by sitting down in the chair across from him.

"So, what is it?" she asked.

"What do you mean?"

She looked directly into his eyes. "You don't seem sad, so I don't think you were just dumped or anyone you know has died. You seem a little nervous, but not enough to be planning to rob the place. You don't appear to be waiting for someone. You don't strike me as shy, and you're very attractive, so I don't think you're here for a hookup, and you ordered a soft drink instead of alcohol."

"Do you always sit with your customers and analyze them?" Ron asked with a smile.

"Only when it's slow and I get bored."

Ron looked around at the relatively crowded bar. "You call this slow?"

"No, but my shift is over and I thought I'd rest my feet a bit before I left. My name is Sunshine, but everyone calls me Sunny. My parents were leftover hippies. It could have been worse; they named my sister Moonlight. And don't get any ideas. I'm not leaving with you."

143

"My name's Ron, and I wouldn't expect you to."

"So, what's your story?"

Ron removed his phone and showed Sunny the photo of Jim Jones. "I'm looking for this man."

Instead of looking at the photo, Sunny studied Ron's face and then glanced at his body. "I didn't see that one coming."

"Not that." Ron laughed. "I'm working with an attorney and we're investigating this man. We have reason to believe he's been picking women up in bars and raping them."

Sunny looked at Ron's phone, tapped the screen because it had gone to screensaver, and then scrutinized the photo. "I don't recall seeing him in here. The picture isn't real clear, and with the sunglasses I can't see his eyes. You can tell a lot about people from their eyes."

"He usually wears his sunglasses in the bar, no matter how dark the bar is."

"Now that I would remember, because I would want to see his eyes. I haven't seen anyone in this bar who kept their sunglasses on. I've been working here for years, mostly this shift and the later one. Let me go ask the other workers."

"Thanks."

Ron drank his Pepsi and did some people-watching while he waited. Most of them appeared to be having a good time, laughing and drinking. A few sat alone just drinking. It struck him as sad, and he decided he never wanted to be one of those. He really wanted to meet someone that he could spend more time with, but he wasn't really lonely. He had his family and friends, and kept busy with hiking, surfing, geocaching, and softball. Now all he needed was a regular job and a girlfriend.

His thoughts were interrupted when Sunny

returned alone. "No one has seen anyone in here wearing sunglasses," she said. "Sorry."

"Thanks for checking." Ron gave her one of JP's cards. "This is my boss, JP. Please call him if you see the man in the photo."

Ron continued his search through several El Cajon bars but found no one who recognized Jim Jones or had any patron with sunglasses, except some kid celebrating his twenty-first birthday who had big lenses shaped like birthday cakes. After his fourth bar in El Cajon and three in Lakeside, he went home with virtually nothing to report.

Chapter 28

The Parker Case

Sabre called JP from Bob's office. She was outside the conference room waiting for everyone to arrive for the meet and confer on the Fowler case. Bob had filed a demurrer on behalf of the father on the case and Irene had joined in for the mother. A demurrer basically admits that the facts in the case are true, but says, "So what?" The contention of the parents was that even if Lester had had sexual contact with Mary Margaret, they were married, so it wasn't illegal. California required a meeting between the parties on the issue prior to bringing it before the judge.

"Did you get an appointment with Sheila Krueger, Sarah Parker's paternal aunt?" Sabre asked.

"I did, but I'm not entirely sure what I'm looking for," JP said.

"Sarah's father wants custody of his daughter, but Judge Hekman isn't going to do that right now because of his recent jail stint and his drug history," Sabre said. "His second choice was for her to live with his sister Sheila. Sarah lived with her for a while when this case first came into the system. She was detained with the father at the aunt's home until her father violated the court order, was caught with drugs, and claimed they were his sister's."

"Nice guy."

"Yeah. Sarah was removed from the home and put in foster care for a short time and then she was returned to her mother. Sarah likes her aunt and wants to live there, but she wants her little brother with her. Sheila is willing to take him, but since she's not related to Denny, she needs to be approved by DSS. The big question is whether or not she can protect the children from Russell Drake, Sarah's father. DSS is doing their evaluation, but I want to see what you think."

"I'll do what I can."

"JP, I know you're crazy busy with all these cases right now and I expect you have others that I don't know about, but it'll all break pretty soon. I just have so many new cases that need so much attention."

"It's all good. I don't have much else I'm working on and I enlisted your brother to help. He's going to be hitting the bars in search of Jim Jones. We'll git 'er done."

"Good, Ron needs the work."

~~~

Sheila Krueger and her husband Paul sat across from JP in their living room. It was a beautiful two-story home in Rancho Peñasquitos.

"I understand you're a teacher, correct?" JP asked.

"Yes," Sheila said, "I teach high school English at Mt. Carmel High. My husband is a pharmaceutical salesman, and he works from home a lot. We've arranged for daycare for Denny, and Sarah will be in school most of the time while I'm working."

"How close are you to your brother?"

"We were very close as kids and have for the most part remained so, but once he got into drugs, our relationship changed, because I lost trust in him."

"Other than the drugs, what kind of father is he?" JP knew if he just asked if she would protect the children, she would say yes, so he wanted to hear more about their relationship.

"He's a good, compassionate man when he's clean. He's a good worker and a good father, but he's

147

weak. He has been fighting his addiction since he was in high school."

"And if he tested clean, would you be in favor of Sarah living with him?"

"He would have to be clean for a very long time to get my trust. In the past, he has stayed clean for almost two years and then started up again. I'll keep helping him if he really wants help, but I'm not sure he'll ever be able to raise his child. I didn't think Sarah should be with him the last time."

"But you let him live with you," JP said.

"They were going to let him live with the child alone. I thought it would be better if I was here to keep an eye on things. I realize I failed by not recognizing he had drugs in the house, but I assure you I won't fail again."

"Russell told the court he was moving in with you."

"So I heard, but it's not true. Russell asked to move in and I told him no. After that trick he pulled last time, I don't need the trouble. I also told him the only way I would take Sarah is if he was *not* in my home."

JP turned to Paul, who had remained silent. "How well do you get along with Russell?"

"I'd say we're good friends—when he's not using. He really is a fun, easy-going guy to be around, but I share my wife's concern that he has an addiction he can't beat. He's not the same person when he's using drugs."

"Do you have any children?" JP asked them both.

"No, we were never blessed with children," Sheila said. "I love my niece to death, and Denny is a very sweet little boy. I love him too. When they were living at home with their mother, Denny would go out with us sometimes when I'd take Sarah for visits. I've taken them both twice now since they've been in foster care. We don't want to see them split up, and we'd love to have them both in our home."

"Would you feel comfortable supervising visits with Russell?"

"Absolutely, and I have no trouble reporting him if I suspect he's using. Look, he isn't going to intentionally hurt his daughter. He loves her very much, and she loves him. Sarah needs to spend time with him, but not alone. If the children are here, we can do family things together and make it more normal for Sarah."

Paul spoke up. "We talked about it, and if there is any concern, we can work his visits around my schedule so I'm here as well. We're willing to do whatever it takes to have our niece and nephew with us."

Chapter 29

The Fowler Case

When Sabre walked into the room where the meet and confer was being held, all of the interested parties were already there. On one side of the conference table was Deputy County Counsel Linda Farris sitting next to the social worker. On the other side were Seth Fowler with Bob, and Mrs. Fowler with Irene. In most mediations and as minor's counsel, Sabre would have preferred to take an end seat so as not to show partiality to either side, but she chose to sit with County Counsel. She had taken a stand on this issue and had no question in her mind that this case needed to be heard in front of a judge.

A demurrer to a case basically doesn't argue with the facts, but says the facts, even if found to be true, do not state a legal cause of action. The Fowlers were arguing that the minor was married and therefore no molest existed. Sabre's position, as well as that of DSS, was that the marriage wasn't valid, so a molest *had* taken place by an adult on a child under the age of fourteen.

Deputy County Counsel Linda Farris said, "Bob, you filed this demurrer. Would you like to begin?"

"Sure," Bob said. "As you know, our position is that the marriage between Lester Gibbs and Mary Margaret is a valid one based on the First Amendment and therefore there is no basis here for a petition. Mary Margaret is a married woman and therefore not under the jurisdiction of the juvenile court."

"But there was not a *valid* marriage," Linda Farris said. "There was no marriage license and no court order allowing an underage child to marry."

"It is our position that we do not need the marriage to be sanctioned by the state. The church sanctioned it, as it has many other marriages in this parish. It is a basic tenet of the Square With God Church."

"We disagree," Sabre said.

"Do you agree that if there was a valid marriage, this case should be dismissed?" Bob asked.

"I agree that if there was a valid marriage prior to any physical contact by Mr. Gibbs with Mary Margaret, then no molest occurred."

"Do you have evidence that a molest occurred prior to the wedding?"

"Not at this time."

"So, the issue is still whether or not there was a valid marriage?" Bob asked.

"That is correct, and I contend there was not," Sabre said.

"Same here," Linda added.

"Then I guess we're done here. The law requires that we meet and confer, but we are too far apart to come to any agreement, right?"

"Agreed."

"I'll state that in my pleadings to the court." Bob stood up and walked out. The others followed.

Chapter 30

JP sat at his computer trying to get to know Harley Lindgren and Vanna Norstrom. He hated to take the time right now, but he knew this was as important to Sabre as her cases. If her mother was at risk, he needed to do something to stop it.

He took another look at Harley's family. He wanted to know as much as he could about him. JP always worked under the assumption that the more you know about a person, the easier it is to make the tough calls. It was often the smallest thing that led him to evidence or answers he needed. He had found a lot of information on the two older children, but not much on the youngest daughter. He made a timeline. Harley's youngest daughter was only four years old when her mother passed away. She had a stepmother from the age of eleven through fourteen, and then her stepmother was killed. She was a few months shy of eighteen when Harley married Vanna. DMV records showed her address on her license was the same as her father's at that time, but it appeared that she had graduated from high school and could have possibly been in college.

JP was deep into Lindgren history when his phone rang. It was an area code he didn't recognize. He figured it was probably a sales pitch, but he answered it in case it wasn't.

"JP Torn."

"Are you the private investigator?"

"Yes, sir."

"I'd like to hire you."

"To do what?"

"Surveillance, for starters. My name is Jim Knight and I'm on the Board of Supervisors for Blacksburg

University in Anchorage, Alaska. We have reason to believe that someone is stealing from the university."

"Are the police involved?"

"Not yet. We have some suspects, but we want to be sure before we go to the authorities."

"Why me?"

"Because you came highly recommended from a friend in San Diego. We're looking for someone who wouldn't know anyone here and has your skill set. Besides, we believe you would fit in well."

"Who is the friend?"

"I'd rather not say, but he has close ties to the San Diego Sheriff's Department."

"I'm not sure my investigator's license would be good in Alaska."

"I've already checked on that. Alaska does not require a state license, and we can take care of the local concerns."

Shocked by the call, JP didn't say anything for a few seconds.

"We can pay $200 per hour, plus all expenses including room and board. What do you say?"

"I need to think about it."

"We need someone right away. We can get you on a flight tomorrow."

"I'm pretty busy right now."

"I don't mean to put pressure on you, but time is of the essence for us. I can give you twenty-four hours and then I'll have to move on to the next one on the list. I just want you to know you are our top choice."

JP wondered if this guy was for real. He hoped so. He had always wanted to go to Alaska.

JP spent the next hour researching Blacksburg University and Jim Knight. The school appeared to be a legitimate private university, and Jim was a member of the board. He felt himself wanting to discuss it with

Sabre, but for now he decided to put it out of his mind and get back to the task at hand.

Lots of questions filled JP's mind about Harley Lindgren and his family. He didn't rule out the possibility that the daughter wanted to get rid of her new stepmother. Upon further investigation of the daughter, he found a misdemeanor drug charge shortly after her eighteenth birthday. It appeared she was now living in Fresno, California and working at Walmart. None of which really made her a killer. He picked up his cell and called DuBois.

"What do you know, McCloud?"

"You said there weren't any other suspects in the Vanna Norstrom disappearance, right?"

"Right. We considered a few, but nothing seriously."

"What about the youngest daughter? What do you remember about her?'

"She was a typical teenager, kind of mad at the world, but she had more reason to be than some. She had suffered so much loss already in her life, but she had a father who seemed to be there for her, and her siblings were supportive."

"Was she ever a suspect?"

"No. We checked her alibi for the time when Vanna left the house. She was babysitting for her older sister at the time. She stayed there for several days. I don't think it could've been her."

"Thanks. I couldn't find the trail."

"Have you discovered anything else?"

"Not really. I met Helga Norstrom. She didn't really want to talk about her sister's disappearance. I guess that's normal after all this time, but I'm going to follow up to make sure she isn't hiding something. I'd like this to be anyone except Harley. He has a date this Friday with Sabre's mother. I can't watch them except from afar because she knows me."

"Where are they going?"

"Out to dinner, I think, but I don't know where."

"Find out and I'll take my wife out for the evening—on you."

"It's a deal."

"I know Vanna had some mental health issues. How bad was she?"

"She spent some time in Camarillo State Hospital when she was a teenager. She was self-mutilating and kept hurting herself. She couldn't have anything sharp in her room, no scissors, pencils, pens, even paper clips, or she would hurt herself. She jumped from the balcony twice and broke her arm the first time, her leg the second time."

"How does a patient jump twice? Didn't the staff figure it out the first time?"

"Exactly. That's when her parents took her out of there. There were a lot of problems at the hospital at that time. I don't know if they were directly related to funding cutbacks, or if it was just poor management, but the hospital closed a few years later."

"Did she have any other hospital stints, public or private?"

"I don't think so, but according to her sister, she was on medication."

"And Harley didn't know that?"

"He says he didn't, not until empty pill bottles were found in the house."

"Do you think maybe she killed herself?" JP asked.

"We certainly considered that, but we've never found a body either. You'd think we would have by now."

"Unless she kept going on that train. Her body could be a long way away."

"That's true. There are body parts found all the

Teresa Burrell

time out in the desert, many of which are never identified."

"I saw that Vanna's deceased parents were in show biz in Sweden and apparently quite famous. And Helga lives in a very expensive home in Orange County. Did Vanna have money of her own?"

"Not that we could tell. The parents' money was left in a trust. Helga is the trustee and also the conservator for Vanna."

"So Vanna didn't have control of any real money?"

"McCloud, I know where you're trying to go with this, but we investigated the money angle from all sides. When we discovered Lindgren had two dead wives before the third one disappeared, the alarms started ringing. When he married the first time, his bride had nothing, and he had very little. They were young and hadn't really established themselves yet. Everything his second wife had went to her son. Vanna was more of a risk to Lindgren than he was to her. He foolishly didn't do a prenuptial agreement and he had a lot to lose."

"Did he have a prenup with the others?"

"No, but he had accumulated a lot more wealth by the third wife."

"So there's no pattern of 'marrying for money' with him?"

"No, and there's no money motive for Helga to kill her sister either. Upon Vanna's death, anything due her was not going to Helga, but to some charity in Sweden."

"Thanks, DuBois. I'll keep digging."

"Let me know the time and place for Friday night and I'll be there watching Sabre's mother. Although I can't imagine anything will be out of order. Even if this guy has been killing his wives, you have a long way to go before we get to that stage."

"I know, but I still feel better knowing someone is watching," JP said. "Do you think he might recognize you?"

"I doubt it. It's been a long time since I saw him, and even if he did, I don't imagine he would think anything of it. I'm just a man out to dinner with his lovely wife. And if he did recognize me, his date still won't know who I am. It might be a good thing anyway if he did."

"How's that?"

"If he's up to something, he might back off if he thinks we're onto him. That's what you want, right?"

"Right—unless he's one of the good guys."

"In that case, he won't be concerned."

JP continued to research Harley Lindgren. He discovered an attempt by Lindgren to get an annulment from Vanna about five years after she disappeared, but it was denied. A month ago, he filed for divorce.

Chapter 31

The Lynch Case

Sabre was alone in her office working at her desk. Normally, Elaine, the receptionist, worked until five, but she had an appointment and had to leave early. The other two attorneys who had offices in the old Victorian home were not there either. Hugh was gone a lot because of a big civil trial he was involved in, and David spent most of his time working his ice cream business. Sabre wondered why he even kept his office there because it wasn't unusual for him to only appear once a month.

Sabre seldom stayed late at her office because of a stalker who had once frightened her, but it had been years and she had learned to not dwell on it as much as she used to. That, coupled with the rape that took place one night, two buildings over from hers, made JP and Bob continue to voice concern. Sabre had come to terms with it. She had decided she couldn't live in fear, and sometimes she had work that needed to be done at the office.

Tonight, she was waiting for JP and Ron to meet with her. She decided she'd better go check the front door before JP arrived. He would be upset if she was alone with it unlocked. She stood up and stepped out of her office. She was almost to the front door when it flew open and Todd Lynch barged in.

"What the hell is the matter with you?" he shouted as he came toward Sabre.

Her first instinct was to run, but she had nowhere to go. He stood between her and the door, and she knew she couldn't make it to the back door. Even if she did, he would catch her in the parking lot. She stood her ground and said, "Calm down."

"Don't tell me to calm down, you stupid bitch."

Sabre tried to step to the side and move toward the door, but he moved in closer and blocked her way. He was getting so close, she took a step back, but it put her against the wall.

"What is it you want?" She tried to sound calm, but she could feel her voice shake, which only seemed to encourage him, so she tried harder to relax.

"I want my kids, and I want them now."

"That's up to the court." This time she didn't hear the shake in her voice, but she still felt it in her body.

Todd leaned in closer to her. She could feel his breath on her face. "Step back," she said, managing a little more resolve.

He didn't move. "Why are you trying to ruin my kids' lives? I haven't done anything wrong. They should've been living with me in the first place. That stupid mother of theirs is nothing but a druggie. You'd rather they were with a washed-up whore than with me."

"What are you talking about? I never recommended the children go home with their mother." Sabre shifted to the right again, trying to work her way toward the door, but Todd slammed his left hand against the wall, preventing her from moving. He seemed to be careful not to touch her. After a few seconds, he pulled his hand from the wall and suddenly clasped his hands together tightly in front of him, still only inches from her face. His face reddened with anger. His fingers began to turn white from the pressure.

Trying to sound in control, Sabre said, "Let's sit down and talk about this rationally."

Todd glared at her, but started to relax his hands. The color began to return to his fingers as he unclasped them. He took a short step backwards, but was still about eighteen inches from Sabre.

"And what's wrong with putting the boys with their grandmother?" he said in a tone not quite as loud as before.

"You tell me," Sabre said.

Just then JP burst through the open door. He took one step toward Todd and reached out to grab him when Sabre yelled, "No, JP. Stop."

Todd swung around and raised his hands, palms outward, blocking his face. "I was just leaving," he said.

JP let him pass as Todd dashed out the door, bumping into Ron on his way out.

"Are you okay?" JP asked.

"I'm fine."

"Do you want me to go after him?"

"No, I'm good. He didn't touch me, just yelled a lot."

JP wrapped his arms around her. "You're shaking. Are you sure you're alright?"

"I'm okay. I'm just a little frightened and a lot ticked off. Let's go sit down."

Ron closed the front door and turned the deadbolt. They all walked back to Sabre's office.

"What happened?" JP asked, once Sabre sat down.

Sabre began to recount the events, and the more she explained, the angrier JP and Ron became. JP paced the floor. Ron seethed. "You two need to calm down, or I'm not telling you anything else. You're making me *more* nervous instead of helping me."

"That son-of-a—"

"JP, please sit down," she said looking at him, then at Ron. "And *you*, breathe."

"Are you going to call the cops?" Ron asked.

"No, he didn't lay a hand on me, even though I

could tell he wanted to. He was so angry that he clasped his hands in front of him and held them there so tight that I thought he might break a bone."

"He did what?" JP said. Sabre could hear the anger in his soft voice.

Sabre demonstrated.

"That's what his brother says he does to his kids. It's a behavioral modification technique to get them to behave. He learned it from his mother who did it to them when they were young. Apparently, she used some pretty harsh punishment to train them so it would work. I think that was more of a threat to you than an effort to control himself."

"Maybe. I'm just glad he's gone and you two are here."

"Are you sure you don't want me to call the cops?" JP asked.

"No, but I need to call the social worker and let her know what happened. That way, it will get into the report for court."

Sabre picked up the phone and called the social worker. While she was on the phone, Ron went to the back room and got each of them a bottle of water.

Sabre hung up the phone, took a deep breath, and said, "Okay, you two get me up to speed on what you know about my cases. I need to think about something besides Todd Lynch, although he's not the only unhappy parent I'm dealing with right now."

"Did someone else threaten you?" JP asked.

"No, I have all these strange cases with strong-willed, angry parents, which isn't all that odd. It's just that I don't usually have this many at once. And then this thing with our mother." Without pausing, she said, "Ron, do you have anything new on Jim Jones?"

"I hit quite a few bars in East County and got nothing."

"Which means he probably doesn't frequent East County bars," JP said.

"I'm going downtown tonight, and if I have time, I'll go to some of the bars at the beach." Ron looked at the time on his cell phone. "I need to go. I told Mom I'd be home for dinner."

"Find out where she's going to dinner Friday night with Harley," JP said.

"That's my plan." He hugged Sabre and left.

Sabre and JP went through every case he was working on and discussed what he had learned.

"You met the LaFiura family when you were in Pasadena investigating Lynch, right?" Sabre asked.

"I only met Marilyn. I don't think her husband and children were home. I didn't go inside, so I can't be sure. Why?"

"Heather Lynch asked that their home to be evaluated for placement of the boys. I talked to the boys about it. Nolan and Drew were thrilled. Evan didn't seem to care much one way or the other. He just wants to be with his mother."

"But won't that make it harder for them to see their mom?"

"Heather's moving to Pasadena too, if her children do. She has a friend she can stay with there, and her sister has also opened her home to her. Heather wants to get away from the influences she has here and would already be gone if her children weren't in foster care."

"I just want that Todd guy gone," JP said.

"What did you think of Marilyn LaFiura?"

"She talked a lot, but she seemed genuinely concerned about the children."

"She's an Avon representative and an author, so she works from home. Her husband, Andrew, is a fireman."

"Good, then he should be able to handle Todd. My first impression of Marilyn is that she would be protective. That's all I got."

"The social worker evaluated the home today, so if that's the recommendation and Todd's not in agreement, I'm sure we'll be hearing about it soon."

"I got some more information on Harley Lindgren and Vanna Norstrom," JP said when there was a lull in the conversation. He filled her in on what he had learned.

"And he filed for divorce just a month ago?" Sabre asked.

"Yes."

"About the time he met my mother?"

"I didn't know exactly when they met, but I do know he filed for divorce around the same time he joined the online dating service. He listed himself as 'widowed.'"

"Do you think my mother is safe with this guy?"

"As long as she doesn't marry him," JP said. When Sabre didn't laugh he said, "Too soon?"

"Yeah."

"Until we can sort this out, Ron and I have worked out a schedule to keep an eye on them. And Detective DuBois is going to dinner Friday night at the same restaurant if Ron can find out where they're going."

She furrowed her brow and tightened her shoulders. "Why? Does he think Lindgren will hurt her?"

"No, he's just going to observe, and I think to get a free meal out of me. We're just taking precautions."

Sabre let her shoulders drop to a relaxed position. "You're right. I'm being silly. It's just that I'd like to be spending more time with my mother right now so we could talk about him, but I'm so busy and stressed out."

JP walked to her, took her hand as she stood up, and wrapped his arms around her. "Do you want to go to dinner and spend the evening together?"

She looked up at him. "I would so love to do that, but I'm going to get take-out and spend the rest of the night preparing for my hearings tomorrow. I'm sorry."

"No worries," JP said.

"I wouldn't be very good company anyway," she said, as she stroked his arm. "I'm already distracted because Mary Margaret is going to church tonight. I hope it all goes well."

"What could go wrong?"

"Not much, I guess. She'll be supervised by someone from DSS and they know she's not to be alone with either of her parents. I don't want her to accidentally see Lester. Although he's not supposed to be there, you never know."

"Do you want me to go?"

"I don't think you'll be too welcome there."

Sabre gathered her files and JP took them from her. She locked up and they walked to her car.

"Thanks for watching over my mom," she said, and then kissed him goodnight.

JP followed her home and made sure she got inside safely. Before he drove away, he picked up his cell and made a call. When the voicemail came on, JP said, "Jim, this is JP Torn. I won't be taking the job in Alaska, but thank you for the offer."

Chapter 32

Ron sat at the dinner table with his mother, anxious to ask her about Harley, but he didn't want to sound too concerned. Instead, he quizzed her about her day.

"Has that neighbor's cat been back?" he asked.

"The one that got locked in the garage yesterday?"

"Yes, that one."

"No, he hasn't been back. I haven't seen him today at all. I think maybe they're keeping him locked inside."

Ron took a couple of bites of his meatloaf. "Did you play bridge today?"

"Yes, I told you I was going to play bridge when I left this morning. And before you ask, my partner and I came in second."

"You mean you lost?"

"Yes, but it sounds better to say it my way."

A few seconds of silence passed before Ron said, "I saw there was a new plant on the shelf out back."

"Yes, I picked it up from the nursery on my way home from bridge today," Beverly said. She set her fork down on the side of her plate. "What is it you really want to know?"

Ron blurted, "Where are you going with Harley on Friday?"

"I knew there was something on your mind. I could always tell when you wanted to do something you were afraid to ask about. You'd give me the third degree on every innocuous thing you could think of before you got to the real question." Beverly smiled and looked at him with compassion. "It's so good to have you back home, Ronnie."

"It's good to be here, Mom. Now tell me already."

"We're going to C Level on Harbor Island. Sabre

and JP went there recently, and she said it has a gorgeous view."

"Sweet. That place isn't cheap, I guess I'll give him that. It does have a spectacular view of the water, the city, and Coronado Bridge. Have you been there before?"

"No, I've never been, so when Harley insisted that I pick some place nice, I did. I also looked it up online and I was quite impressed."

"Is he picking you up?" Ron asked, afraid of the answer. If he was, Ron planned to follow them.

"No, I'm meeting him at the restaurant. Not because I'm concerned, but I knew you and Sabre would have a fit."

"What time?"

She sighed, but then answered, "At seven o'clock."

"Mom," Ron said, trying to sound nonchalant, "how well do you know this guy?"

"We've gone to coffee three times, and we've had four or five phone conversations. We've exchanged life histories. He is very polite, has a good sense of humor, and I like him."

"How many times has Harley been married?"

"Three. Two are dead and one disappeared. He has three grown children from the first marriage: a lawyer, a teacher, and his youngest who has recently moved back home and enrolled in college. He owns a very successful real estate business, so I expect he is financially comfortable. He hasn't shown me his bank statements or his stock portfolio, but he does drive a new Mercedes." She paused. "But then you already knew all this, didn't you?"

"I didn't know about the Mercedes, or his daughter moving home."

"So Sabre is investigating him?"

"A little," he said sheepishly. Then he added with

more fervor, "You met him online. It's not like you know someone who can vouch for him." He reached across the table and touched her hand. "We just want you safe, Mom."

"I know, and I appreciate that. I think if you met him, you'd feel better about him."

"Good idea, Mom. When can we do that?"

"Let me get through our first date. I don't want to scare him off."

They finished their meal and then both stood and picked up their plates. "Oh, and we've had sex twelve times in the back of his Mercedes," she said seriously.

"Eww! Mom!"

She roared with laughter. "I'm kidding. You know your mother better than that, but you deserved it. You should've seen the look on your face."

"You got me good, but do me a favor, okay?"

"What's that?"

"Pull that on Sabre when you get a chance, but say twice instead of twelve. It'll make it more believable."

Ron chased his mother out of the kitchen. They had an agreement that if she cooked, he did the cleanup, and vice versa. At first, she tried to do it all, but she finally quit fighting him on it, which made him feel better about staying there. He didn't want to be a burden on her. Before he started the dishes, he called JP with the time and location of his mother's date.

"Are you going to the bars tonight?" JP asked.

"Yeah, I think it's a good night to go downtown and try the Gaslamp Quarter."

"That's a lot of bars. Maybe I should go with you. We can split up and hit more that way. Maybe it'll give us time to do another area as well."

"Do you have time?"

"There's not a whole lot I can do elsewhere

tonight. Sabre's too busy, it's too late to go to Orange County and follow up on Vanna, and I'm sick of sitting at the computer. If I'm going to work, that means going to church or the bars. I choose the bars."

~~~

The Parker Case

JP and Ron made a plan before they left. They were familiar enough with the Gaslamp to know which bars were where. They decided to each take at least two smaller bars and one large one, and then meet in front of The Tipsy Crow on Fifth Avenue.

JP started at the south end of the Gaslamp, near Market. His first stop was The Field Irish Pub, which was literally brought over in pieces from Ireland and reassembled. It was dark and cozy, and known for its good food. It was busy, but it didn't take long to find out that a guy who wore his wire-rimmed sunglasses the entire time had been there several months back. He struck out at the Barleymash and Werewolf bars, but he wasn't sure if they were too busy to notice the guy or if he hadn't been there.

JP tried a couple more bars on the side streets with no luck until he reached The Reef, a small dive on Market. He discovered Jim Jones had been there as recently as the night before. MJ, the bartender, was certain that was him in the photo JP had on his phone.

"Did he leave with anyone?"

"I'm not sure. He seemed to be hitting on one of our patrons."

"Did they leave together?"

"I think so, but I can't be certain. I was about to go see if Dandee needed another drink, and they were both gone."

"You know her?"

"Just from coming in here. You get to know the names of the regulars. She's been here a lot the last couple of weeks. She used to come in every few nights and then she stopped for about six months until a few weeks ago."

"Do you know anything else about her?"

"Only that she's troubled. She seems to be drinking her sorrows away right now."

JP handed her his card. "Please call me if she comes back in. We'd like to stop this predator."

"You got it."

JP stopped at two more places before he reached The Tipsy Crow. Ron was coming out of the bar.

"I got nothing in there," Ron said, "but I found one place that had seen him, and one that was a strong maybe, both dives. The bigger places were a bust."

"Same here," JP said. "That seems to be his pattern. How long ago was he here?"

"They were both pretty vague, three months, six months, maybe a year."

JP shared what he had found out. Dandee appeared to be their most likely chance of talking to another victim.

"Do you want to hit the bars at the beach?"

"You go ahead. I think I'll call it a day. I'm tired as a two-dollar hooker on dollar day. Let me know what you find."

Chapter 33

The Fowler Case

"How did it go in church last night?" Sabre asked Mary Margaret.

"It went really well. I got to see Penny. She told me about all the things that are going on in the church."

"Like what?"

"Like Dana got caught passing a note to Brayden last week. They got in so much trouble. They had to sit on opposite sides of the circle last night, and they couldn't sit together when we had a snack, or during prayer."

Mary Margaret babbled on about the evening and her time with Penny. Sabre felt good that Mary Margaret had a few moments of childhood. So much of that part of her life was gone.

"It felt so good to be in church again. I know God wanted me there." She looked down at her feet and bit her lip. "I just get so confused sometimes."

"How do you mean?"

"I want to be a good girl and do what's right, but I don't want to be married to Lester. He's creepy."

"I know."

"I want to go home to my parents, but I don't want Lester there. But my father says I need to trust God. He has a plan. Papa says we're legally married in the eyes of the church and it's wrong for me to fight that. What do you think, Ms. Brown?"

Sabre did all she could to keep from saying what she really thought. She didn't like any excuse for child molestation and that's the way she saw this whole thing. Mary Margaret was too young to consent to any of this. For Sabre, it was simple. She was too young to consent to a marriage, they had no marriage license sanctioned by the state, and in the eyes of the law, Mary Margaret was not married. But for Mary Margaret, it was much more than that. She had a moral dilemma she couldn't figure out. She felt guilty for not obeying her parents and even guiltier for not doing what she thought God wanted her to do.

Sabre took Mary Margaret's hands in hers, looked her in the eye, and chose her words carefully. "Mary Margaret, I know life is very unsettling for you right now. I also know how important your church and your beliefs are to you and I wouldn't ever try to take that from you or disparage it in any way. The same with your parents. I would never tell you to disrespect them. What I will tell you is that adults don't always agree on how children should be raised, and the law isn't always black and white. You have stated several times that you don't want to be married to Lester. My job as your attorney is to protect you—as a child, not as a married woman—and I'll keep fighting until we win, or run out of options. Your job is to try to be a kid, and let the adults sort out the legal issues. Once they're resolved, we can figure out where to go from there."

"I try not to think about everything at home. I do pretty good most of the day, but when I go to bed at night, I start to think about the things my father tells me when he visits."

There was a court order that her parents could not discuss the court case with Mary Margaret, or talk about Lester or the marriage. "Has he said anything about the case or about Lester?"

She thought for a moment. "No, he just says to trust God's plan, but I know what he means by that."

"Does your mother say anything?"

"No, she hugs me a lot and tells me how much she misses me."

171

"You seem to be pretty settled in here. Are things going okay?"

"Mr. and Mrs. Venable are very good to me. She loves to bake, and she's really good at it. They're good Christian people. They said if I wanted to and my parents agreed, I could go to church with them on Sunday. They know how much I miss going to church, but they made it very clear that I didn't have to go."

"What do you think about that?"

"I wouldn't mind, but I'd rather go to my own church. Do you think I could go on Sunday?"

"You're not concerned about seeing Lester?"

"I don't have to talk to him or anything, do I?"

"No, you would not. Let me see what I can do."

"Thank you, Ms. Brown."

~~~

Back at her office, Sabre called the social worker on the Fowler case to see if transportation and supervision could be arranged for Sunday morning to take Mary Margaret to church. They agreed that it had to be someone who would sit with her through the services.

When the social worker called back about fifteen minutes later, Sabre called Bob to set the guidelines for the father.

"I'm sure my client will be ecstatic that his little girl can go listen to his sermon," Bob said.

"Just make it clear to him that it is still a supervised arrangement, and the restraining order on Lester Gibbs remains in full force."

"Since he'll be spouting his divinatory words of prudence from the pulpit, he won't have much control over that."

"I understand, but tell him anyway. She'll be sitting with her mother and the DSS supervisor, so I'll make it clear to Irene as well."

"I don't think that'll be a problem."

"I hope it's not a mistake," Sabre said and hung up.

Chapter 34

"Are you sure you don't want some company, Mom?" Ron asked as his mother started out the door for her dinner date.

She walked back to where Ron was standing and put her hand on his cheek. "Ronnie, it's very sweet how you're trying to protect me, but it's getting a little annoying." She gave him a tender look, patted him, and added, "I love you, dear."

He smiled. "I love you too, Mom."

He texted JP: *She's on her way.*

JP: *TY, I'll let DuBois know.*

~~~

DuBois saw Harley waiting outside the restaurant when Beverly arrived. She left her car with the valet. Harley greeted her and escorted her inside the busy restaurant. Since C Level didn't take reservations, they put in their name for a table and waited at the bar.

DuBois approached the maître d' and flashed his badge. "See that couple over there at the end of the bar?"

"Yes," he said.

"The name on your list is Lindgren. We need to be seated close enough to them to be able to observe them. Can you do that?"

"Is there going to be trouble?"

"No, nothing like that." DuBois palmed him a twenty-dollar bill. He didn't usually tip when he was investigating, but this felt a little different, and he was pretty sure it would get him a lot closer.

"I'll take care of it, sir."

DuBois and his wife went to the other end of the bar, where they could still see the couple. They were close enough to see them but not hear them. Twenty minutes passed, and they were not seated. Beverly and Harley nursed the first drinks they bought, chatting like two young kids. Thirty minutes later, they were all still waiting. DuBois' wife was getting a little anxious. "I'm hungry, Vinny," she said.

"I expect it's taking a little longer because they're trying to get two tables near each other. I told you I had to do some surveillance."

"Not until we were almost here. I might've known, when you said we were going to this fancy restaurant."

"Come on, you're always wanting to go out to different places. Just enjoy it."

"You're right. It's just nice to get you out of the house."

Another ten minutes passed before Beverly and Harley were shown to their seats. Then a waitress led DuBois and his wife onto the patio area and seated them adjacent to the windows that enclosed the patio, giving them a full view of the city skyline and Coronado Bridge. Directly behind them, adjacent to the windows as well, were Harley and his date. Harley was closest to their table. DuBois wished the couple were in the opposite seats so he could observe Harley's facial expressions. Since that wasn't an option, DuBois sat with his back to Harley's, hoping he could hear what Harley was saying. It worked.

"I'm proud of my daughter for going back to school. I never thought I'd see the day."

Harley continued to talk about his family while DuBois listened, until finally he heard his wife say sharply, "Vinny."

"What?"

"You haven't heard a word I've said, have you?"

"What is it?"

She handed him the wine list. "I'm having a glass

of wine. Are you going to join me?"

Just then the waitress came over and took their orders. Vinny ordered the fish and chips, and his wife ordered the special, which was a combination of different seafood. They each ordered wine.

DuBois did his best to have a conversation with his wife and listen to Harley throughout the meal. It worked most of the time. He had gotten pretty good at making listening noises over their forty-three years of married life. He looked at his wife. She had aged right along with him, and put on some weight, as he had, but she still looked beautiful to him. They'd had some rocky spots in their marriage, most of them due to his other spouse—the sheriff's department. He knew it wasn't easy being a cop's wife. Retirement was right around the corner. He vowed to himself to make it up to her.

Harley's conversation never consisted of anything more than one would expect from a normal first or second date. DuBois made sure the bill was paid early on, and then lingered at the table, waiting for Harley to leave. They didn't seem to be in any hurry. DuBois decided to make his presence known, hoping it would chase him away from Sabre's mother. He stood up and walked to the bathroom, passing the couple, but Harley's back was to him.

When DuBois returned, he caught Lindgren's eye.

"Evening," DuBois said.

Harley nodded and said, "Detective."

Harley didn't hurry to leave. It was another twenty-three minutes before they finally got up and left the restaurant. DuBois and his wife did the same. Once outside, Beverly and Harley waited for the valet to bring their cars around. It was perfect, since DuBois had found a parking spot on his own that was fairly close. He and his wife walked to their car, pulled out of the spot, and waited at the end of the lot until Beverly drove by. JP had described the car and given him the license plate number, so he was certain it was her. He had no idea where Harley was.

He followed Beverly's car onto the freeway in the direction of her home. He continued to watch to make sure Harley wasn't following them, but was certain he was not. He called JP.

"We left the restaurant. I'm following Sabre's mother home."

"Thanks. Ron is at home, so she'll be fine once she's inside. I'll text him and let him know she's on her way. Did you learn anything?"

"Not really. I could hear a lot of their conversation throughout dinner and it was all very innocent. Mostly talk about his work, her bridge games, and how he'd like to learn to play someday. A lot of chatter about their children. Nothing unusual. Just two people getting to know each other. There was one thing."

"What was that?"

"Toward the end, I made my presence known. I walked right past him, looked him in the eye, and greeted him. He responded, and he knew who I was."

"Maybe he was just being friendly."

"No, he called me 'Detective.' And he didn't seem surprised. Did Beverly know I was going to be there?"

"No, she knows we've been checking on him, but no details."

"We were all at the bar for over half an hour where I couldn't hear any of their conversation, so he might have spotted me earlier."

"He's a businessman. He's used to greeting people and remembering faces."

"Or maybe it's a cat-and-mouse game, and he wanted me to know that he knew who I was," DuBois said.

Maybe, JP thought, as he hung up.

Chapter 35

According to Ron, his mother had a wonderful time on her date and was determined to continue seeing Harley Lindgren. The only way to really know if Lindgren was involved in Vanna Norstrom's disappearance was to find Vanna—or her body, which seemed an unlikely task since the police hadn't been able to get very far. JP had the feeling that Helga knew more than she was telling and hoped to get some direction from her, so he decided to spend his Saturday in Orange County.

During the drive to Tustin, he thought about how he would approach her. He had a hunch she was hiding something. *Perhaps Vanna was alive, and Helga knew where she was. But why would she keep that hidden? What did she have to gain? Maybe she was just being a loyal sister.* JP decided to approach her again and see if he could gain some insight.

It was barely eight o'clock when JP arrived, and no traffic was going into the gated community. He waited about fifteen minutes before he was able to follow someone through. It was still too early to knock on her door, so he parked where he could see if anyone came or went. He saw no activity.

At 9:15 he rang the doorbell, hoping he wasn't waking her up. Apparently, he had not, because when she answered the door, she was dressed up as if she was going out.

"Oh, it's you," she said grudgingly. "What do you want this time?"

"Just a few more questions, ma'am. I see you're headed out again, so I won't take much of your time." He paused to see if she would volunteer where she was going. When she didn't, he said, "Do you have any reason to believe your sister is alive?"

She frowned at him. "Mister..." She paused. "What is your name again?"

"JP Torn." He thought about making up a name, but since he had never said he was a policeman, he decided it was better this way. If this went much further, he would probably have to reveal who he was anyway.

"Mr. Torn, I have every reason to believe my sister is dead. She left eleven years ago with no money and hasn't asked me for a dime since. My sister and I were real close, so even if she didn't need money from the trust, she would've gotten ahold of me if she could." Her face filled with sorrow. "I know I wasn't always the best big sister. I wasn't always there for her when we were younger. I should've been more understanding about her illness, but we got closer as we aged." She stopped speaking for a second, then said, "Do you have something new that makes you think she's alive?"

"No, ma'am, but it's possible she's in some institution and they don't know who she is."

"That detective checked out every hospital, clinic, and mental institution in a two-hundred-mile radius and couldn't find anything. He did it again a year or so later. You should have that in your records."

"Yes, of course, but it's been almost ten years since that was done, and she could be in another state."

"Look, Mr. Torn, my sister is *dead.* Your coming here is just getting my hopes up, so unless you have some new information, please don't come back."

JP didn't blame her for getting upset. He realized he might have gone too far, and he probably would've handled things differently if it weren't for the safety of Sabre's mother, but he couldn't help feeling a chill when Helga said the word *dead.*

JP left, waited for Helga to leave, and followed her to Fashion Island in Newport Beach, where she went straight to Neiman Marcus, or as Bob referred to it, Needless Markup. It wasn't a store JP had ever been in, partly because he hated to shop and partly because it was out of his budget. While he waited, he jotted down her license plate number, GST 023, more out of habit than anything. He was going to call his friend Ernie or DuBois and ask them to run it, but decided it was a waste of time.

Helga exited Neiman Marcus carrying three large shopping bags. Her next stop was a designer denim boutique called 7 For All Mankind, where she left with one more bag about the same size as the others.

When she drove to a place called Basin Street Hair Salon, JP followed her. When she didn't come out after ten minutes, he drove back to her neighborhood and started knocking on doors in search of someone who had been there long enough to know Vanna. The first three neighbors he spoke to had lived there less than ten years, and none had gotten more than a hello from Helga. The fourth house was an older couple named Anastasia and Ervin Lott, who invited him into their home after he told him who he was. He explained that he was a PI and he was trying to find Vanna.

"That poor girl," Anastasia said. "Do you think there's a chance she's still alive?"

"I don't know, but either way, we'd like to know." As JP walked in, he said, "Your home is very beautiful." He looked around the living room and through the huge window at a view of the city. "Nice view too."

"Yes, the homes up here are situated so they all have beautiful views," Anastasia said. "It's not beachfront, but we decided we didn't want to be at the beach. It's too busy and noisy most of the time."

"Well, it's very nice, ma'am. And you said you

moved in when the houses were first built?"

"That's correct. We were the first to buy, before they were even finished. There were only twelve homes built in the community. The Norstroms bought the last home, which was the model."

"That was in the 80's?"

"Yes."

"So the girls were young?"

"They were teenagers when they moved in. Vanna was sixteen, and Helga was eighteen."

"Did you know the parents very well?"

"They spent a lot of time in Sweden. They were in show business, you know. The girls pretty much lived there by themselves. I mean, the parents would come for a weekend here and there, or occasionally one of them would be here for a week or two, but it was never very long before they'd be gone again. The girls traveled a lot too, especially Vanna. She spent a lot of time in Sweden or on the road with her parents."

"What were the girls like when they were young?"

"They were complete opposites. Vanna was lively, outgoing, a little wild, I think. Helga was far more reserved, kept to herself, read a lot, but she had to be more level-headed because she had the responsibility of caring for Vanna. I think it was hard on Helga, keeping all the young men away."

"Helga had a lot of suitors?" JP asked.

"No, they were there for Vanna. Although Helga was the prettier of the two, Vanna always had the more gregarious personality. I always thought Helga—"

"Anastasia," Ervin interrupted, "don't be telling things you don't know."

"Tsk. It wasn't easy for Helga, that's all."

JP figured she was probably talking about the mental issues so he asked, "Were you aware of any mental problems Vanna had back then?"

"Yes, her mother confided in me once over a bottle of wine. Even though she wasn't here that often, I got to know her fairly well. We had a lot in common, both in the biz and all, although her talent was very different from mine. I acted some myself, you know, but I wasn't really that good at it. That's how I met Ervin. He was a movie director, but even as much as he loved me, he had to admit I wasn't that good. But he married me, so I got the best role in the end."

"And she's been playing the part of a good wife ever since." Ervin smiled and winked at her. "She's the best actress for the part I could have ever cast."

JP thought it was very endearing, the way this couple in their eighties still seemed to be in love. He hadn't seen much of that in his family, certainly not with his parents.

"Anyway," Anastasia said, "she told me Vanna had spent a few months in Camarillo, but she had improved a lot. I don't think she could handle her and that's why she stayed away so much. Helga had far better control over Vanna than either of her parents did, but it was hard on her. She gave up her life for Vanna."

Ervin frowned at his wife.

"Well, she did, Ervin. That's not gossip. It's just what it is."

"Did you see Vanna around here near the time she disappeared?"

"The cops talked to everyone in the neighborhood when they were investigating, otherwise I probably wouldn't remember. I hadn't seen her the night she was supposed to go to Helga's. It had been several months since I had seen her go into that home. We hadn't spoken in a few years prior, so I knew little about her at that time."

"What about Helga? Do you talk much?"

"Not really."

"What do you mean *not really?*" Ervin said lightheartedly. "You haven't spoken in fifteen or twenty years. Not even so much as a greeting. You only know what she's doing because you watch out that window."

Anastasia pointed to the bay window in the front of the living room. "As you can see, I have an excellent view of their front door. It's not that I try to watch, but sitting here, I can't help but see."

The Lott house sat on higher ground than the Norstroms', and they were almost directly across the street. "You do have a good view of the front door."

"And the master bedroom," Ervin muttered.

"Oh, pish, posh," Anastasia said to Ervin. "Anyway, as the years went on and Vanna became an adult, Vanna came and went, and Helga became more of a recluse. She seldom went anywhere and never had company except for Vanna. After Vanna disappeared, Helga hardly came out of her house for over a year, but then I think she started seeing a therapist."

Ervin snickered, but kept silent.

She waved her hand at him, making a dismissive motion.

"You never mind, Ervin. It gives me something to do." She turned her attention back to JP. "Anyway, as I said, I think she was getting professional help because she started going out three times a week at two o'clock in the afternoon. She did that every week for over a year, and then it decreased to once a week. After a while, she started going out at other times of day, and she started dressing better. She even started getting her hair done. Now she pretty much comes and goes."

Anastasia pointed to the window. "Look, there she is."

JP watched as the garage door opened across the street, and a Mercedes pulled into the garage. The trunk popped open and Helga removed several packages. She walked around her car toward the front of the garage and the door closed behind her.

"She shops a lot," Anastasia said.

"Does she ever have company?"

"She never used to, but I think she recently got a new male friend."

"You mean, like a boyfriend?"

She looked at Ervin before she answered. "I don't know about that. I can't say I've seen anything romantic, but he's called on her for the last three Saturdays." She glanced at the grandfather clock in the corner. "He should be here in about an hour." She stood up. "Will you excuse me for a moment, please?"

"Certainly," JP said. He visited with Ervin while she was gone. They talked about sports and about his career as a director. He had funny tales to tell about Robert De Niro and Christopher Walken, and several others. He was in the middle of a story about young Tom Cruise, aka Thomas Cruise Mapother IV, when his wife returned.

When he finished his story, Anastasia said, "I never tire of hearing about his experiences, especially the early days. It got rougher as time went on; there was so much competition, and it got real cutthroat. Ervin retired a lot earlier than he had planned, but I'm glad he did. We had plenty of money for what we wanted to do, and we've had a lot of wonderful years together."

"It's nice to see," JP said. "I'd better get going."

"Would you like to stay for dinner? We have plenty, and I'm a much better cook than I was an actress."

"That's true," Ervin mumbled.

Anastasia waved her hand at him again. "If you stay, you'd be able to see the man who calls on Helga," she said with a grin.

JP thought about it, but he wanted to get a photo if

he could, and hopefully a license plate number. He didn't want to do it in front of them and he could possibly have a better vantage point from his car. Besides, he didn't want to intrude.

"Thank you, ma'am, but I really better go. I appreciate the information and I enjoyed our visit. It made me happier than a hog in mud." He gave them his card and left.

Chapter 36

J P sat in his parked car a few hundred feet south of the Lott home. He had a good view of Helga's house. At 5:28 p.m. a silver Camry passed him, drove to the corner, made a U-turn, and then pulled up in front of Helga's home. JP had his camera ready and snapped a photo as a silver-haired man stepped out of the car. He was dressed in a well-fitting suit and walked with confidence toward the front door. The door opened, and he stepped inside. For a second, JP thought the man leaned in for a kiss, but he couldn't be certain.

The car had no front license plate, which wasn't unusual in California even though it was required by law. JP drove forward, made a U-turn in the same spot the Camry had, and pulled up to the curb on the opposite side of the street, putting him behind the Camry. He felt a little conspicuous with only two other cars on the street, but this put him in a better position to see the plates and to follow when they left, and he was not visible from inside Helga's house. With the help of his binoculars, he was able to see the plate. He wrote the number down on his notepad and waited.

By six o'clock, JP was getting restless. He called his friend Ernie Madrigal, explained what he was doing, and asked him to run the plate. By six-thirty he was beginning to wonder if they were going out at all, but he continued to wait. He hoped they would leave before the sunset. The later it got, the harder it was going to be to follow them in city traffic.

JP picked up his phone to call Sabre, but before he could make the call, the front door opened and Helga appeared, followed by the silver-haired man. Based on comments Anastasia had made, JP watched for signs of their relationship. Was it a date? Or were they just friends? He wasn't sure that it mattered, but his gut told him it did.

The man walked behind her to his car, reached out and opened her door, and she got inside. They drove off and JP followed, keeping his distance, but close enough to see which way they turned after they passed through the gates. Once he saw them make a right-hand turn, he pulled forward and out of the gate, which did not require a code to open when leaving. He caught up to them at the first traffic light.

The traffic was heavy and JP almost lost them twice before they turned south on Pacific Coast Highway. They stopped at Mastro's Ocean Club, a high-end restaurant on the waterfront, and left their car with the valet. JP held back, found his own parking spot, and waited about five minutes before he went inside.

He glanced into the foyer before entering to make sure Helga wasn't still there. A couple in their thirties were at the counter where a tall man in an expensive suit appeared to be seating people. He led them inside and returned.

"May I help you, sir?" the man asked, eyeing his clothes from top to bottom.

"May I see a menu?"

The man hesitated. "We're by reservation only, sir." Even his voice showed disapproval for JP.

"It ain't for tonight," JP said in a stronger than usual southern accent. "My wife and I have a big anniversary comin' up and I want to see if the food would suit her."

He handed JP a menu. JP looked it over. He thought about asking to have a quick look at the dining area, but decided he would be too conspicuous. The man kept watching him as if he were going to steal his menu.

JP handed the menu back to the man and said, "I 'spect this'll make her as happy as a clam at high tide. See ya next month."

JP stayed on PCH until he reached Dana Point, then took Interstate 5 south toward home. He called Sabre, but she didn't answer. He called Ron and told him what little he had found out.

"You left them at the restaurant?" Ron asked.

"Yeah. I knew I didn't belong there when I saw there were no prices on the menu." They both laughed. "Have you talked to Sabre tonight?"

"No, why?"

"I tried to call her a few minutes ago but she didn't answer."

"I'm sure she's fine."

"I know, but I don't like what's going on with that Lynch guy. He's madder than a bat in a suitcase. I don't want him around Sabre when he blows."

"Neither do I. I thought I'd try the bars in North County tonight, but I'll stop by and check on Sabre first."

JP had an incoming call. "That's her now. I'll call you later." He disconnected and answered Sabre.

"Hi, Sabre. Everything okay?"

"Yeah, I was in the shower when you called. Are you done for the day?"

"Yes, I'm headed back."

"How close are you?"

"I passed Del Mar a few minutes ago. Are you free?"

"As a bird. I need a break, and I'd like to spend it with you. Are you hungry?"

"Just for you, darlin'," JP said. "But I should go home and take a shower."

"You can take one here."

JP hung up and heard his stomach growl, but it was already past eight-thirty and he was anxious to get to Sabre's. He decided he could order pizza if she didn't have anything to eat in her house except salad, which he referred to as rabbit food.

His phone rang, and a San Diego number flashed across the screen. "JP Torn," he said.

"Hello, this is MJ from The Reef. You were in here last night asking about the guy with the sunglasses."

"Is he there?"

"No, but Dandee is. She just came in alone."

"I'll be right there. I'm about ten minutes away."

He called Sabre back and told her. She was disappointed and said, "Maybe we shouldn't be spending so much time on Jim Jones. He doesn't really matter to the outcome of this case unless he turns out to be the father."

"I don't have to go. I'd much rather come see you."

She was silent for a few seconds. "No, I can't stand the thought of that predator out there. If we can do something to stop him, we should. You better go talk to her. Who knows when you'll get another chance."

"Okay, kid. If it's not too late, I'll come by after."

~~~

At MJ's direction, JP found Dandee near the end of the crowded bar. There were no seats available on either side of her, so he stood behind her and ordered a beer. When MJ brought the beer, she said something in a low voice to the man sitting next to Dandee. He stood up and took an empty seat a little further down.

"Can I buy you a drink?" JP asked Dandee.

She looked him up and down and said, "Absolutely."

He signaled to MJ and then pointed at Dandee's empty glass. "Coming up," MJ called out.

"Do you come in here often?" JP asked.

"More than I should, but I've never seen you here before."

"It's only my second time here. Nice bar, though."

"The people are nice."

JP waited until her drink came. "Thanks," she said, "but so you know, as good-looking as you are, I'm not looking for a hookup."

"I'll be straight with you. I'm here to get some information."

"I might have known." She seemed a little disappointed. "Are you a cop? Because I don't need any more trouble."

"No, I'm a private investigator."

She slapped her hand lightly on the bar in frustration. "Tsk. You already have my kids. What more do you want? I'm not using drugs. I just have an occasional drink. That's not illegal."

"Whoa," JP said. "I don't know anything about that. Are you involved with CPS or is it a custody battle with the father of the children?"

"CPS."

"I don't work for the county. This has nothing to do with your case. I didn't even know you had one. It's about a man you met in here a few nights ago. He probably called himself Jim Jones."

"That guy is a real whack job! He thinks he's some kind of an angel or something."

"Did you leave here with him?"

"I must have, but to tell you the truth, I don't remember much. I felt kind of drunk, but I had only had a couple of drinks. I think he walked out behind me, and the next thing I knew I woke up with him in my bed. I told him to leave."

"Did he?"

"Not right away. He kept babbling about how famous he was going to make me when I gave birth to his child who would be the next prophet. He had me sort of pinned down, and he wouldn't let go of me until I told him I had to go to the bathroom. Then I got up and grabbed the baseball bat I keep under my bed and told him to get out. That's when he finally left. He was so scared he left without his stupid sunglasses."

JP showed her the photo on his phone.

"That's him," Dandee said. "Stupid sunglasses and all."

"One more thing," JP said. "Which court is your dependency case in?"

"What does that have to do with anything?"

"Please. It may tell us more about your predator."

"Whatever." She shrugged. "It's in Meadowlark."

~~~

JP reached Sabre's condo at 9:48 p.m. He couldn't see any lights, but if she was upstairs reading or watching television, he wouldn't be able to see that without going around to the back. He sat in the car trying to decide if he should knock on the door, call her, or leave. He didn't want to wake her if she was asleep and since she kept her phone next to her bed, calling would be as bad as knocking. *If she wanted me to come in, she probably would have left a light on downstairs,* he thought. He drove away.

Chapter 37

The next evening, JP was waiting for Sabre at her office when she arrived. They had plans to go over the cases JP was working on and then finally go to dinner. Sabre was a little frustrated that JP didn't make it back to her house the previous night, but she decided not to bring it up. After all, he was working for her and she didn't want to sound petty.

"Thanks for meeting me here at the office," Sabre said. She kissed him lightly, and they went inside.

Sabre pulled her files and sat down at her desk. JP sat across from her. She picked up the first file and said, "Let's start with Parker. What did you find out last night about Jim Jones?"

"The most surprising thing was that Dandee has an active dependency case."

Sabre's eyes widened. "That's interesting. Every other victim we've talked to was also in the system, but that's because we got them from other dependency attorneys. This one came from outside. That seems like a big coincidence."

"That's what I thought, and I don't take much to coincidences. It's only one victim, but still, what are the odds? The thing is, I thought since we had found three or four within the system that once we started investigating, we would find dozens of others that had no connection to juvenile court."

"You know what this means," Sabre said. "He must be connected some way to juvenile court."

"Yes, and he's not picking up random women. He knows they're vulnerable and may even know which buttons to push."

"And where they hang out."

"If he has access to their files, he would have a lot

more information on them as well."

"That's frightening," Sabre said. "Has Ron come up with anything new?"

"He's narrowed Jones' territory. He found no sign of him in any of the outlying areas; nothing in east, north, or south counties. It has all been downtown and Clairemont, possibly the beach."

"That's still a huge area. If he's an employee, he would have to have access to case files. If he works at DSS, it's most likely Linda Vista."

"I asked Dandee where her case is, and she said Meadowlark."

"So, he could be with social services at Lavant Street in Linda Vista."

"Or he could work at juvenile court at Meadowlark."

"It's time to turn this over to the authorities. I'll call and report it."

"I think that's a good idea. There have been too many victims, and most of them sound like they'd be willing to help, especially Dandee. He left her house without his sunglasses, so they have some physical evidence to connect to him. She told me she hadn't touched them. She was tempted to throw them in the trash, but she didn't have the heart to throw away an expensive pair of Ray-Bans."

"Did you get a chance to talk to Sheila Krueger, Sarah's paternal aunt?"

"I did. I met both her and her husband Paul. They really want Sarah. And they want Denny, even though they aren't related to him. They both strike me as no-nonsense kind of people. Sheila loves her brother, but I don't think she'll let him break the rules if they were to be placed there."

"The social worker agrees. I think the problem last time was that Sarah's father, Russell Drake, had control. This time, he won't be living with them."

Sabre set the file she was holding aside and picked up another.

"Lynch," she said.

"Have you had any more problems with him?"

"No. I heard through the grapevine he's boiling mad about DSS putting the kids with his neighbors, Andrew and Marilyn LaFiura. Somehow, I'm getting the blame for that too. I'm not exactly sure why, since the request was made by Heather, his ex-wife, and the evaluation was done by the department. Maybe he found out you went there and spoke to the LaFiuras, or maybe he sees me as an easy target."

"He better not mess with you again or he's gonna find himself a few pickles short of a barrel."

Sabre frowned. "The thing is he's fighting the placement, but if the kids move to Pasadena, their mother plans to go too and live with her sister, Delores Green. Then there is no basis to keep the case in San Diego, which is what he seems to want most."

"Wasn't the Department considering placement with Delores?"

"Yes, but she's too afraid of Todd. She's a single mother and she didn't think she was strong enough to control the situation."

"So this is the second placement he has fought in Pasadena, but he wants the case moved to Los Angeles County?"

"He does. He's been asking for that since the first hearing, but apparently, he wants the children with the LaFiuras even less. Or maybe the only places he'll consider are with him or his mother."

"I just hope they all go to L.A. I'll feel a lot better knowin' he's not doggin' you."

Sabre picked up the next file. "That leaves the Fowler case. Their big argument is that Mary Margaret is legally married and therefore not under the jurisdiction of the juvenile court. We weren't able to come to any agreement at the meet and confer, so the judge will decide on the demurrer."

"And if you lose?"

"If we lose, it's over. If the court rules they were legally married at the time then there was no molest. The cause of action in the petition is for the same date they were married. We have no evidence that supports anything happening before that date. Although, I'd bet my last dollar it did. Besides, if the marriage is valid, juvenile court has no jurisdiction."

"And if you win on the demurrer?"

"Then we're back to the usual jurisdiction and disposition issues, placement, etc."

"Any chance Candace Fowler will leave her husband for Mary Margaret?" JP asked.

"I doubt if she could protect her daughter from the wishes of her husband. He has a pretty strong hold on her. And she has her two boys to consider as well. I'm sure she's afraid he'll get the boys."

"Is there anything else you want me to do on this case?"

"Not at the moment."

"So that's a wrap. Wanna go eat?"

"You bet. Just let me get the files together that I need for court tomorrow." Sabre brought up the calendar on her computer and started to pull the files. "Have you learned anything new about my mother's new love interest?"

"Not that I haven't already shared with you."

"What does your gut tell you? Do you think Vanna is alive or dead?"

"I don't know, but I think both of those Norstrom girls, Helga and Vanna, are a bit left of center. I have to wonder what kind of childhood they had."

"It sounds like they had to fend for themselves at a

pretty young age. Who knows what else they went through?"

Sabre stood up and started to reach for her stack of files. Just as she did, her phone rang. "Sabre Brown," she said. Her face lost color. "What?" she said loudly. She listened. The color came back, turning her face red with anger. "And you're just now telling me?" She listened a little longer, then said, "Text it to me," and hung up.

"What is it?" JP asked.

"Mary Margaret is gone."

"What do you mean gone?"

"The guy who was supervising her visit to the church lost her. During the service, Mary Margaret went to the bathroom and never came back."

Chapter 38

"Let's go," Sabre said.

JP took her stack of files from her and followed her out the door. "Where are we going?"

"We're going to talk to the guy who lost Mary Margaret."

"I'll drive," JP said. "Where to?"

Sabre checked her text messages. "DSS in Linda Vista."

"It's Sunday night. Aren't they closed?"

"They opened the building for the social worker."

They got in JP's pickup. "Dang it!" Sabre said as she slammed the door.

"Easy on the door. It ain't the truck's fault," JP said.

"Sorry. I didn't mean to slam it. I'm so frustrated. Mary Margaret has been gone for almost three hours and I just heard about it."

Sabre's phone rang. The ringtone was a Leonard Cohen tune. She hit the speaker button. "Hi, Bob. I take it you heard about Mary Margaret."

"I got a call from Seth Fowler. He's pretty upset at you and the social worker."

"Because we let her go to church?"

"No, because you're fighting the whole thing. He said if his daughter was with her husband like she should be, she wouldn't be in danger now."

"Right," Sabre said. "Did he say anything about Lester?"

"I asked him if he thought Lester might have taken her. He said he didn't think so, but my money is still on Lester."

"Mine too. Have you talked to Irene?"

"Yes, she said Mrs. Fowler is upset, but she trusts that God will keep Mary Margaret safe."

"Did Seth tell you what happened?"

"He didn't seem to know much. Do you?"

"No, but we're on our way to speak to the DSS worker who was supervising. I'll keep you posted."

Sabre had calmed down a little by the time they reached the Department of Social Services. Only four cars were parked in the lot, one of which was a 1970 Chevy Chevelle LS6. JP admired the car as they walked past it.

Upon checking their ID, a security man let them inside the building and led them to an office. Two women and a young man, who looked to be about twenty-five, were in the office. Sabre recognized the social worker, Misty McMorrow, and her supervisor, Maxine Quinn. Sabre had known Maxine for a lot of years and had great respect for her.

"Thanks for coming, Sabre."

Sabre introduced JP, and Maxine introduced the young man as Kyle Greene. Kyle stood up and shook Sabre and JP's hands. He had very short blond hair, was about six feet tall and beefy, some muscles, but looked like he enjoyed his food as well. Kyle sat down and began wringing his hands.

"I know you've told this story a dozen times," Maxine said, "but please tell Sabre what happened, from the beginning."

"We got to the church about five minutes before the service started. Mary Margaret's mother was waiting outside for us as was previously arranged. They hugged and then we walked into the church and sat up close to the front. Not the first row, but a couple rows back. Mary Margaret sat between her mother and me. About an hour and fifteen minutes into the service, Mary Margaret said she had to go to the bathroom." Kyle popped a knuckle.

"And you let her go alone?" Sabre asked

incredulously.

"No way. We left the church together and she led me outside to a restroom on the side of the church. I couldn't go inside with her, of course, so I waited outside." He sighed and popped another knuckle, appearing to be completely oblivious to his habit. "Here's where I messed up. I had to go too, so I dashed into the men's room. I figured I had plenty of time because men are always quicker than women, right? I came right out and I waited for her. Several minutes went by and I started to get concerned. I waited a few more minutes and then I knocked on the door. No one answered. I knocked again. Nothing. Finally, I pounded. When I got no response, I opened the door, which I may get in trouble for, but I didn't know what else to do. The room was empty. I'm so sorry."

"What did you do then?"

"I looked around outside, hoping she was out there, but she wasn't, so I went back into the church to see if she was with her mother. She wasn't. Mrs. Fowler saw me and followed me out and helped me look. Then she went back inside to see if Mary Margaret was sitting anywhere else. I kept looking outside."

"Did you ever see Lester Gibbs?" Sabre asked.

"I didn't know what he looked like, but I asked Mrs. Fowler and she said she saw him leave the church shortly after the service started and she didn't notice if or when he came back."

"But he was there when it was over?"

"Yes, she pointed him out when he came out of the church." Another knuckle popped.

"Did you talk to Lester?"

"No, that's when I called Misty, and shortly after, the cops came."

"Who was there when the cops arrived?"

"The pastor, Mrs. Fowler, Lester, and a couple with a young girl named Penny."

"That was Mr. and Mrs. Cunningham," Misty said. "Penny wanted to see Mary Margaret, so they were looking for her. When they found out she was missing, they stayed to see if they could help."

"I don't think I have any more questions," Sabre said. She looked at JP. "Do you?"

"Kyle," JP said, "is that your muscle car out there in the parking lot?"

"That's my pride and joy," he said, looking a little brighter for the first time since they had arrived.

"Is it a 454?"

"Yup, but the experts claim the output is closer to 500 horsepower. I've got it to hit 60 miles per hour in 5.2 seconds."

"Did you know that until 1970, GM wouldn't allow any other Chevy to carry a horsepower rating higher than the Corvette? I don't know why they finally did, but the Chevelle LS6 was quite a car. Yours is in great shape too."

"Thanks," Kyle said.

Sabre frowned at JP for getting off the subject.

JP said, "Do you mind showing it to me?"

"No, not at all." He turned to Maxine. "Am I done here?"

"Yes, you may go, but keep your phone near you in case we have any other questions."

Kyle seemed to relax once the men were outside. He spoke excitedly about his car.

"Look, Kyle. I know you might be reluctant to say too much in front of your supervisors, but what you tell me won't be repeated."

"Okay."

"Did anyone ask you to let Mary Margaret get

away?"

"No," he said quickly.

"Did Mary Margaret give any indication beforehand that she wanted to run away?"

"No, she didn't say anything like that. In fact, she spoke very little. She seems kind of shy."

"Think carefully, Kyle. Is there anything else you remember?"

"I don't know if it's important, but just before the cops got there, I saw Mrs. Fowler glare at Lester."

"Like she was angry with him?"

"Yes, but then the pastor put his arm around her and kind of turned her so she wasn't facing him. At least, that's the way it looked to me."

Chapter 39

The Lynch Case

Attorney Wes Hodges was inside the courtroom when Sabre walked in. "Great," he said, "just the person I wanted to see."

"Good morning, Wes. What's on your mind?"

"My client is dead set on his children living with family."

"You mean *his* family. He certainly doesn't want them with the maternal aunt."

"Why don't you want them with their grandmother?"

"Because she's not very grandmotherly. What's wrong with the LaFiura family?"

"Plenty," Wes said, but didn't offer any further explanation.

"Doesn't he want this case transferred to LA County?"

"Yes, he does, but not at the expense of his children."

"Is there something about the LaFiura family that I should know?"

"I'm sure you've done your research."

Sabre figured he must be bluffing, acting like there's some big secret, but she didn't know for sure. DSS had done their investigation and JP had as well, once they were considered for placement. Neither had found anything that made them inappropriate for detention of the children.

"If you were to agree to detain the children with the grandmother, maybe together we can convince the social worker. Otherwise, I'm going to have to convince the judge."

"Perhaps if we had a different judge, but there's no way Judge Hekman is going to approve the grandmother's home," Sabre said with the utmost confidence.

Just then Judge Federico Castro walked in through the back door and took the bench.

Wes gave Sabre a sheepish smile and said, "We have a new ball game."

"Good morning, Your Honor," Sabre said.

"Good morning, counselor." He smiled at Sabre. "How are you this morning?"

"Very well, thank you. So nice to see you on the bench this morning."

"It's good to be here."

Sabre turned to Wes, grinned, and said, "Give it your best shot."

"That I will." He left the courtroom.

Sabre didn't feel as confident as she looked. Judge Hekman could make some strange calls, but Sabre had no idea what Castro might do. She knew he was very pro-family, as was she, but sometimes he made some unpredictable orders.

"Are you ready, Ms. Brown?" the judge asked.

"Ready, Your Honor."

He turned to Mike McCormick, the bailiff. "Please see if the other parties are ready to go. I don't want to be dragging this morning calendar into the afternoon."

McCormick left the courtroom and returned with the attorneys, Wes Hodges and Regina Collicott, and their respective clients, Todd and Heather Lynch.

"It appears we have two issues in this case this morning, detention of these boys and change of venue. It also appears that the mother plans to move to Pasadena, the father already lives there, and if the children are detained in Pasadena, I'll be inclined to change venue. So, let's deal with detention first." He

Teresa Burrell

looked at Deputy County Counsel Linda Farris. "What is the Department recommending?"

"We evaluated the home of Andrew and Marilyn LaFiura and found it to be quite satisfactory. Marilyn works from home and can transport the children to and from school. Andrew is a fireman who works a three/four-day shift. He's willing to supervise the visits."

The judge turned to Regina Collicott. She stood up. "Regina Collicott for the mother, Heather Lynch, who is present in court. We are in full agreement with the recommendations."

"Mr. Hodges?" the judge said.

Wes stood. He was a big man whose presence exuded power. His voice matched his looks. "My client does not think this would be an appropriate place for the children when there is a perfectly good grandmother willing and able to take the boys. The law favors placement with family when possible. This grandmother has raised two stable, successful boys, my client and his brother who is a CPA in Costa Mesa."

Suddenly when it's convenient the brother isn't homeless, Sabre thought.

Wes continued. "The grandmother doesn't work outside the home, so she would be available to get the children to school and be there when they return. All of the boys have spent time with her and know her, unlike the LaFiura family whom only Drew really knows."

Judge Castro looked at the attorney for the Department. "Has the grandmother been evaluated?"

"Yes, Your Honor," Deputy County Counsel Linda Farris said. "We do not think it is an appropriate placement. We believe she would hand the children over to her son."

"He's a non-offending parent," Wes interjected. "Todd Lynch is not the reason this case is in court. There is no evidence of abuse or neglect by my client.

In fact, he fought vigorously for custody of his boys in order to protect them. He contends that if family court had given him custody, we would not be here today."

"And yet they didn't," the judge said. He turned to County Counsel. "Why are you not recommending return of the children to their father?"

Sabre wondered if he had read the file. She stood up. "Your Honor, the children do not want to live with their father."

"That's a lie," Todd said, loud enough for everyone in court to hear.

Wes leaned over and whispered to his client. Todd sat silently with his arms crossed.

Sabre continued. "The children do not want to live with their grandmother either. They appear to be afraid of both their father and their grandmother. As far as the grandmother, Ruth Lynch, being an appropriate placement, we would agree with the Department. She does not seem to really want the boys, but she would take them for Todd. She told my investigator, and I quote, '...they won't be any trouble. Todd will make sure they stay in line. He always does.' I don't think she fully understands that she would need to be the caretaker and not their father. Also, Ian Lynch, Todd's brother, has been estranged from his mother for about five years. He does not see his mother as a good placement for the children."

The judge addressed Todd Lynch. "Do you want these boys home with your mother?"

"I'd rather have them with me, sir," Todd said, "but if I can't, then my mother would be a good place for them."

Sabre was getting concerned about what Castro might order. She wanted to tell him more about Todd's recent behavior, but she didn't dare interrupt him.

"Why do you think your children are saying they

don't want to live with you or their grandmother?" the judge asked.

"They're not," he said angrily. His attorney glared at him and he toned his voice down. "I don't believe that at all, unless someone has convinced them of it. Their grandmother isn't a 'cuddly, bake cookies' kind of grandmother, but they love her and she loves them. Both she and I are stricter than their mother. I'm sure the boys have been getting away with whatever they want with Heather. It's no wonder they don't want to come home."

"So you agree they don't want to go home to you?"

Todd's voice grew louder. "No, I didn't mean that. The social worker, their mother, Ms. Brown...they're all filling my children's heads with lies about me. I love my boys and I want what's best for them. They should be with me. I haven't done anything wrong." As his voice grew louder, Wes put his hand on Todd's arm. Todd stopped talking.

"Why did you go to Ms. Brown's office last Wednesday evening?"

Todd cleared his throat. "To convince her to send the boys home with me or their grandmother."

"Do you suppose she felt threatened?"

"I didn't threaten her," he shouted. "She's lying."

Wes stood up and put his hand on his client's shoulder. "Your Honor, I'm sure you can see my client's frustration. He agrees that these children were appropriately removed from their mother's house. He has been trying to tell judges and mediators that from the beginning, but he feels like no one has been listening. Now that the boys were removed from that environment, he is labeled as the bad guy. He is a non-offending parent, and there are no allegations or evidence of abuse by him. He can't even get unsupervised visits with his boys. He just wants his children back at home where he can see to their needs." Wes sat down.

"I certainly can see his frustration," the judge said. It sounded sarcastic to Sabre, but she still wasn't certain what he was going to order.

"Other than your client's preference to have the children with family, do you have any specific objections to placement with Marilyn and Andrew LaFiura?" Castro asked.

"My client believes the children need a strong father figure in the home and Mr. LaFiura is a fireman who is gone three full days a week, and sometimes for long periods when he is fighting fires. Also, if the court orders supervised visits and Mr. LaFiura is the supervisor, his visits would be severely limited."

The judge perused the file. Then looked at the Deputy County Counsel. "The grandfather is not alive, correct?"

"That's correct, Your Honor," Linda Farris said.

"And there's no father figure in the grandmother's home, right?"

"That's correct, Your Honor," Linda said.

Attorney Wes Hodges stood up again. "Your Honor, my client understands there is no father figure in his mother's home, but Mr. Lynch would be there a lot more often, and consequently, the children would have their actual father. He is willing to concede to supervised visits if the children were detained with his mother. It would be a more natural setting, and a lot more comfortable and less disruptive for the boys."

"Anything further?" Castro asked, looking directly at Wes Hodges.

"Would you like me to make my argument for change of venue at this time, Your Honor?"

"No need," the judge said.

Sabre started to stand up. She needed to make

sure this judge knew how angry this father was, and that he needed counseling before these boys would be safe at home with him. The problem was that she didn't have a lot of specifics, but the reactions of the boys were enough for her.

Judge Castro looked at Sabre and shook his head. "I know your position, counselor."

Sabre sighed with relief and sat down.

Judge Castro made his orders. "The children will be detained with Mr. and Mrs. LaFiura in Pasadena, California." Todd's face reddened and Wes once again tried to calm him by gripping his arm. The judge didn't look up as he continued with his orders. "The father will have supervised visitation with Mr. Andrew LaFiura as the supervisor. The times and places to be arranged by the Department of Social Services. If Mr. LaFiura is unable to supervise, the Department will use a supervisor of their choice until this matter is sorted out. The court grants the father's motion for Change of Venue to Los Angeles County once the children are moved to Pasadena. All other orders remain in full force and effect."

Chapter 40

The Fowler Case

The counsel table was filled from left to right with Deputy County Counsel Linda Farris, Sabre, Candace Fowler, her attorney Irene Serlis, Bob, and his client, Seth Fowler. Judge Hekman was on the bench.

"We're here for the demurrer today. I see the pleadings were filed by Mr. Fowler. The meet and confer was unsuccessful, is that correct?"

All the attorneys agreed.

"What is the position of Mrs. Fowler?"

"She is in agreement with the father, Your Honor. However, Mr. Clark will be making the oral argument."

"And I see that both the minor's attorney and county counsel filed responses. I'm willing to hear from both of you, but please do not repeat the same arguments. Saying it twice doesn't make it any more plausible. Who wants to take the lead?"

Sabre and Linda looked at each other. "I'll be glad to," Sabre whispered to Linda. Linda nodded. "Fine with me."

"I will, Your Honor," Sabre said. She was very vested in this and wanted to make a clear record. She trusted Linda would pick up any points that she might miss.

"Very well, then, Mr. Clark?" Judge Hekman said.

"Your Honor," Linda said, "did you get a chance to see the supplemental report this morning?"

The judge opened her file and read. "Are you serious?" she said.

"Yes, Your Honor, the minor, Mary Margaret, went missing from church yesterday."

"And she hasn't been found?"

"No, Your Honor. We don't know if she was kidnapped or if she ran away. The parents have been very cooperative."

"The entire congregation of the Square With God Church has formed a search party, Your Honor," Irene said. "They were out until late last night, and those who could were back out again this morning. The parents stopped only to come to this hearing."

"Would you like to continue this to another date?" the judge asked.

"We discussed that, Your Honor," Bob said. "Our clients would like to go forward with the hearing, if the court permits."

"Very well, then. Mr. Clark, would you like to start?"

Bob stood up. "Thank you, Your Honor. Let me start by saying that my client does not believe his rights come from the U.S. Constitution, but rather from Almighty God. However, I know the court wants to hear the law and it is our contention the law supports his position. The First Amendment to the U.S. Constitution has a double aspect with regard to religion. First of all, it prevents compulsion by law of the acceptance of any creed or the practice of any religion. It permits freedom of conscience and freedom to adhere to any religious organization or form of worship. Secondly, it safeguards the free exercise of the chosen form of religion. My client is merely exercising his First Amendment right."

Sabre stood up. "May I, Your Honor?"

"Go ahead, counselor."

"We agree that the First Amendment grants those rights. However, the first aspect is absolute, the second is not. A person's conduct must remain subject to regulation for the protection of society. If it were otherwise, one could excuse any behavior by claiming it was the expression of a professed religious belief."

Bob said, "According to *United States v. Ballard,* (1944) 322 U.S. 78—"

"Please dispense with the cites or we'll be here all day. I can see them in your pleadings."

"Thank you, Your Honor. In *Ballard,* while a court can inquire into the sincerity of a person's beliefs, it may not judge the truth or falsity of those beliefs. My client wholeheartedly believes that God wants Lester Gibbs and his daughter to be wed. In fact, God spoke to him and told him so. He also believes that the government does not overrule the will of God. The marriage of two people is a holy sacrament, not a governmental contract."

"Forgive me, counselor, but I'm obviously not familiar with the practices of this church. As for the sacraments, I know the Roman Catholic Church has seven of them. I know some Protestant churches have two, Baptism and the Eucharist. So, I need you to school me here. What sacraments does this church practice?"

Bob whispered with his client. "They have three, Your Honor, the two you mentioned and Holy Matrimony."

"Okay, please proceed."

"It is my client's contention that God, not the state, sanctions marriage. The government can't compel affirmation of a religious belief according to *Torcaso v. Watkins,* nor penalize or discriminate against groups or individuals due to their religious beliefs as found in *Fowler v. Rhode Island.*"

"Is that a relative?" Judge Hekman asked facetiously.

"Not that we're aware of, Your Honor. However, I'm sure my client would appreciate any Fowlers before him setting a precedent. My client should not be penalized for his religious beliefs, and religious belief is absolutely protected."

"We agree that religious belief is absolutely protected," Sabre said. "However, religiously-motivated conduct is *not*, according to *Sherbert v. Verner*. Such conduct 'remains subject to regulation for the protection of society,' as determined by *Cantwell v. Connecticut*. According to *Wisconsin v. Yoder*, religion clauses only serve to protect those claims *rooted* in religious belief. We contend that marriage to a twelve-year-old is not rooted in the religious beliefs of the Square With God Church."

Bob responded, "The issue is not the age of the bride, but rather that the church has the right to marry whomever God compels them to marry without permission from the state in the form of a license or a court order. Even the State of California does not have any minimum age whatsoever for a minor to marry. Technically, a six-year-old could marry."

"If they had a court order," Sabre said, shaking her head. "This minor did not. There is a proposed bill, SB 273, right now, to regulate child marriage, due to the deleterious effects created from young marriages, especially to older men."

"As Ms. Brown said, it is a proposed bill and is not in effect. As to the *Yoder* case that Ms. Brown mentioned, it was also found that government action that burdens religious conduct is subject to a balancing test, in which the importance of the state's interest is weighed against the severity of the burden imposed on religion. The greater the burden imposed on religion, the more compelling the government interest at stake must be. We contend that if the church has to get permission to marry every time God tells them to, it will create an overwhelming burden on the church and one of its basic tenets."

"The Supreme Court in applying that balancing test has allowed some religious conduct to be banned entirely," Sabre said with more fervor. "The court upheld the law against polygamy; it upheld mandatory participation of Amish in the Social Security system; it upheld compulsory vaccinations for communicable diseases; it upheld license requirement for religious parades; and it permitted the state to prohibit parents from allowing their children to distribute religious literature when necessary to protect the children's health and safety. It would certainly apply to the marriage of a twelve-year-old girl for her safety and well-being. Studies have shown that women who marry as girls face greater vulnerability to domestic and sexual violence. They have more medical and mental health problems. They have an increased high school dropout rate, increased risk of future poverty, as well as up to 80% divorce rates."

"That has not been the experience of the couples who have married within the Square With God Church. Quite the contrary. The divorce rate is extremely low, as are mental health problems and the high school dropout rate."

"Your Honor, in the well-known *Reynolds v. United States*, the Supreme Court held that Congress could constitutionally apply to Mormons a prohibition against polygamy, and, in so doing, promulgated a basic test for the constitutionality of state legislation. If the court does not allow more than one wife, it certainly would seem that it wouldn't allow an adult to marry a twelve-year-old."

Sabre took a deep breath and tried to calm herself because her arguments were getting too passionate.

"Really?" Bob shook his head at Sabre.

"Counselor, make your point," Judge Hekman said.

Bob cleared his throat. "*Reynolds* is a case from

1878 which, if it were tested today, would likely be overturned."

"But it hasn't been overturned, has it, Mr. Clark?" Hekman said.

"No, Your Honor," Bob said. "Not yet."

Sabre continued. "It is still the law. The Supreme Court held in *Reynolds* that 'the history of the laws against polygamy showed that the condemnation of the practice was a matter of the gravest social importance.' It found in polygamy 'the seed of destruction of a democratic society.' It viewed the practice as 'highly injurious to its female adherents.' Allowing a marriage or even the illusion of a marriage to a twelve-year-old is certainly injurious to that child. It strips her of her basic freedom."

Bob responded, "In that case, the Court also compared polygamy to human sacrifices and funereal immolation of widows, which is a little extreme and archaic. On the other hand, in *People v. Woody*, the Supreme Court found that there was an unconstitutional infringement of the freedom of religion guarantee of the First Amendment of the Constitution of the United States. In *Woody*, a group of Navajos met in an Indian hogan in the desert to perform a religious ceremony that included the use of peyote. The Indians were arrested and convicted for the unauthorized possession of peyote. The Court concluded that 'since the defendants used the peyote in a *bona fide* pursuit of religious faith, and since the practice does not frustrate the compelling interest of the state, the application of the statute improperly violated the First Amendment's guarantees of freedom of religion.'"

"Your Honor," Sabre said, "that case can be distinguished because the Navajos had a long history of the practice of peyotism. It is essential to the ceremony of the Native American Church, a religious organization of Indians. It is documented as such as far back as 1560. The sacramental use of peyote composes the cornerstone of their religion."

"Just as marriage initiated by God Himself does in the Square With God Church, or as the bread and wine does in other Christian churches."

"To the American Indians, peyote is more than a sacrament. The court determined that it was so engrained in the practice of their religion, to prohibit it would result in a prohibition of the practice of their religion. It then went on to the second step, to determine if there was a compelling state interest that would override the defendant's First Amendment right. The Supreme Court found there was not."

"We would contend, Your Honor," Bob argued, "that if the court does not allow marriage initiated by God, it would also result in a prohibition of the practice of my client's religion. After all, what is more powerful than the Word of God? In *Reynolds*, at the time, the court considered polygamy a 'serious threat to democratic institutions.' This is quite the opposite. Marriage is a basic foundation of family and our democratic society. We want that upheld. In *Woody*, the Supreme Court realized that religions are practiced differently, and we have a basic right under the Constitution. The difference between the *Reynolds* case and the *Woody* case is eighty-six years of living in a democratic society under our great Constitution of the United States."

Sabre rolled her eyes. "The Supreme Court distinguished *Reynolds v. United States* from the peyote case for two fundamental reasons. First was the degree of abridgment of religious freedom. They determined that polygamy was a basic tenet in the theology of Mormonism, but it was not essential to the practice of the religion. On the other hand, peyote is the sole means by which defendants are able to experience their religion. Without it, they could not practice their faith. Second was the degree of danger to state interests. In *Reynolds,* it far exceeded that in the peyote case. *Reynolds* is the case that needs to be applied here because of the extreme danger put on children. As in *Reynolds,* it is a 'serious threat to democratic institutions and injurious to the morals and well-being of its practitioners.'"

"The determination of who is to marry whom is a basic tenet of my client's religion," Bob said, making another attempt to argue his client's point. "Mr. Fowler regularly receives the word of God directing him to arrange the marriage of two persons, and in this case, God, Himself, directed the reverend to marry Lester and Mary Margaret. Not permitting him to do so would be keeping him from practicing his religion."

"Are all marriages arranged in that manner, Mr. Fowler?" Judge Hekman directed her question to Bob's client.

Mr. Fowler said, "All marriages within the church are sanctioned by God, not the state. I will not perform a ceremony if the couple feels they need permission from the state."

"Why is that?"

"Because if God has not told them to marry, then they should not marry."

"So, sometimes God tells the couple and sometimes He tells you. Is that correct?"

"Yes, God does not limit His voice to me alone, but I always consult Him in such matters."

"Your Honor," Sabre cut in, "another thing that is considered by the courts is the history of the tenet. Whether or not the religion has a long history of these marriages being arranged, and if these marriages were successful. There is little history of the tenets of this church because it was established only eighteen years ago."

"Exactly," Bob said. "The tenet of the church is as old as this religion itself. It began day one. They have a history of successful marriages by those who follow the tenets of this religion, with no harmful consequences, including that of my client and his wife. They have been married for thirteen years and are still married and happy today. We ask that the court allow my client to practice his religious freedoms given to him by the United States Constitution, find that a valid marriage exists between Lester Gibbs and Mary Margaret Fowler, and grant our demurrer." Bob sat down.

"Ms. Brown?"

"I would only add, Your Honor, that this practice subjects my client and similarly situated minors to abuse, deprivation of their right to education, and circumstances similar to indentured slavery without presenting opportunities for independence. This is particularly true for my client as she does not want to be married to Mr. Gibbs."

Bob stood. "We object to the last comment Ms. Brown made regarding her client's desires. That is a factual issue, which we would contest given the opportunity."

"I will not take that into consideration in making my ruling, Mr. Clark." She turned to County Counsel. "Ms. Farris, what is your position?"

"I concur with minor's counsel and request that the court deny the demurrer."

"Ms. Serlis?"

"I concur with Mr. Clark."

"Thank you." She looked down at her notes and then back up again. "I'll let you know when I've made my decision." She looked at the parents. "I hope they find your daughter really soon. You must be very worried."

"So is her husband," Mr. Fowler said.

"I'm sure he is," Hekman said. She tapped her gavel on the sound block. "Court is adjourned."

Chapter 41

JP waited in Miles Cunningham's office with Miles' wife, Julie.

"Miles will be here in a second," Julie said. "Can I get you something to drink?"

"A water would be good."

"I'll be right back," Julie said and walked out.

The office was simply decorated. Miles's desk was tidy, with only a computer, a pen holder, an 8 x 10 photo of his family, and one basket with a couple of files. The only things hanging on the walls were a painting of the Star of India, a framed California insurance license, and a certificate of some sort purporting to recognize his excellence in sales.

Miles and Julie walked into the office. Julie handed JP the water, and Miles greeted him and took a seat behind his desk. "I expect this is about Mary Margaret being missing. What can we do to help?"

"I'm sure you've spoken to the police, but I have a few questions."

"Of course."

"Did either of you see Lester Gibbs leave the church during the service?"

"No," they both said.

"Did you see Mary Margaret and her supervisor leave?"

"No, I'm afraid not," Miles said.

JP looked at Julie when she didn't answer right away. "I didn't either, but Penny did."

Miles looked surprised. "Why didn't you tell me that?"

"She told me last night just before she went to sleep. I didn't think it was important."

"What did she tell you exactly?" JP asked.

Teresa Burrell

"She said she saw Mary Margaret leave, and that's when she asked me if she could go to the bathroom. I told her to wait, that the service wouldn't be much longer."

"Do you know if she saw Lester leave?"

"I don't know."

"I'm not accusing your daughter of anything, but sometimes kids don't realize the consequences for their actions. Do you think there's any chance Penny planned to help Mary Margaret run away?"

They both sat silent for a second, exchanging glances. "It's possible," Julie said. "Penny really felt bad for Mary Margaret. She kept asking us how she could help."

"If Penny knows where she is, she needs to tell. If Mary Margaret ran away, she's probably still safe, but that can change depending on where she's hiding."

Miles sighed. "We understand."

"Can I speak to Penny?"

"Of course, but she's not here right now," Miles said. He turned to his wife. "What time do you pick her up today?"

"She gets out of school at 2:30 today, but she has a dance class right after, so we won't be back here until about four o'clock. You can come by then."

~~~

JP spent the rest of the morning interviewing everyone he knew who was connected to Mary Margaret, but made little progress. He decided to concentrate his efforts on Lester Gibbs, even though the police had searched his apartment and found nothing.

JP had called Merlot Group Home and found that Lester was not working, so he parked near his home to see if he came and went. Lester left about noon, went through the drive-through at Jack in the Box, and then returned home. JP was still sitting in front of Lester's house when Sabre called.

"How did the hearing go?" JP asked.

"I don't know. Hekman took it under advisement, but I can't imagine her not ruling in our favor."

"When will you know?"

"Whenever she has decided. There's no hurry as long as Mary Margaret is gone since we can't do anything else on the case until she's found. Have you learned anything new?"

"No. I spoke to the foster parents and they said there wasn't any indication that she might be running away."

"Did anyone besides Mrs. Fowler see Lester go in or out of the church?"

"No, but most of them didn't see Mary Margaret or her supervisor leave either. I guess they were pretty intent on the service. I spoke to Miles and Julie Cunningham. They didn't see anyone leave the church during the service, but Mrs. Cunningham said that Penny saw Mary Margaret leave. I expect she was watching her friend more closely than the adults were. She also said that Penny asked to go to the bathroom, and she told her to wait."

"Do you think Penny and Mary Margaret planned something?"

"I asked the Cunninghams, and they think it's possible. I have an appointment to talk to Penny at 4:00. Want to go?"

"I'll see you there."

~~~

Sabre hoped Penny didn't feel too intimidated surrounded by so many adults. She didn't appear to be, but Sabre didn't know her well enough to be sure. Penny was safely positioned between her mother and father on the sofa in the living room. JP and Sabre sat in armchairs a few feet in front of them.

Miles spoke first. He had assured Sabre and JP that they hadn't questioned Penny any further. "As I told you, Penny, Ms. Brown and Mr. Torn are going to ask you a few questions about Mary Margaret. They really need to find her to make sure she is safe. You need to tell them the truth. Do you understand?"

"Yes, Daddy, I will," she said confidently.

"Penny, you saw Mary Margaret in church yesterday, right?"

"Yes, I wanted to talk to her, but I didn't get to."

"I understand that you asked your mother if you could go to the bathroom at some point during the service. Was that when Mary Margaret went out?"

"Yes, I thought maybe she was leaving and I wanted to see her before she left."

"So, you didn't know she was going to the bathroom?"

"No."

"But you asked your mother if you could go there."

"Yes, because I knew she wouldn't let me go outside to say goodbye and I miss Mary Margaret a lot." Her mother took Penny's hand and gave it a little squeeze.

"Did you know she was not coming back into the church?"

"No, but I was afraid she was leaving with her supervisor."

"When you saw her last Wednesday evening at church, did you talk about her coming to church on Sunday?"

"I told her to come if she could. She said she'd try."

"And she didn't say anything about running away?"

"No. Do you think she did?"

"Run away?" Sabre asked.

"Yes."

"We don't know what happened. That's why we're asking so many questions. If she did run away, do you have any idea where she might be?"

Penny glanced around at the adults. "I don't know where she is. I wish I did. I would tell if I knew, but I don't."

"I need you to think carefully, Penny. Did Mary Margaret say anything that might make you think she was leaving the foster home?"

Penny didn't answer right away. She took a deep breath. "She missed her mom and seeing me, but she liked her foster parents and she didn't mind living there. She was afraid she might have to go live with Brother Gibbs and she hated that." She paused. "I would've helped her if she had asked me to, but she didn't. I wish she would've because then I'd know where she is now."

"I wish she had too," Sabre said.

"Penny," JP said, "did you see Lester Gibbs leave the church yesterday during the service?"

She shook her head. "No, but I never look at him. He's creepy." She shuddered.

Miles's face turned red. "Penny, has Brother Gibbs ever done anything to you?"

"No, but he looks at me funny." She gave a quick, disgusted snort. "He looks up and down, like from my toes to my head, when he talks to me and other girls. All the girls hate it."

Miles's nostrils flared and he took a deep breath. "Penny, you do not have to talk to him or be around him at all. If he comes near you, you go to the nearest adult. Do you understand?"

"Yes, Daddy, I will. We've all gotten pretty good at

avoiding him." She started to choke up when she said, "Except for poor Mary Margaret, because he'd come to her house."

"Penny," Sabre said, "I know Mary Margaret has told you things in confidence, but it's important that we know everything so we can help your friend. I'm going to ask you a couple more questions and I need you to be honest with me, okay?"

Penny looked at her father.

"You need to tell them everything you know, Penny," Miles said. "It's the only way to help Mary Margaret."

"Did Mary Margaret ever tell you that Brother Gibbs touched her inappropriately?"

Penny's face flushed and she gazed at the floor. "She said he touched her 'who-hah.' That's what she called her private parts." She looked up. "And that he kissed her on the lips with his mouth open. She said she wanted to throw up."

Sabre noticed Julie's grasp on her daughter's hand tighten, and her father's jaw clench.

"Was that before or after the wedding?"

"About a week or so before. I didn't see her after the wedding until last week."

"Thank you, Penny. You've been very brave."

Penny snuggled up to her mother, who wrapped her arms around her and held her. Miles stood up, as did Sabre and JP. He walked them to the door.

"I'm sorry Penny had to go through that," Sabre said. "I know it made her uncomfortable."

"It did. And I feel so bad for Mary Margaret, but I keep selfishly thinking how glad I am that nothing happened to Penny."

Chapter 42

Bob and Sabre sat in the hallway at juvenile court waiting for their last case to be called.

"My client is chomping at the bit to get the ruling on the demurrer," Bob said.

"You'd think he'd be more concerned about his missing daughter," Sabre said.

"I know you don't like him much, but he is genuinely concerned about Mary Margaret. He's been searching every day with a group from the church."

"You're right. I'm being unfair. How's the mother handling it?"

"She's been staying close to home with the boys."

"She's probably afraid to let them out of her sight."

"Yes, and she's hoping Mary Margaret will show up."

"You know Hekman isn't going to rule on the demurrer until Mary Margaret is found, right?" Sabre said.

"I know. I'm sure she doesn't want to make this ruling at all, and as long as the minor is missing, she doesn't have to."

"There's no downside to her putting it off, really. And you know she isn't going to rule in your favor."

"Not likely." Bob stood up and stretched.

"Even if she thinks the law is on your side, she's likely to rule against you in order to protect the child. Unless, of course, it was overwhelming, which it isn't. In fact, the law's not on your side."

A heavyset bearded man in a leather vest walked past them. As he passed, they could see the back of the vest, which had a skull with horns and a red and yellow headdress in the shape of wings on the back. Above the skull was a half-circle with the words "Hell's

Angels" in red on a white background.

"One of yours?" Sabre asked.

"No, but I'd like him to be. I bet he can spice up a case," Bob said. "I think that's Wagner's client. If he's the one I think he is, his ex-wife's boyfriend molested his kids. How long do you suppose that guy will last on the streets—or in prison?"

"Not long."

"Anyway, I thought I made a pretty good argument on the Fowler case."

"You did. It just wasn't good enough."

"We'll see. The fat lady isn't singing yet."

"She may not be singing, but the band is playing. Hekman doesn't care if they rule against her on an appeal. At least the minor would be a little older, maybe even of age, by the time it got through the whole process. And she's going to do what's in the best interest of the child; I'm betting that's not to be with Lester the molester."

"What do you think happened to Mary Margaret?" Bob asked.

Sabre shook her head. "I don't know. She's not real bold and has been pretty sheltered. She doesn't strike me as the type to run away."

"She ran away on her wedding night."

"That's true, but she was really pushed to the limit."

"Do you think something happened that pushed her over the limit again?"

"I thought about that, but there doesn't appear to be anything. She had a visit with her parents and her brothers earlier in the week, and that went fine."

"She's been going to school," Bob said. "Maybe something happened there."

"JP checked into that. There was nothing unusual he could ascertain. I thought maybe she saw Gibbs and got spooked, but JP couldn't find any evidence of that either. Then I thought maybe her friend Penny helped her and was hiding her, but she swears she didn't. Her parents have been very cooperative. If Penny is hiding her, it's not at their home, and they're watching her carefully."

"What does JP think?"

"He's betting on Lester. JP's been watching him for days. The cops aren't sure if it's a kidnapping or a runaway teen, but their main suspect is Gibbs. They searched his apartment and his car, but didn't find any sign of her."

"Maybe he kill—"

Sabre cut him off. "I can't think that way. Besides, why would he? And how did he dispose of the body? At best, he only had a few minutes when he left the church and came back."

Irene Serlis walked up to where Sabre and Bob were sitting. "Hi, guys."

"Hi," Sabre said. "We were just talking about Mary Margaret."

"Do you know something new?" Irene asked.

"Nothing. How is Mrs. Fowler holding up?"

"Surprisingly well, actually. As much as she is controlled by her husband, she's stronger than I gave her credit for. I expect she has rallied for her sons."

"Good for her," Sabre said.

The bailiff came out of Department Six and called, "Hernandez."

"That's me," Irene said. "Later."

"You like magic, right?" Sabre asked.

"It's alright, why?"

"I have six tickets to see the Great Silent Thunder at the Sports Arena on Friday. JP, Ron, and my mom are going. I thought maybe you and Marilee would like to go."

"I'll check with Marilee, and unless she's figured out a way to have a date with George Clooney, she'll want to go. She loves magic shows."

"You tell her if she gets that date with Clooney, I'll join her, and the rest of you can go to the show."

Sabre sat there quietly for a few minutes.

"What is it?" Bob asked.

"Nothing. I was thinking about Mary Margaret." She stood up. "Excuse me a minute."

Sabre walked outside and called JP.

"Hey, kid," JP said. "I'm sitting here at Lester's. Dang, this guy is boring. He hardly goes anywhere."

"He's not going to work?"

"No, it appears he has been suspended pending an investigation. Someone reported him."

"That's right," Sabre said. "I talked to Maxine Quinn, the DSS supervisor and she was taking care of it. I'm glad he's not with those young girls anymore. That makes me feel a little better."

"Me too."

"Have you found out who the anonymous caller was who reported the Fowler case?"

"No, everyone I've asked denies it. All we know is that it came from the phone at the church. But does it really matter who made the call?"

"I think whoever called in the initial abuse may be the same person who helped Mary Margaret run away."

"What can I do?"

"I want you to forget about Lester for a while and go to the church."

"And do what?"

"For now, just watch who comes and goes, and keep an eye on the pastor's house as well. I'm going to see if Irene will go with me to talk to her client. I have a hunch."

"Do you think Mrs. Fowler was the reporting party?"

"No, I think it was one of Mary Margaret's brothers."

~~~

Sabre went back to where Bob was sitting. "Is Irene still in there?"

Just then the courtroom door opened and Mike Powers walked out with a very unhappy client. Mike tried to console him as they walked past, but he wasn't successful.

"Bob, I need to take care of something. Can you appear on this case for me? We're in agreement, just submit on the recommendations."

"Sure," Bob said, looking inquisitively at her. "Are you okay?"

"Yeah, something has come up on another case and I need to follow up on it."

Bob walked into Department Six. Sabre waited outside for Irene and explained to her what she thought was going on.

"We need to find Mary Margaret if we can," Irene said, "but I don't want to implicate my client."

"All I want is for Mrs. Fowler to give us permission to speak to her sons."

"Seth will never allow that."

"I know, that's why I didn't ask Bob, but Seth isn't home right now. We could go there and talk to your client before he gets home."

"At least if her brother is helping her, she's probably safe."

"We don't know where she is, and her brother isn't exactly free to come and go a lot. It's not like he could be checking on her very often. We need to know."

229

When Irene didn't respond right away, Sabre added, "I don't mean to put pressure on you…"

"Yes, you do."

"Okay, I do, but if I can't talk to the boys, I'll have to call the social worker and tell her what I think. They'll follow up, but if Mr. Fowler is home, it'll be a real scene, and probably not a pleasant one for your client." Sabre knew Irene didn't like the way the pastor controlled her client. That, coupled with a missing twelve-year-old, was probably enough to get Irene to cooperate.

Irene hesitated for a few seconds and then sighed. "I guess we have to do something if we can. We can't just leave that little girl out there."

Chapter 43

Candace Fowler opened the door just enough to see who was there.

"Candace," Irene said, "we'd like to talk to you a minute about Mary Margaret."

"I'm sorry, my husband's not home."

"That's okay. It's you I need to talk to. May we come in?"

She twisted her lips from side to side. "My husband doesn't like me to have guests when he isn't home."

"But I'm not a guest. I'm your attorney, and we really need to talk."

Candace opened the door and stepped back, letting them inside. They all stood there for a few seconds before Candace said, "Please, have a seat."

"Thank you, Mrs. Fowler," Sabre said. "You know we all want what's best for your daughter, don't you?"

She nodded.

"Then we need to find her and get her off the streets. We will protect her," Sabre said, trying to keep any comments away from the alternatives. "We know who called Child Protective Services."

Irene frowned at Sabre. She had stretched the truth a little, but she didn't know how else to get her to talk. They were both surprised when Candace started to cry. Her sons must have heard her because they dashed into the living room. The younger boy climbed up on the chair beside her. The older boy towered over her until he knelt down by her side.

"Are you okay, Mama?" the older boy asked.

She sniffed and tried to compose herself. "I'm fine." She cleared her throat. "These are my sons, Zeke and Jacob," she said as she glanced first at the older boy, and then at the younger one.

"Hi, boys," Sabre said. "Your mama is being very brave." Jacob gave his mom a hug. Zeke said hello, but the concerned expression on his face didn't change.

"Mrs. Fowler, would it be okay if I asked your sons a few questions?" Sabre asked.

"I don't have to talk to her, do I?" Zeke asked his mother.

"Maybe I should talk to my client alone for a minute, Sabre," Irene said.

Candace took a deep breath. "No, this has gone on long enough. I don't know what I was thinking, but I never thought it would get to be such a mess."

Zeke stood up. "I'm the one who did it."

"Did what?" Sabre asked.

"I called CPS and I'm the one who helped Mary Margaret."

Jacob snapped his head up at Zeke and gave him an incredulous stare. Zeke frowned at him.

Candace reached for Zeke's arm and gently pulled him down on the arm of the chair. "It was all my idea," she said.

Irene stopped her again. "Are you sure you want to do this? If you tell me in confidence, it's very different from what you say in front of Sabre. The attorney/client privilege does not exist if you speak when there are witnesses. I think we should talk alone."

Candace shook her head and kept talking. "When their father finds out what happened, he's going to be so angry. But I can't let my boys keep lying to their father." She took another deep breath. "A couple of weeks ago, Zeke came to me and told me that he had seen Lester doing something to Mary Margaret. I made the mistake of telling Seth. He said he would pray on it and God would tell him what to do. The next thing I knew, we were planning a wedding."

"And Mary Margaret, did she want to get married?" Sabre asked.

"No, she begged me to stop it. I should've done something then, but I didn't."

"But you helped her when she ran away from Gibbs on her wedding night, right?"

"Yes, she got away from him and ran all the way home. He came by looking for her and I would've hidden her, but her father knew she was here. I'm not sure, but I think Seth had called Lester and told him."

"Why didn't you call CPS then?"

"We don't have a house phone, only the phone in the church, and my husband's cell phone. Besides, if the call came after the wedding had been announced, it could've been anyone in the congregation. So we devised a plan to get through the night and then get help. Zeke told Mary Margaret to scream if she needed him. The boys' room was right next to hers, and Zeke stayed awake all night listening for her."

Sabre looked at Zeke. "Did she ever call for help during the night?"

"No, but once she spoke a little loud. She did it intentionally so I could hear her. She threatened to scream if he did anything and he promised to leave her alone until they got in their new home. Mary Margaret came out in the middle of the night to go to the bathroom and I checked on her. She said Gibbs was asleep and he hadn't done anything, but she was afraid to sleep. When the sun came up, I heard the door open again and she came out. We both went into the kitchen and stayed there until everyone else finally joined us."

"And then you all went to church?" Sabre asked.

"Yes, that's when my husband announced the marriage."

"How did the congregation take it?"

"Not well. They scattered pretty fast after the service. Usually, everyone hangs around and socializes a bit, but they couldn't seem to get away fast enough. A few gave us some disbelieving stares, others made the obligatory congratulations to the couple."

"When did you make the call?"

No one spoke for a few seconds. Then Jacob said, "I did it."

"Jacob always runs around playing after church, so we knew Seth wouldn't miss him," Candace said. "Zeke and I kept Seth occupied. Jacob didn't have as much time as we had hoped because, as I said, the crowd left early, but he got it done."

"And then you helped Mary Margaret run away from foster care?"

"Yes, she was afraid and so was I," Candace said.

"But she was safe in the foster home," Irene said.

"She never felt safe. I tried to reassure her, but most of the time Seth was with me and he was so sure we would win at court. He kept saying that they'd have to let her come home soon."

"But you said you wanted the motion as well," Irene said. "I could've fought him in court. I still can."

She shook her head. "I couldn't go against my husband in court. You don't know him."

Sabre turned the subject back to Mary Margaret. "Where is she?" The mother and the two boys exchanged glances, but no one answered.

Sabre's phone beeped with a text from JP.

--Fowler's here.

"Your husband is home," Sabre said.

Candace jumped up. "You have to go."

"Where is Mary Margaret?"

"She's out back in the fort."

"I need to take her with me," Sabre said. "It'll be a

lot easier than if CPS comes back here. They'll probably bring the police with them."

Irene looked directly at her client. "She's right. If we take her in, it'll be a lot easier on you and the boys."

"What will I tell Seth?"

"You don't need to say anything yet. Let us work it out."

A new text came in from JP:

--He's going into the church.

Sabre shared the text with the others.

"Please go," Candace said. "Seth always goes to church to pray before he comes into the house, but he won't be long. Go to the alley behind the church. We'll send Mary Margaret out there when it's safe."

Sabre didn't want to leave without her. She feared that Mary Margaret would run again, and then she would be out on the streets without a safe place to hide.

"Please," Candace begged. She glanced toward the back of the house and back at them again.

Sabre looked at the scared faces on the three of them and left.

Chapter 44

Irene and Sabre dashed to the car, checking behind them for Fowler. As Irene started to pull away from the curb, Sabre said, "There he is. He's coming out of the church." Her phone beeped with a message from JP with the same information. She texted back.

--*Watch the house. Let me know if anyone comes out.*

The next text she got was a "thumbs up" symbol.

"Where did he go?" Irene asked.

"There's a gate by the side of the house where the fence juts out. He went through there."

"So he's in the back yard."

"That's probably the way he goes to his house from the church. I saw Candace looking toward the back of the house when she knew he was home."

"He's a creature of habit and pretty set in his ways."

Irene drove around to the alley behind the church and the Fowlers' home. A six-foot wooden fence surrounded the large back yard with a gate that led to the alley. Two enormous southern magnolia trees loomed upward from inside the fence. Sabre looked for the fort, but only the roof was visible because it was blocked by the fence and the border of tall Italian cypress trees that lined the fence between the house and the church. The trees also surrounded the small parking lot behind the church, except for a gap left for people to leave the parking lot and drive into the alley at the opposite end from the house.

"Where should I park?" Irene asked as she drove past the back fence to the house. "If we stop here, we can't see anything, and if we park behind the cypress trees, the car is too visible."

"Keep going. We'll turn around and stop on the other side. Right there." Sabre pointed to a spot next to some trashcans.

Sabre and Irene sat there, watching and waiting in silence. Irene broke it. "I hate to see these kinds of things."

"What do you mean?"

"I hate to see churches involved in young marriages, or possible molest issues. This sort of thing gives people a reason to blame the church or God. I hate that. I go to church and I believe in God and I hate that when this hits the media, it'll give us all a bad name."

"They come in all shapes and sizes. Scout leaders, school teachers, priests," Sabre said. "It's not about religion, or church, or God. These people don't represent their organizations, they're the exceptions, the dregs of society. And there's always going to be some of those."

"I know."

They kept watching the yard and the church. While they waited, Sabre called JP to let him know what was going on. After about ten minutes, Irene checked her phone for the time.

"Do you have to go?" Sabre asked.

"I have to pick Binky up at daycare."

"I can wait here and you can go if you want," Sabre said.

"Where are you going to wait?"

"I'll stand there between the fence and that cypress tree."

"It's going to be dark soon."

"Then I'll have JP come and wait with me. Candace is probably waiting for it to get dark so Mary Margaret can sneak out. If she doesn't come shortly after dark, I'll have to call CPS."

237

Sabre got out of the car and walked around to the driver's side. "Get going."

"Are you sure?" Irene asked.

"I'll be fine. The sun is still shining, I have my phone, and as soon as it starts to get dark, I'll have JP leave his post and come to me."

"Let me know if Mary Margaret comes out."

"I will."

"And, Sabre, if she doesn't come out and you have to call CPS, please let me know first. Maybe I can get back here and do a little damage control for my client."

"Absolutely."

Sabre walked over to the fence and stood between it and the row of cypress trees. She stood on her tiptoes, but she still couldn't see much. She looked for something to stand on, but there was nothing in sight. She jumped up once to see the fort, but she decided not to do it again in case Fowler was in the backyard. She saw enough to know that Mary Margaret would have to cross the yard, either to the back gate that went into the alley or the side into the church parking lot. She didn't expect she would do either until dark.

Sabre called JP and told him that Irene had left.

"I'm coming back there," he said.

"No. I'm fine. Give it a little longer. I don't want you to miss them if they go out the front."

"You're about as stubborn as a Missouri mule halfway home after plowin' all day."

"I love you too," Sabre said.

JP didn't respond right away and Sabre realized what she had just said. But she was joking. Neither of them had ever said those words seriously. She wished she had chosen a different response.

"Be careful," JP said and hung up.

Sabre stood there listening for any backyard activity, but none came. The alley was quiet as well.

The garages to the houses were on the street side. The alley bordered the back yards and a couple of sheds. No one appeared on foot and only one car passed through in the twenty minutes she had been standing there. It was getting late, but the sky was still lit with the setting sun when she heard a vehicle. Sabre peeked around the fence and saw JP park, get out, and walk toward her, carrying a pair of binoculars.

"Hey, darlin', you want some company?"

"Sure do." She kissed him. "I don't know how you can stand to do surveillance. I'm bored to death."

"It's not a lot of fun," JP said. "Until it is." He looked over the fence and assessed the situation. "It's getting dark and hard to see even with the binoculars. The patio light helps. Do you think she'll come out?"

"I don't know. She may as well, now that we know her mother was involved." She took out her cell phone. "I better call CPS. I can't risk her getting out on the streets, and I'm afraid if she gets spooked, she may run out the front."

JP put his hand over hers, covering her phone. "I got that covered."

"What did you do?"

"I called Ron. I knew you'd be worried about that. Besides, your brother needs the work."

She wrapped her arms around him and gave him a long, lingering kiss. "You're the best."

JP pulled away. "Did you hear that? I think the back door opened." He looked over the fence, then shifted a few feet to his left so he could see the door. "It's a kid," he whispered.

"Short or tall?"

"Short."

"That's Jacob."

"He's carrying a bag and walking toward the fort." JP moved to his right and tilted his head. "He went

239

inside."

A few minutes passed. "What's happening?" Sabre asked.

"Nothing," JP said. "Wait. Jacob's coming out without the bag. He went inside the house and someone shut the patio light off."

"Maybe so she could leave without being seen," Sabre said.

"There's a street light on the other side of the house that gives some light to the back side of the fence. She'll be more visible if she goes out the back gate."

Another ten minutes passed with JP periodically looking over the fence until the back door opened again.

"Who is it?" Sabre asked, this time jumping in an attempt to see, but all she got was a glimpse of a shadow.

"I think it's the older boy. He's taller, but not tall enough and too slender to be Fowler, but I can't be certain because it's too dark where he's standing." JP was silent for a few seconds. "A young girl just came out of the fort carrying the bag."

"Is it Mary Margaret?"

"I don't know. I've never met her, but how many teenage girls do you suppose they have hiding in their fort?"

Sabre smacked him playfully.

"She's walking toward the patio. She and the young man are walking toward the gate."

Sabre dashed off alongside the fence toward the church. The kids turned the corner and met her. "Thanks, Zeke, I'll take it from here. You better get back inside before you're missed."

Zeke hugged his sister. "It's going to be okay. Just have faith."

"Come on, Mary Margaret," Sabre said. "Your brother's right. It's all going to be okay."

Mary Margaret didn't respond, except for a few light sobs. Sabre just let her get it all out.

Chapter 45

JP drove Sabre and Mary Margaret to Sabre's office to get her car. On the way, Sabre called Irene and then the social worker. The social worker agreed to meet them at Polinsky Receiving Home where Sabre would explain everything. All Sabre told her on the phone was that Mary Margaret had run away, then turned herself in.

Sabre didn't question Mary Margaret while JP was in the car, and the girl had volunteered very little. She did tell them that the bag Jacob brought her contained a sandwich, an apple, and a bottle of water. Her mother was concerned she might not get any dinner.

Once they were alone, Sabre needed to find out what had happened so she would be better prepared for the hearing that would take place now that her client had been found. After some small talk, Sabre asked, "How did you get away from your supervisor?"

"My mother made sure the bathroom window was open. I was going to climb out the window, but then I heard the other bathroom door open and I peeked out. Kyle was gone, so I grabbed the bag of food my mom left for me, and I went out the front door and ran to the parking lot. I crouched down and moved behind the cars until I got to the alley. It's not a very big lot, so it didn't take long."

"Where did you go?"

"I snuck in the back gate and went into the fort, but then Jacob came and told me I had to leave because they were looking for me. He told me that Mama said I could come back after they checked the house because that was the first place they would look."

"Then what did you do?"

"I ran for a couple of blocks until I saw a church

and I went inside. It was beautiful. The windows were so pretty when the light shined through them, and the altar was amazing. For a minute, I thought God had performed a miracle and put me in an old church like in the history books. I'd never been in another church before. I didn't know they still had churches like that. It was so different from ours. Then I felt bad for thinking our church was dull—but it's not really, it's just different. Anywhere where God is can't be dull, right?"

"Right," Sabre said.

"After a while, I realized that God took me there to keep me safe."

"How long did you stay there?"

"They were having a service, so I sat there until it was over, and when all the people started leaving, I hid. Then I just hung out there the rest of the day. Once, a man came in through the back, and I almost got caught. He looked around, and then locked all the doors. I didn't know if I would be able to get out, but it was dark by then and I didn't really want to go anywhere. It wasn't so bad. I had the food and water Mama had left for me. There were bathrooms inside, and I took a couple of cushions off of a pew and put them in a corner to sleep on."

"And you went back to your house in the morning?"

"I walked back there. It took me a while because I got a little lost once, but I found it. I saw Papa's car was gone, so I went in the side gate and in the back door. I've been in the fort ever since."

"Mary Margaret," Sabre said, "can you tell me why you ran away?"

"I was afraid I'd have to go back to Brother Gibbs."

"I told you I would do everything I could to keep that from happening."

"Yeah, but you didn't say you could for sure. And

my dad said he was going to win. He sounded way more sure than you did." She paused. "He said he would win because he had God on his side."

Sabre was always careful to not get into any kind of religious discussion with her clients, especially the minors. She respected the parents' religious views, just like any other choices parents made, as long as it didn't amount to abuse or neglect. But she had to say something to this scared young girl.

"Mary Margaret, here's what I think. If your father has God on his side, so do you. And, you also have the Department of Social Services, me, your mother, and the law on your side. Together, we're a force to be reckoned with."

"Can you make him stay away from me?"

"Gibbs?"

"Yes, I don't want to even see him."

"Have you seen Gibbs since you've been in foster care?"

"I saw him walk by the school a couple of times, and once when my foster parents brought me home from school, I saw him in his car near their house."

"Did you tell anyone?"

"No."

"We have grounds now to get a restraining order against him, so he won't have the right to come near you, your home, or your school. In the meantime, you'll be safe at Polinsky. But you need to promise me that if you ever see him again, you'll report it to the nearest adult in charge and have them call me or the social worker. Okay?"

"Okay."

"I have a few more uncomfortable questions, but I need to ask." Sabre glanced at Mary Margaret. When she didn't object, Sabre said. "I know you told Penny that Gibbs did something to you before the wedding.

She never would've said anything except she was worried about you. Can you tell me what happened?"

Mary Margaret was silent for a few seconds before she spoke. "Brother Gibbs touched me down there." She glanced toward her crotch. "But I didn't want him to. He just did it anyway."

"Did it happen more than once?"

"Yes, whenever we were alone, he would do it. I told him to stop, but he wouldn't. It just kept getting worse."

"And what about your mother? Did you tell her?"

"I didn't tell Papa or Mama because Brother Gibbs said I was a bad girl and I would be kicked out of the church. He said my parents would be shamed and they would hate me and send me away. I was afraid I'd never see my brothers again." She looked up. "I don't know how they found out, but that's when Papa said I would have to marry him to save my soul because I was soiled."

"Soiled?" Sabre spurted. Then she bit her lip to keep from saying what she wanted to say.

"But I didn't want him to touch me. He just did it anyway."

Sabre took a breath and spoke softly again. "Did you tell your father that?"

"Yes, but he said if I didn't really want him to I could've stopped him, and that if I was a good girl, I would've asked God for help. And now, the only way to fix it was to get married."

Her gaze turned downward.

"It's going to get better," Sabre said. "I promise you." She didn't usually make promises to kids when dealing with the law because she knew she couldn't be certain of the outcome, but she had to give this little girl some hope. She didn't know for certain what ruling she would get on the validity of the marriage, but she had enough now to get Gibbs for the molestation charges with or without a marriage. And she was determined to see that happen.

Chapter 46

Irene and Sabre sat outside of Department Four waiting for the special hearing that was set to inform the court about Mary Margaret's return.

"How's Candace doing?" Sabre asked.

"She's afraid of what will happen when her husband finds out she *defied* him," Irene said. "Her word, not mine."

"Have you seen the special hearing report?"

"No, I didn't see anything in my mailbox."

Sabre handed her a single sheet of paper. Irene turned it over as if she was looking for more, then said, "This is it?"

"Yup."

"All this says is that Mary Margaret ran away from the church while her supervisor was in the bathroom and that she turned herself in."

"That's what happened, right?" Sabre smiled.

"That's what happened."

"If this goes to trial, we won't be able to keep it from the court, but for now at least, we're good."

Bob walked up with his client, Seth Fowler. "We're ready," Bob said.

The social worker, who approached behind Bob, said, "You might want to see this first." She handed them each a blue document, which the attorneys all knew was the paper used for a petition. She also gave them another report. "We amended the petition to include the dates three weeks prior to the wedding when Lester Gibbs was molesting Mary Margaret."

Seth Fowler grabbed the paperwork from Bob. "That's disgusting!"

"If that's so disgusting, why would you let him marry her?" Sabre muttered.

"That was God's way of saving her. Besides, my daughter wouldn't do that."

"Your daughter *didn't* do anything." Sabre spoke loudly and clearly this time. "Gibbs did."

"Okay," Bob said waving his hand. "I need to speak to my client." Bob directed Seth away from the group.

~~~

The parties were all seated at the counsel table with their attorneys and the case was called to order. Introductions were made for the record.

"I'm glad to see Mary Margaret is back," Judge Hekman said. "Is she at Polinsky?"

"Yes, Your Honor," Deputy County Counsel Linda Farris said. "However, the foster parents are willing to take her back into their home, and Mary Margaret would like to go there."

The judge turned to Sabre.

"I agree, Your Honor."

Bob said, "Our first choice would be home with the parents, but short of that, we have no objection to the foster home."

Irene said, "No objection, Your Honor."

"How do your clients plead on the amended petition?"

The parents both entered denials and kept the original trial date.

"I've made my decision on the demurrer," Judge Hekman began. "Obviously, with the amended petition, the demurrer does not apply to Count II of the petition stating molest took place prior to the wedding. I'm sure no one in this courtroom would make that argument." The judge glared at Bob for a brief second.

"That's correct, Your Honor, but we would still

contest Count I. Of course, your decision on the demurrer will make a great deal of difference on how we proceed at trial."

"I understand that, Mr. Clark, and therefore, I've made a decision. As you all know, even if this practice of marrying in the church without a state-issued license or, in the case of a minor, court approval, were a valid religious one, the First Amendment is not absolute. The state has compelling reasons for requiring court involvement. In addition, I'm not convinced the child's agreement was obtained without duress or coercion. Marriage is defined as a voluntary agreement, making the child's consent paramount. It appears this child did not want to marry at all. Any countervailing religious interest here does not measure up to the state's interest or the 'best interest of the child' standard. Therefore, I'm denying the demurrer and ruling the marriage invalid."

Sabre looked at Candace to see her reaction. She saw her mouth curl up ever so slightly on the sides. She fought the smile and quickly looked blank, a look she had probably practiced many times.

Chapter 47

Sabre, JP, Ron, Beverly, Bob, and Marilee walked up to the Sports Arena. Ron and his mother were at the back of the pack.

"I've always wanted to see this guy," Ron said. He gave his mother a quick squeeze. "I'm glad you came, Mom. It'll be fun."

"You just want to keep an eye on me. I know your tricks."

"There is that, but I also didn't want to be a fifth wheel. You make a great date."

"You need to find yourself a nice girl. How am I ever going to have grandchildren if you don't find someone soon?"

"Sabre could have children too, you know."

"I'm not holding my breath for that. I've always thought I stood a better chance with you, Ronnie. Sabre's always been so career-minded."

"She has a career, and I don't even have a real job. I guess I'd better get one of those before I think about having kids."

"I didn't mean that, Ronnie. I'm sorry."

Ron forced a smile. "I know you didn't, Mom. It is what it is. I'll find something soon."

They walked into the arena and took their seats in the front row. "Wow, we couldn't ask for better seats," Bob said. "It helps to have connections."

"For sure," Sabre said.

The lights dimmed and music blared from the stage. With the curtain still closed, a deep voice announced, "The Greatest magician in the world, the one and only, the Great Silent Thunder." A thunderous sound and the opening of the curtain revealed the magician with his black tails and hat, his face painted half white and half kelly-green. He lifted both arms in the air and then slowly took a bow. The crowd roared.

When the noise died down, the great magician did a few sleight-of-hand tricks that required no words and then turned to his female assistant. He pointed at her and then at someone in the audience. The assistant walked down the steps and toward the person. The assistant raised her hand above the man's head and pointed at him. The magician put his hand out, palm up, and raised it up in a rising motion. A young man about six feet tall stood up. The magician nodded, and the assistant escorted the man to the stage. He then signaled for the crew to bring out a tiger in a cage. They rolled it out on a platform, so the distance from the floor to the top of the cage was about seven feet.

He pointed at the man and then at the cage as if he were signaling him to get inside with the tiger. The man shook his head. The crowd laughed. Silent Thunder motioned as if he were cradling something and petting it. Then he pointed to the man and the tiger again. The man shook his head once more. Finally, the magician put his hands out in front of him, palms up, and shrugged.

Silent Thunder walked the man over to the cage and showed him the only opening to the cage was in the front. The tiger roared and the man jumped back. When the magician directed him to stand near the edge of the cage, the man took a step away so he wasn't so close. The crowd laughed and applauded. The magician positioned the volunteer so his back was to the cage, just off to the side.

The assistant brought out a curtain on a cable, and both of the men inspected it. They moved it around and fluffed it out showing the crowd it was an ordinary curtain. Silent Thunder handed one end of the cable to the man, placing it in his right hand, and made a motion with his hand to raise it up, which the man did. Silent Thunder pointed at his eyes with his index and middle finger and then at the audience. He motioned twice. The man nodded that he understood.

The magician took the other end of the cable, and proceeded to encircle the cage with the curtain, which completely engulfed it. He paused next to the man for about one second, then he dashed back around the cage, dropped the curtain, and the tiger was gone. He opened the cage door, reached in, and removed a little orange kitten, which he handed to his helper. The crowd roared.

As the volunteer walked to his seat, Silent Thunder wrapped himself in the curtain and suddenly he was on the other end of the stage. The curtain dropped to the floor in an empty heap.

When the applause died down, Silent Thunder indicated he needed another volunteer. He pointed toward Sabre and her group and sent his assistant into the crowd. As she got closer to the group, he pointed at JP. The young woman stood next to JP and pointed at him. The Great Silent Thunder nodded. JP protested.

"Come on," Bob said. "Don't be chicken."

"No, I'm not going up there."

"Do it," Ron said.

"I'd rather be beat with a sack of wet catfish."

The woman looked confused.

"That's a 'no'," Bob said.

The assistant stepped back and pointed at Sabre. The magician nodded. Sabre stood up and followed her onto the stage. The stage hands rolled out a 4 x 4 x 6-foot windowless box with a door on the front. Sabre inspected it for openings and trap doors. She found none.

Silent Thunder took two ropes from a table and handed them to his assistant. He clasped his hands in front of himself and she tied them together. Then he cocked his head to one side, looking at Sabre. The assistant held up the rope. Sabre put her hands out like the magician had and the assistant tied them together.

"I don't like that," JP said.

"You don't like other men tying up your woman?" Bob teased. "Imagine that."

"No, I guess I don't."

"It's just a show," Ron said. "They'll go in the box, and in a few minutes, they'll both reappear somewhere else in the room. I've seen this trick on YouTube, but I have no idea how he does it."

"Still don't like it," JP muttered.

The assistant opened the door to the box. Sabre stepped inside first and then the Great Silent Thunder. A scrambling noise came from the box and then silence. All eyes were fixed on the box.

"What's taking so long?" JP asked.

"It's a show," Bob said. "The longer he makes the audience wait, the more the anticipation builds."

Another minute passed and JP shifted in his seat as if he was going to stand.

"Where are you going?"

"On stage, to see what's going on. This is taking way too long."

"You're going to ruin the trick."

"I'm supposed to care?"

Bob glanced at a huge security guard standing near the exit. He nodded toward him. "You may want to care about *him*?"

JP shot a quick glimpse his way. "If he wants a fight, he better pack a lunch and bring a flashlight."

As JP stood, the assistant walked to the opposite end of the stage toward the Great Silent Thunder, who was sitting on the wall by the steps. Surprise emanated from the crowd followed by loud applause.

The magician stood up and looked around. He stretched his hands out in a swooping motion, then scanned the audience. He looked back at the stage and out into the audience again.

"Where is Sabre?" JP asked.

"Will you relax? She's going to pop up any minute now."

The magician swooped his arms out again. The spotlight scanned the room. The assistant moved back toward the box, but before she got there, JP had run up the six steps and onto the stage.

"What are you doing?" she asked.

"Getting my girlfriend."

"Stop. You'll ruin the trick."

"Does it always take this long?"

"No, but we were told to wait."

"Then you do that," JP said and opened the door of the box.

Sabre was lying on the floor in a heap, her hands still tied together. Scattered on the floor were a rope, a top hat, and a pair of white gloves.

Chapter 48

"We need the paramedics," JP yelled.

JP checked her pulse. It was light, but she was breathing. Before he could do much else, two men in uniform appeared and asked him to step out. The box was too small for all of them. JP wanted to pick her up and bring her out, but without knowing what had happened, he didn't want to risk hurting her.

Bob and Ron were already on stage when JP came out. The murmur from the crowd seemed extra loud, and security guards were running onto the stage. JP hurried over to where the magician was standing, his mouth agape. Bob followed him. Ron stayed near his sister.

"What happened?" JP asked.

He didn't respond, keeping in character. He nodded his head toward the side of the stage, then stepped back behind the curtain. JP and Bob followed.

JP reached up and grabbed the magician's collar. "If you can talk, you better start now."

Bob reached out and touched his friend on the shoulder. "JP."

The magician took a deep breath. "I don't know," he said with a heavy accent.

"What do you mean, you don't know? You were in there with her."

"Actually, I wasn't."

"I saw you go inside."

"No, you saw someone dressed like me go inside. There are two of us."

"Where's the other one?"

"He should be in the dressing room, but I don't know for sure. I've been here the whole time. Your friend should have reappeared in the audience shortly after I did, but she didn't."

"Check on Sabre," JP said to Bob as he saw a policeman approaching them. "I'll be back."

JP went through the back curtain where he encountered a very young security guard. JP would have guessed he was still in high school if he had seen him on the street.

"You can't be back here. You need to take your seat."

"That's my girlfriend out there. I just want to know what's going on."

"I'm sorry, sir."

"Look." JP raised his voice. "There's another magician dressed like Silent Thunder in the dressing room. You can be the hero here. Let's find him and see what he has to say."

The kid hesitated, but only for a second. "Right this way." They stepped around the corner and the young man knocked on a door. No one answered.

"Open it," JP said, and started to reach for the knob.

"I'll do it."

He opened the door. Lying on the floor was another magician in tails, wearing a green and white face mask. His top hat was across the floor. He moaned. The young security guard stood there dumbfounded. JP took advantage of the moment and dropped down to check on him. "Are you okay?"

"I think so." He sat partway up and reached for the back of his head. "My head hurts."

"What happened?"

"I think Thunder hit me with something."

"Thunder?"

"My partner—the other magician."

The young security guard suddenly thought he should be in charge. "We'd better call the paramedics, and...and...I should radio this in."

"You should do that," JP said.

While the guard got on the radio, JP remained with the magician. "What happened to the woman inside the box?"

"I don't know."

"What do you mean?" JP raised his voice.

"I was never in the box. This happened before I could go do it."

Just then the paramedics walked in with two security guards and a uniformed policeman.

JP stood up. "He said someone hit him on the head. I was just trying to get him to lie still." JP rushed out and back to the stage where he saw the paramedics rolling Sabre away on a stretcher. Ron, Bob, and Marilee stood to the side of the stage. More police and security had gathered. Most of the audience remained in their seats as they had been asked to do.

"Is she conscious?" JP asked.

"No," Ron said.

"Where are they taking her?"

"I told them she has Kaiser, but the paramedic said they were taking her to Scripps Mercy on Fifth because it was closer. Mom went with them."

"Where are you going?" a policeman asked as they started out the back door not far behind Sabre.

"We're the victim's family and we're going to the hospital." JP pulled his card out of his pocket and handed it to the officer.

Bob handed him one as well, and said, "You'll find us there if you need us."

~~~

Marilee had gone home. Bob and Ron waited with JP at the hospital. JP couldn't sit still, so he paced in front of them. "Did the paramedics say anything?"

"Not much," Ron said. "Sabre gets a little claustrophobic, so at first I thought she just passed out, but then she didn't come to."

"What the hell happened?" JP said.

"Did you see the *other* magician?" Bob said.

"What other magician?" Ron asked.

Bob explained what Silent Thunder had told him and JP.

"Yes, I saw him. He'd been hit over the head and was lying on the floor. He blamed Silent Thunder—the other Silent Thunder."

"So they're pointing the finger at each other?"

"Looks that way," JP said.

A balding man about 5'8" with a mustache and short beard and a woman about 5'5" with curly brown hair and hazel eyes walked toward them. Each produced a badge. The man said, "I'm Detective Eugene Fontenot, San Diego PD. This is my partner, Detective Addie Lewis."

"You were all at the magic show?" Eugene asked in what sounded like a Louisiana accent.

"Yes," Bob answered.

"We'll need your full names."

Bob gave them the information they requested, and Eugene wrote it down. "What is your relationship to Sabre Brown?"

"I'm her friend and colleague." He nodded his head toward Ron, who was sitting next to him. "Ron is her brother, and JP is her friend and private investigator."

"Can you tell us what happened?"

"We were watching the show and the magician's assistant came down off the stage to get a volunteer," Bob said.

"Did Ms. Brown volunteer?" Addie asked.

"Not exactly. The assistant tried to get JP up there

first, but he refused."

"Why's that?" Addie said directly to JP.

"I don't like that sort of thing."

"Then what?" She turned back to Bob.

"The assistant moved on to Sabre."

"Did you encourage her to go up there?" Addie asked JP.

"No, I did not. If you're suggesting that I had anything to do with this, you're barking up the wrong tree."

"Just trying to get the facts."

"We don't even know what's wrong with her," JP said. "I'm assuming by your questions that someone did something to her?"

The detectives exchanged glances, then Addie spoke. "Someone gave her a shot of midazolam."

"What's that?" JP asked.

"It's a sedative they use for surgery," Bob said. "It can also be used to induce loss of memory, and I think it's used for epilepsy patients."

"Oh, my God!" Ron said. "Can it be fatal?"

"If the dosage is too high or if it's mixed with alcohol or certain other drugs."

JP's face turned red with anger. He didn't speak.

"How is she?" Bob asked.

"She's not conscious, but she's alive."

"Do you know anyone who might want to hurt her?" Eugene asked.

"Yeah," Bob said. "She's a juvenile court defense attorney. She primarily represents abused children. She has angered a lot of parents over the years."

Ron nodded in affirmation.

"How about recently?"

Bob and Ron both looked at JP.

"I can give you the names of the cases we've been working on."

Addie said, "Let's sit over here and you can give them to me." She and JP walked over a few rows where there was extra seating and a little more privacy.

JP gave her the information starting with Todd Lynch. Even though that case had closed, JP thought he was the most likely suspect, especially in light of his behavior in her office the other night. Next, he told them about the Fowler case. "The father just lost a motion in court and new petitions have been filed against him. I expect both Seth Fowler and Lester Gibbs are not too happy with Sabre right now."

"Angry enough to try to kill her?"

"I don't know, but Fowler sure had his knickers in a knot when he lost in court yesterday. He had himself pretty well convinced he would win."

When they were finished, JP said, "Sabre's mother is in the ER with her, but we haven't heard anything. Can you check to see what's going on?"

"We're going back in there when we're done here. We need to talk to her when she wakes up. I'll let you know if there's any change."

Chapter 49

Sabre had stabilized but had not regained consciousness. Ron, Bob, and JP decided to go to her office and try to figure out who had drugged her. Sitting in the waiting room was not getting them any closer. Sabre's office was close to the hospital and it also gave them access to her files if they needed them.

"We need to figure out who is angry enough at Sabre to go this far," JP said as they gathered in front of a whiteboard.

"Lynch is the first one I thought of," Ron said.

"Who's Lynch?" Bob asked.

"The guy who got in Sabre's face last week at court. He came to her office and did it again."

"He's a very angry man," Bob said.

"There's not a lot we can do about him, but the cops are checking him out," JP said. He walked over to the whiteboard and wrote *Sabre*. Underneath her name, he wrote, "Lynch, Fowler, Gibbs, Drake, Jim Jones."

"You think our ghost lover might be involved?" Bob asked.

"Can't rule him out. If he knows we're on to him, he could be scared."

"Who's Drake?" Ron asked.

"Russell Drake. He's the father on one of our cases. He's seeking custody of his daughter, Sarah Parker."

"Is he angry at Sabre?"

"I don't know, but we've been investigating him, and he may not like that. Also, he recently bought his daughter a magic kit. I'm not discounting anything *magic*."

To the right of Sabre's name, he started another column with the heading, *Silent Thunder*. "Whoever did this had to know Sabre would be at the magic show. It was calculated. Do either of you know where Sabre got the tickets?"

"She said she got them in the mail from Silent Thunder, Inc.," Bob said. "The note said it was a 'thank you' for representing his nephew a while back. She didn't think anything of it. She receives thank you notes all the time from relatives or from parents who clean up their act and appreciate what she did for them."

"When she's not getting threats," JP muttered. "Did it say who the nephew was?"

"I don't think so."

"I'll get that note to the detectives tomorrow. Maybe they can get something from it. There has to be a connection between those tickets and this attack."

"They weren't just any tickets," Ron said. 'They were front row seats. Whoever got them had to have good connections. Most performers save those seats for special guests or for big promotional giveaways."

"Like perhaps Silent Thunder himself—the one with the nephew Sabre represented," Bob said.

"That's too easy," JP said. "Why would he send tickets to his show, along with a note identifying himself, and then try to kill her at the same show?"

"And which one did it?" Ron asked. "Remember there are two of them."

JP's eyes widened. "Or maybe there are more than two. Maybe someone dressed the part. With the costume and the face make-up, they only had to be about the same size and familiar with the act to get away with it. He never gets close enough for most people to see his face, and he doesn't talk, so there's no voice recognition. That's how he gets away with having a double."

"And anyone who knows that could do the same," Bob said.

"So, again, there has to be a connection to Silent Thunder. Someone who knows there are two of them, and has access to the tickets."

"And meets the same general description, height, weight—although if he was thinner he could pad his suit, and if he was shorter, he could wear lifts in his shoes."

"So he can't be taller or heavier." Ron pointed to the board. "Who in that list could it be?"

They all stared at the whiteboard.

"Dang," JP said. "The only one it rules out is Lester Gibbs. He's too big."

"Even the Jim Jones ghost fits," Ron said.

Ron grabbed for his cell phone when it rang. JP and Bob stopped talking as Ron said, "Mom?" He listened while she spoke. "Okay, we'll be right there."

JP was already half way out the door when Ron hung up and said, "She's awake."

~~~

Beverly met Bob, Ron, and JP outside the emergency room. The two detectives stood about ten feet away.

"The doctor is examining her again and the detectives are waiting to talk to her," Beverly said.

"Did you get to talk to her at all?" Ron asked.

"Yes, and she's going to be fine. She's groggy, but coherent."

"Did she say anything about what happened?" JP asked.

"No, and I didn't ask," her mother said.

JP walked over to the detectives and told them how Sabre obtained the tickets to the magic show. "I don't have the envelope or the note, but the procedure in Sabre's office is for Elaine, her receptionist, to open the mail and do the filing. I can call her in the morning if you'd like."

"How about you just give me her phone number and I'll follow up," Addie said.

"That'll work too." JP gave her the number, although he had every intention of contacting Elaine first thing in the morning himself.

An orderly came out and told Beverly she could go in. Everyone followed her. Just before they reached her room, Eugene said, "We need to talk to her."

"Give us a minute and we'll clear out," Bob said. Addie and Eugene stood just outside her cubicle. The curtain was open and Sabre could see them all. Ron stepped forward to her bedside and took her hand.

"Is this the welcoming committee?" Sabre asked.

Ron squeezed her hand. "You were supposed to disappear or something, not get drugged."

"That would have been too easy," she muttered.

"What did the doctor say?"

"He said I'm going to be fine. They want to keep me here until everything is out of my system, but I'm okay."

"There're two detectives here who want to talk to you, so I'm going to take Mom home and we'll see you tomorrow. Okay?"

She gave a slight nod. Ron kissed her on the forehead. "Love you, Sis." Their mother and Bob did the same.

She smiled at JP when he came forward. He reached down and gave her a quick kiss on the lips. "You had us pretty scared."

The two detectives came in. "These are Detectives Addie and Eugene, San Diego PD. They want to talk to you."

Eugene glanced at JP.

"He's staying," Sabre said.

Eugene shrugged and said, "Fine. Can you tell us what happened?"

Sabre explained how she was picked to go up on the stage. She was still groggy, so her accounting of the events took a little longer to tell, but she got through it.

"I was a little concerned about getting in the box because I tend to get a little claustrophobic, but I figured it would be quick, so I got inside. I panicked a little when the door closed because it was dark inside. I kept telling myself to breathe. I heard a noise and I realized it was the rope dropping to the floor." She paused. "I thought the magician was going to untie me. I even turned so he could get to my hands, but instead he grabbed me and covered my mouth so I couldn't scream." She stopped and took another breath. "I remember kicking him and trying to pull away. I got one good kick against the wall, and then I felt something jab me in the arm and I must have passed out."

"Can you remember anything else? Maybe about his hands when he put them over your mouth. Were they rough or soft?"

"Soft, I think. I didn't feel any calluses or anything."

"So his gloves were already off when he covered your mouth?"

"Yes."

"Did you feel a ring, maybe? Or a certain smell? Maybe tobacco or whatever?"

"I didn't feel a ring, but he could have had one. And he smelled like..." Sabre closed her eyes for a minute and took a deep breath. "...like mango."

"Mango?" Addie asked.

"Yeah, mango."

"Does that mean anything to you?" Addie asked.

"No."

Teresa Burrell

They asked about the show tickets and Sabre told them the same thing JP had. "Do we have your permission to get the note from your secretary?"

"Of course. It's been handled a lot, so I doubt if you'll get any fingerprints or anything though."

"Probably not, but we'd like to see it just the same."

"You think whoever sent the tickets is the one who tried to kill me." It was more of a statement than a question.

"Maybe, but it could be that whoever did this wasn't after you," Eugene said. "It may not have mattered who was in the box. He could have had a completely different motive. We don't know, but for now, you are what we have to go on."

"Okay."

"I know your work can create a lot of enemies, but is there anyone who has threatened you recently?"

Sabre told him about Lynch, but she wasn't able to provide any more details than JP had already given them.

"Has anyone threatened you outside of work?"

"No, but other than the time I spend with JP, which has been very little lately, there isn't much else other than my work."

The detectives asked a few more questions, but Sabre didn't have anything of importance to add. They wished her well and left.

JP pulled up a chair next to her bed and sat there looking at Sabre.

"I'm okay, you know," she said. "Or at least I will be really soon."

"I know, and you're right, we haven't had nearly enough time together."

"I've been trying to remedy that," Sabre said. "I guess this is one way to do it."

"It's not exactly what I had in mind, but I'll take what I can get."

Chapter 50

"How is she doing?" Ron asked.

"I talked to her doctor about an hour ago. She's going to be fine," JP said. "They'll be releasing her this afternoon."

Ron looked around. "When did they move her to this room?"

"About four o'clock this morning. She slept pretty well, except when the nurses were pokin' and proddin' her. They kept checking her blood pressure, which has been steady all night."

"So, what's the plan?" Ron asked.

"I'd like to go take a shower. Can you stay? I don't want to leave her alone."

"That's why I'm here. Did you get any sleep at all?"

"No, he didn't," Sabre said.

"Good morning, Sis. And how would you know that if you were sleeping?"

"Because every time I woke up, he was staring at me." She turned to JP. "Go home and get some rest."

"That's probably good advice," Ron said. "I'll call you when they release her, or better yet, I'll bring her to you."

"What do you mean?" Sabre asked.

"You're staying at JP's this weekend. We've already decided."

"I don't need a babysitter."

"Yes, you do," JP said. "Someone tried to kill you. Until we know who, you're not staying alone. If you're not coming to my house, then I'm going to yours."

"I guess you're right. Besides, I can't fight both of you."

~~~

268

On his drive home, JP called Elaine, Sabre's receptionist, and told her what happened.

"Did you keep the envelope and the note?" he asked.

"Yes, I filed them."

"So you know where they are?"

"Yes, Sabre has a whole folder of correspondence she's received after cases have closed. Anything before then would be put in their open file, but if it comes in later, it all goes into the miscellaneous folder."

"I expect the detectives will be contacting you soon about the tickets and the note."

"Should I give them everything?"

"Yes, it might help them. Sabre already gave them permission, but do me a favor."

"Sure."

"Before they take them, please take a photo and text it to me. Just don't handle them any more than you need to."

When JP got home, he fed Louie and crashed on his bed, where he remained until Ron called him about three hours later.

"They're releasing her," Ron said, "but as you know that process can take a while. We should be there in an hour or two. She wants to stop at her condo and pick up a few things."

"Text me when you leave the hospital. I'll meet you at her condo. I want to check her place out before she goes in."

"Do you think someone might set a trap for her?"

"I don't know what to think."

JP hung up, took a shower, and sat down at his computer. He wasn't sure where to start, but he had to figure it out. He thought about what the detective had said, that it might not be connected at all, but he didn't believe it. He was pretty sure Eugene didn't either. He picked up his cell and called Ian Lynch.

"This may seem like a strange question," JP asked, "but did Todd ever show any interest in magic?"

"When we were kids, my dad used to pull quarters from behind our ears, and he thought that was pretty cool. You mean something like that?"

"Yeah. Or did he go to magic shows, or have a magic set, anything?"

"I can't remember either of us ever having a magic set. We saw a magician at a circus once, but Todd was more interested in the elephants than the magic show."

"Have you ever heard Todd mention the Great Silent Thunder?"

"No."

"Do you know who he is?"

"No, but I'm guessing from your questions that he's a magician."

"Yes, he is. He recently performed a show in San Diego, but he's world-renowned."

"Sorry, never heard of him."

"Do you know if Todd would have any connection to show events? Maybe some way to get free tickets?"

"Maybe. He's a sales rep for Xerox and his clients would occasionally give him tickets for things, but they were mostly sporting events, football or baseball. Keep in mind, I haven't been around him for the last five years. Things could be different now."

"Thanks," JP said. "Please call if you think of anything else."

JP's phone beeped and he checked his text.

Ron: *We're leaving hospital now.*

JP: *Ok. See you at Sabre's.*

"Come on, Louie, let's go for a ride."

JP and Louie reached Sabre's before Ron arrived. He punched the code into the keypad on the garage and let himself in. Louie darted from room to room looking for Sabre. JP looked around for anything unusual, but found nothing out of the ordinary. He heard a car pull up and the garage door open as he started upstairs. Louie looked back at the door and then upstairs, seemingly uncertain of which way to go. Finally, he ran up the steps. Again, JP didn't find anything out of place or any hint that someone might have broken in.

JP started back down again, just as Ron and Sabre came inside. Louie ran full bore down the steps and up to his guests, where he flitted from one to the other, seeking attention.

When JP reached Sabre, he gave her a kiss. "How are you feeling?"

"Almost normal," she said. "I'm not surprised to see you here. Did you find evidence of any intruders?"

"No, it's fine as cream gravy."

Sabre gathered some clothes and her make-up bag and they left. They stopped by her office and picked up a few files. JP and Louie went in first, making sure everything was okay.

"What did you expect to find?" Sabre asked on their way out.

"I don't know, but I'll know it when I see it."

"Maybe they weren't really after me, like that detective said."

"I hope that's the case, but until they catch him, or we figure it out, I'm not letting up."

Chapter 51

The next morning, JP pulled out of his driveway and away from his house, heading down the steep but short incline toward Mission Gorge Road. He pushed on the brake and his foot went to the floor. He kept his foot off the accelerator, downshifted to low, and pumped the brakes, but still didn't feel any resistance.

"Hang on, Sabre! The brakes are out!"

Sabre braced herself and JP stepped on the emergency brake just enough to make the truck jump, slowing it some. Then he pushed a little harder. Mission Gorge Road was coming up fast and JP had to make a right turn or drive into oncoming traffic. Trees blocked his vision on his left but he could see cars passing on the busy street in front of him. He pushed the emergency brake all the way down as they hit Mission Gorge. The truck skidded onto the avenue with JP pulling the steering wheel to the right to avoid as much traffic as possible. His truck came to a stop partway into the street. Sabre sighed just as a horn blared and a red Ford F-150 swerved to go around them, but the Ford skidded and slammed into the front of JP's truck, spinning them around and into the side of the hill.

There was a loud bang and for a few seconds everything was white. The smell of talcum powder filled the air. The dust from the deployed airbags made it hard to breath, but the air from his broken window was helping the powder dissipate. JP turned the key in the ignition to off.

"Are you okay?" Sabre asked as she coughed.

"Yes, are you?"

"I think so."

"Do you hurt anywhere?" JP asked.

"I feel like I was punched in the face." She wiggled around, moving her arms and legs. "My limbs all seem to work."

JP tried to open his door, but couldn't. "Can you open your door? Mine won't open."

Sabre reached for the handle and opened the door, but it didn't open very far. The truck was sitting at an angle with the passenger side higher than the driver's side, making the heavy door hard to maneuver. She unlocked her seatbelt and used both arms to push the door open. The air flowed in, clearing out more of the powder.

JP leaned over, trying to assess what Sabre was stepping into, but he couldn't see much. "Can you get out without hurting yourself?"

"It's a bit of a drop, but I think I can," she said turning back toward JP. "You're bleeding." Sabre's mouth dropped open and she gasped. "Oh, no!"

"I'm okay," JP assured her.

Sabre gulped, then took a deep breath. "You have a piece of glass stuck in the side of your head."

JP started to reach up. "No, don't! Leave it alone. Let's get you out of here first."

"Go ahead. I'll be right behind you."

Sabre looked down, trying to figure out how to get out without the door slamming against her. The truck was sitting about a foot higher than normal. Even when it sat flat on the ground, it was difficult for her to get in and out.

"What's the matter?" JP asked.

"I don't know if I can hold the door open and get out at the same time. I'm afraid it will slam shut and it might make the truck move with you in it."

"Can you see what the tire is sitting on?"

She leaned over as far as she could. "No, sorry."

"Close the door," JP said. "I'm going to move over

as close as I can and hold the door for you, but our combined weight might make the truck drop so hold on." He pulled himself up in the seat and slowly scooted toward her. JP leaned over to where he could get some leverage on the door. When the truck didn't move, he slowly pushed the door open far enough for Sabre to get through.

Sabre turned, gave him a quick kiss, and jumped. The truck shifted a little but didn't drop. "The tire is on a rock," she said. "Be careful."

"Stand back," JP said. Sabre took a couple of steps backward as JP opened the door and jumped, letting the door slam shut as he did. He lost his footing and rolled just as the truck slid off the rock. It bounced a little before it came to a standstill.

A couple in a Honda Accord stopped to help. They jumped out and ran toward them. The woman said, "I called 9-1-1. Is there anything else I can do?"

"Do you have any water?" Sabre asked. "Maybe a towel or something?"

The man in the Ford F-150 had exited his truck and walked toward JP and Sabre. He couldn't have been more than eighteen and his lips were trembling.

"Are you hurt?" JP asked.

"Not really, but my dad's going to be furious."

"I'm sorry," JP said. "My brakes went completely out. Are you sure you're okay?"

He stared at JP. "Better than you, dude." He pointed at JP's head. "You have glass coming out of your head. That's jacked up."

"You'd better call your parents," Sabre said, and took hold of JP's arm. "I think you should sit down. You're still bleeding."

"I feel okay."

"Because you're running on adrenaline."

The woman returned from the Honda carrying two

bottles of water and a white bar towel. The man with her brought a folding chair. He opened it up and sat it on the side of the road. "I think you should sit, sir," the man said to JP.

JP started to object, but Sabre said, "Please, JP."

He sat down and the woman gave him a water. "Drink it," Sabre said.

The woman handed Sabre one as well, along with the bar towel. "You too."

Sabre took a drink, then poured some water on the towel.

"Let me get some of that blood off so we can see how badly hurt you are." She very carefully dabbed at JP's face, turning the towel red. They all looked up when the sirens came into range. Within minutes, there were two police cars, an ambulance, and a fire truck surrounding them, and they were whisked off to the hospital once again.

The medical team examined Sabre and discovered she only had a few bruises and a sprained ankle, which she thought she got when she jumped from the truck onto a loose rock.

JP took a little longer. The doctor removed the glass from JP's head and cleaned him up. Fortunately, the glass didn't go very deep or hit any major arteries. Other than the head injury and some sore muscles, JP appeared to be unscathed.

Ron was waiting for them when they came out of the ER. "I thought you might need a ride home."

Chapter 52

Sabre insisted on going back to work after their trip to the hospital, so Ron drove them to JP's house. They cleaned up, and JP drove Sabre to juvenile court, where Bob was waiting for her. Sabre's cheek was bruised and she had a burn mark on her arm from the airbag. JP had a 4 x 4-inch bandage on the side of his head.

"Nice bandage," Bob said to JP. "How's your head?"

"I feel like they tried to hang me and the rope broke—dang lucky. The chunk of glass didn't penetrate much, but it bled a lot, especially when they pulled it out. They ran a bunch of tests, stitched me up, and sent me home."

"I'm glad it wasn't any worse," Bob said.

JP pecked Sabre on the cheek. "Call me when you're done here."

"I'd like to go see Mom," Sabre said. "You and Ron will probably be working late anyway." She turned to Bob. "Can you take me to my mom's?"

"Sure."

"Are you sure you don't need your car?" JP asked.

"No, I'll be fine."

"Call me when you get to your mother's. I'll have a better idea of how late I'll be, but I'll come pick you up when you're ready."

~~~

Bob and Sabre walked to Department Four, went inside and sat down in the back, and waited for their next hearing.

"Fowler has already taken steps to file an appeal

on Hekman's ruling on the demurrer," Bob said.

"Do you think he can win on appeal?" Sabre asked.

"He has an outside chance."

"I don't think any California court would rule in his favor."

"I think Fowler knows that, and he's fine with it. At this point, I don't think he wants to win in California. What he wants is a chance to get to the Supreme Court where he believes he can win."

"He's not going to win on this one. He has the wrong set of facts. Maybe if he was dealing with an adult he could get there, but not with a twelve-year-old."

"That's what I told him, but I won't be handling the appeal, so it's not my problem," Bob said. "Speaking of problems, Fowler has bigger ones than that. Did you hear he was arrested?"

"For what?"

"Child endangerment—for putting Mary Margaret at risk."

"That seems like a stretch. I can't imagine they'll get a conviction."

"That's what I thought." Bob shrugged. "But you never know."

Sabre picked up her cell phone and stood up. "I had a message from the social worker, but I didn't get the chance to call her back. I bet that's what it was about." She made a call as she walked out of the courtroom.

Sabre returned shortly and sat back down next to Bob.

"So what did you find out?" Bob asked.

"You're right about Seth Fowler, but there's more to the story. They also arrested Gibbs for lewd and lascivious acts with a minor under the age of fourteen."

"That's no surprise."

"No, but get this. Your client worked with Gibbs when they lived in Texas over ten years ago. They were both fired."

"Your point?"

"They worked at a group home for teenage girls and were fired because several girls reported inappropriate behavior.

~~~

After the accident, JP had had his truck towed to his house. When he returned from dropping Sabre off, he found Ron examining his truck.

"It's pretty messed up," Ron said.

"Yeah, I don't think it's fixable."

"What did you want me to look at?" Ron asked.

"Check the brake lines."

Ron got down on his knees behind the front tire on the driver's side. He turned on the flashlight on his phone and looked under the truck. "Damn, this line has been cut."

"Exactly."

"The back too?" Ron asked.

"Yup."

Ron walked around to the back and checked it anyway. "You're right. What do you make of it?"

"I think whoever did this was also the one who attacked Sabre."

"So, if they're after Sabre, they know she's staying here with you."

"Yup."

"What now?" Ron asked.

"I've called one of the detective who's working on the Silent Thunder issue. She'll be out here soon. In the meantime, we need to figure out who could be after her. Did you bring your computer?"

"I did."

"Bring it in. We'll start going over everything on Sabre's cases and pin this down."

Ron brought his Apple laptop inside and set it up on the dining room table, not far from JP's desk.

JP's phone rang, and he answered it. When he hung up, he said, "We can take Jim Jones off the list."

"What happened?"

"I made some calls earlier to see if they found Jones. The cops got the fingerprints off the sunglasses he left behind at Dandee's house, and when they ran them they didn't find a criminal record. But since we had narrowed it down to a likely worker at CPS in Linda Vista, they compared the prints to those employees. Turns out he's a data entry worker, and had access to hundreds of names, addresses, and whatever else he needed to prey on these women."

"If he hadn't left his sunglasses behind, he might never have been caught."

"Exactly. No one ever reported him and he couldn't understand why he was being charged with rape because he never forced any of them."

"He drugged them. That's the same thing," Ron said, raising his voice. "I take it he's in custody?"

"Yes, they arrested him on Thursday, so unless he has an accomplice, which is unlikely, he's not our magic connection. Besides, it appears he didn't even know we were onto him."

"Who does that leave us?"

"Assuming it's a recent case, which it may or may not be, we have Seth Fowler and Russell Drake, Sarah's father. And I haven't ruled out Todd Lynch."

"Me neither. I really don't like that guy."

"Here're my notes and the reports on Lynch." JP handed some paperwork to Ron. "Read through these and see if I might have missed something. Then do whatever you can to find any social media sites that I haven't uncovered. Read his posts on the ones I have, or any new ones you find. You may have to go back a few years. Google his name and see if that leads you to anything connected to magic. I'll do the same with Seth Fowler."

They both worked diligently until the doorbell rang, and Louie barked.

Detective Addie Lewis was at the door.

"Come in," JP said and introduced her to Ron.

Addie smiled at Ron, then turned to JP. "Tell me what happened."

JP explained how he started down the hill, and when he tried to apply the brakes, they didn't work. He told her the lines looked like they'd been cut.

"Would you like to see them?" Ron volunteered.

"Please."

Ron and Addie walked out. JP stayed behind and continued with his research.

Ten minutes later they returned. "You're right, those lines were definitely cut," Addie said. "When did you last drive your vehicle prior to the accident?"

"Sunday night we went out and got some food and brought it back here."

"What time was that?"

"We were back here by eight or so."

"And you didn't drive it again until the accident?"

"No, the line had to have been cut sometime between eight last night and nine this morning."

"And you never heard anything?"

"I think it happened around midnight."

"Why's that?"

"Because Louie started barking. I got up and looked around, but I didn't see anything. The neighbor's dog was barking too, so I figured Louie just joined him."

"Did you go outside?"

"Not very far. Louie does this a lot, so it wasn't unusual."

She asked him a few more questions, taking notes as she did.

"Do you have anything new on Sabre's case?" JP asked.

"We've about ruled out Russell Drake, the father on the Sarah Parker case. He's even less likely if these two events are connected."

"You don't think they are?" Ron asked.

"I think they probably are, but we can't be certain yet."

"Why is Drake no longer a suspect?" JP asked.

"He has an alibi for Friday night, although it is somewhat tenuous. He was with some woman who vouched for him, which may or may not be true. Yesterday, we verified he was in Fresno Sunday night with his mother. He's still there. It's possible he drove back to San Diego sometime in the night, then went back again, but it's not likely."

"Have you got anything on Todd Lynch?" Ron asked.

JP noticed Addie smiled every time she looked at Ron. He glanced at her left hand—no rings.

"We spoke to him on Saturday. He was extremely polite, almost sugary sweet, not at all like others have described him. I wasn't impressed with his constant comments about what a dangerous job we have, and how brave we are. It all seemed like an act to me. He had no alibi for Friday night. He said he was home alone watching television. We'll see if he has an alibi for Sunday night."

Addie turned to go, then looked back at JP and then Ron. Her eyes lingered a second longer on Ron.

"Let me know if you find anything else."

"I will," Ron and JP said in unison.

JP tipped his head and stared at Ron.

"What?" Ron asked.

"She was flirting with you."

"You think?"

JP nodded.

Ron smiled. "She *is* cute."

Chapter 53

Ron and JP continued to search the internet for any connection between Sabre's clients and magic, or more specifically the Great Silent Thunder. They found nothing.

"I still think Lynch is involved," Ron said. "It's too bad his boys are gone or Sabre could ask them if Todd was into magic."

"Yeah, she can't do that now," JP said. "But I have an idea." He picked up his phone and called Marilyn LaFiura, the new foster mother. He put it on speaker so Ron could hear.

"Hello, is this Marilyn?" JP asked.

"Yes, who's calling?"

"I'm JP Torn. We met a little over a week ago. I told you I was the investigator for Heather Lynch in their divorce."

"Yes, I remember you."

"I know you are aware of the juvenile court case now because you have the children, correct?"

"Yes, they're here and doing very well."

"Good. I thought you would make a good foster parent for those boys."

"Thank you. They've been here a week now, and of course my son Andrew is thrilled, and so is Drew. The other boys seem happy to be here as well. My husband has supervised one visit for the father. Todd wasn't happy about that, but he dealt with it. They let me supervise the visit with the mother. That went well."

"Did—"JP started to ask a question.

"They both came to the house for their visits. We thought it would be easier on the boys that way. Besides, they both know us and where we live anyway, so there was no point in trying to go elsewhere for the visit."

"But—" JP tried again.

"Todd lives a little too close and he has tried to just stop in, but Andrew, my husband--not my son, put the kibosh on that."

Ron snickered as JP tried to get a word in. Finally, JP interrupted her. "I appreciate the information, but I have a question about something else. I was hoping you could help out."

"Sure, what's that? If it's—"

JP jumped in. "Do you know if Todd ever had any connections to a magician? Or did he ever do magic with the boys, maybe?"

"I don't think he knew any magic, but a couple of years ago, he got some free tickets for a show at the Magic Castle. He took Drew, Andrew, and Nolan. The boys loved it. They had the best time. Heather stayed home with Evan. He was too young to appreciate it, and I don't think she was that interested in going."

"Do you know if there was a magician there called Silent Thunder?"

"That doesn't ring a bell, but they have tons of magicians at the Magic Castle. They do acts in every room, even the bar. They also have a stage where they have the main show. Different magicians perform there all the time. You know you can only go there by special invitation."

"Do you know where Todd got the tickets?"

"Well, you have to be a magician and belong to their club to get tickets, so he must have gotten them from someone who was a member. He said he got them through his work. That's all I know. I had no reason to question where he got them. Why do you ask?"

"It's just something we're following up on," JP said. "Do you happen to know what date it was?"

"Not off hand, but I can check. I think I have the ticket in one of my scrapbooks. I love to do scrapbooking and I've made up albums for both of my children. They love looking back at the old photos and stuff. It's like they get to experience it all over again. When they're older, I'll give them their albums. I'm not sure when to do that yet, but probably not until they're married and more settled down. Right after high school is too soon. They won't fully appreciate them yet. Even college might be too soon. I think they'll make special wedding gifts. Don't you?"

"That would be good timing," JP said. "Do you mind checking the date on the ticket?"

"No, not at all. Give me a minute."

Ron was laughing so hard that JP clicked the speaker off on the phone so Marilyn couldn't hear him. JP frowned at Ron, but he had a hard time not laughing himself.

A few moments later, Marilyn came back on the phone and gave him the date. JP thanked her and hung up before she could say anything more.

"She's a nice woman, but she could talk the legs off a chair," JP said, shaking his head. "We need to see if Silent Thunder was at the Magic Castle that night."

Ron was already tapping away at the keyboard. It didn't take him long to see who was starring that night.

"I found it," Ron said, then sighed. "He wasn't performing on the main stage. But that doesn't mean he wasn't there."

JP started looking for Silent Thunder's appearances. He looked up from his computer. "No, but this does. According to this, he was performing in Europe all that week."

"But there are more than one of them. What if he was in both places?"

"You have a point there. We might make a

detective out of you yet, Ron. We need to shift our focus a little. Instead of concentrating on Sabre's clients, perhaps we need to find out everything we can about Silent Thunder."

"Great idea," Ron said. "And if we find anything, it'll give me an excuse to call Detective Addie."

"You dog."

The room was silent except for the clicking of keyboards while both men tried to find out everything they could about the Great Silent Thunder.

"There are thirty-five Google pages on this man, but it's mostly different events he has performed at," Ron said. "Wow. I've never seen this before."

"What is it?"

"When you click on the last Google page, it says: *In order to show you the most relevant results, we have omitted some entries very similar to the 350 entries already displayed. If you like, you can repeat the search with the omitted results included.*

"Did you click on it?"

"Yes," Ron said, and he continued to click through the pages. "Now I have seventy-four pages."

"You start at the beginning. I'll start at the end. We need to check each one to see if we find anything relevant."

About forty-five minutes later, Ron said, "I've got nothing. I can't even find this guy's real name. There's no Wikipedia on him and no social media."

"And the earliest show listed on here is about twenty years ago, which probably has more to do with the internet than when he began."

"Wait. I might have something," Ron said. "There's a guy who blogs about mysterious people. He claims he's done a lot of research and this blog post is called A Magician Who Calls Himself Silent Thunder." He read from the blog:

The Great Silent Thunder has done a magnificent job of hiding his identity from the world. He is called Silent Thunder because he doesn't speak during his performances, and you never see his face either because it is covered with a mask. Many have speculated as to why that is. Some have suggested he is mute. Others have theorized he did it because he wanted to travel from country to country and he didn't speak but one language. If he didn't talk at all, it didn't matter what country he was in. Some say it's because he is a woman and that she thought it would be more difficult to gain fame as a woman.

I have reason to believe that most of those theories are correct, except I don't think he is mute. Although, I can't prove it, I think there is more than one Silent Thunder. It would not only explain some of his tricks, but it also explains why he hasn't aged in the last sixty-plus years.

"That's not news. We discovered that in one show."

"Wait, there's more. Let's see what else it says."

I'm disappointed I can't provide you with the name of the first or even subsequent Silent Thunders, but I haven't given up yet. I've become a Silent Thunder groupie, and with each show, I get a little closer to the truth.

Silent Thunder's career started over sixty years ago. The first show I've been able to verify took place on July 7, 1956 at a 200-seat cabaret theatre in Paris, France called Lavoir Moderne Parisien. I have reason to believe his career began in another country, most likely Sweden.

Ron and JP exchanged glances.

"Do you think?" Ron asked.

"It's possible."

Chapter 54

Sabre and her mother sat at a small table in a local coffee shop called Wholly Crepe drinking coffee and sharing a "Monkey Turtle" crepe that consisted of pecans, marshmallows, banana, caramel sauce, chocolate sauce, and whipped cream.

"You're living a little on the wild side," Sabre said, "eating dessert in the afternoon. Aren't you afraid it will ruin our dinner?"

"That's why we're sharing it, dear," Beverly said. "I wanted you to see this place. I know how much you like crepes, and they make the best."

"I like this side of you, Mom."

"I'm trying to relax more, not be so anal about everything. I know I need to let loose."

Sabre studied her mother. "Not too loose. Okay, Mom?" Sabre said.

"Not much chance of that."

"You seem happy. Tell me about Harley."

"He's a good guy." Her eyes smiled when she spoke about him. "I know he has some unusual things in his past, but it could happen to any of us."

"I'm sure he's fine, Mom. Just give JP a little more time to investigate. He's kind of busy right now trying to find out what happened at the magic show."

"I want you to meet him," Beverly said. "I've decided to have a barbeque on Saturday. I want you and Ron there, and JP, of course. We've invited Harley's children. We expect two of them will be there."

"So it's already planned?"

"Yes, it is."

"Isn't it a little early for this, Mom? You two have only had, what? One formal date?"

"We want it all out in the open. It feels like we're

sneaking around trying to see one another."

"But, Mom, the whole family, really?"

"His children are just as concerned about *me* as you two are about *him*."

"You don't have a trail of dead husbands behind you."

Beverly cleared her throat and looked sternly at Sabre. "You don't have to come if you choose not to."

Sabre didn't want to argue with her mother like she had done so many times growing up. She had been making an extra effort to spend more time with her and to see things from her mother's point of view, but it wasn't easy. She could be in danger. It was different with her father; they had always seemed to be on the same page. How she wished he were here right now to help make her mother see that dating this guy was risky. *That's silly,* she thought. *If Dad were here, she wouldn't be dating anyone.*

Just then a handsome blond man, who appeared to be in his late fifties or early sixties, walked in the door. He was solidly built and stood around 5 feet 10 inches tall, but he had a presence about him that made him appear taller. Beverly's eyes lit up when she saw him.

"I guess you don't have to wait until Saturday to meet him," Beverly said.

"Mother, did you set this up?"

"No," she said indignantly, "I had no idea he would be here."

Sabre believed her because her mother wasn't much of a liar.

Harley stood by the door for a couple of seconds as if he were waiting for someone, then opened the door and an attractive woman about five-foot-six with a blonde bob, blue eyes, and a trim body walked in. He put his arm around her shoulder and guided her to a table in the corner not far from the exit.

Beverly's shoulders drooped, and her smile faded.

"Maybe she's a colleague or a client," Sabre said.

"You're right."

They both had a good angle so they could see the couple, but not hear their conversation. Sabre saw Harley take the woman's hand and squeeze it. She hoped her mother hadn't seen it, but she did.

"He's awfully friendly with his young clients or co-workers."

"Mom, you've only had one real date. You're not exclusive, are you?"

"I guess I thought we were." Her voice broke. "I've been such an old fool. I think we better go."

Sabre laid some cash on the table and they stood to leave.

"Just don't look that way when we leave," Sabre said.

"No, I'm going to look right at him, hold my head high, and act like I don't care."

"You're not good at that sort of thing, Mom. You even had a hard time pretending Santa Claus was real when we were kids. Deceit doesn't work well for you."

"I can do it."

Beverly took a deep breath and started forward looking directly at his table, but when she got closer she turned her head toward the exit.

"Beverly," Harley called to her.

She turned toward him, and he stood up.

"Hello, Bev, it's so nice to see you. Come meet my daughter."

Beverly sighed, smiled, and stepped toward his table. Sabre followed.

"Your daughter?"

She must have sounded stunned because he said, "You didn't think I was cheating on you, did you? That wouldn't make me much of a man now, would it?"

Beverly waved a dismissive hand, but didn't speak. Sabre reached out her hand and said, "I'm Sabre, Beverly's daughter."

"I've heard so much about you," Harley said.

"Likewise."

They continued the introductions and Harley asked them to sit, but Carly Banks, Harley's daughter, got up. "I don't mean to be rude, but I have to go. I have a classroom full of twelve-year-olds who will destroy the school if I don't get back soon. Nice to meet you both." She kissed her father on the cheek. "Thanks, Dad."

"See you later, honey girl."

Sabre glanced at her mother, then at Harley, her eyes wide and her posture stiff. Her father always called her 'honey girl'. She knew it was silly, but for a few seconds Sabre felt resentful that this man used her father's term of endearment. She sat there thinking about and missing her father. She was startled when her phone rang. It was JP.

"Excuse me," Sabre said. She answered her phone and went outside.

"Are you with your mother?" JP asked.

"Yes, we're at a coffee shop called the Wholly Crepe. You'll never guess who else is here."

"Who?"

"Harley Lindgren."

"Stay at the coffee shop until Ron gets there. Can you do that?"

"Yes, but why? What's wrong?"

"We have reason to believe Harley might be connected to the magician."

Chapter 55

JP sat in Detective DuBois' office waiting for him to return from a meeting. He called Sabre while he waited.

"Are you at your mom's?" JP asked.

"Yes, and Ron is with us. All is good."

"I don't know how long I'll be, but I think we're getting closer to an answer."

"I've been looking through the reports you gave me, and I noticed you wrote down a license plate number for Helga Norstrom."

"Yes, but I didn't do anything with it."

"You might want to," Sabre said. "Check to see if it's registered to Helga and if it's a custom plate."

"Where are you going with this?"

"The plate number is GST 023. Do you suppose the GST stands for Great Silent Thunder?"

"You just might have something there, kid."

DuBois walked into his office. JP said his goodbyes and hung up.

JP explained to DuBois what had happened to Sabre and about his brake lines being cut.

"Holy moly," DuBois said. "Why didn't you come to me sooner?"

"Because I had no reason to think there was a connection. Even now, what I have is a long shot. All I know is that this magician *might* be Swedish, and I'm not even certain of that."

"What would Lindgren have to gain by killing Sabre?"

"Maybe he knows we're investigating him and he's afraid we'll find out what happened to Vanna."

"But why wouldn't he just stop seeing . . . what's Sabre's mom's name?"

"Beverly."

"If he stopped seeing Beverly, you wouldn't have a reason to keep investigating."

"I thought about that, but maybe we're closer than even we know and he's scared. I don't know. Nothing seems to fit together. It's like trying to put socks on a rooster."

DuBois smiled. "That's the McCloud I know and love. What can I do?"

"For starters, could you check out this license plate?" He gave him the number. "It should be registered to Helga, but who knows?"

"Sure." DuBois called someone and asked them to run it for him. "You don't suppose Lindgren and Helga are working together, do you?"

"It's possible," JP said. "I'd like to have another look at that file and see if there's something that stands out for me, now that I'm a little more informed."

"By all means." DuBois opened a file drawer and pulled out the file marked Vanna Norstrom and handed it to JP.

"Do you know what you're looking for?"

"Magic," JP said.

JP read through every word in the file that had anything to do with Harley Lindgren, but found no "magic." About halfway through, a document caught JP's eye. It piqued his curiosity because of the language. "What's this?"

"That's the Norstrom family trust. It's written in Swedish, but the translated document should be in there."

JP shuffled through the trust and found the English translation. "You said Helga had nothing to gain by getting rid of Vanna, correct?"

"That's right. Helga was set for life. Vanna, because of her mental instability, had no control over her money. She got enough to live on, and when she died the money went to a charity."

"So, if Vanna had children, they wouldn't inherit?"

"No, but apparently she couldn't have children of her own, and they didn't want to encourage her to adopt because of her mental illness. And since Helga was gay, they didn't expect any grandchildren."

JP jerked his head up. "Helga's gay?"

"Yes, according to everyone we talked to, including Helga."

Then JP remembered the neighbor, Anastasia, started to tell him something about all the men who Vanna had coming around, and her husband Ervin stopped her. Maybe that's what she was trying to tell him.

"I'm a little confused," JP said, and continued to read the translated trust document.

After a few minutes, JP said, "Can I use your computer a second?"

"Sure." DuBois turned the screen toward JP and handed him the keyboard.

JP googled *Harleysk Magisk Cirkel*. "Bingo."

"What?"

"The charity the Norstroms left their money to is the Swedish Magic Circle, a national organization for magic in Sweden."

"But what does that really tell us?"

"I'm not sure. You said Vanna's father, Arne Norstrom, was in show business. Do you know what kind?"

"Not really. It was never an issue."

"Could he have been a magician?"

"I suppose."

JP continued to search, but found nothing about Mr. Norstrom. His wife, Ulrika Terese Norstrom, was quite a famous actress. After reading numerous newspaper and magazine articles, the few that were in English, JP found one with a one-liner about her husband, *the struggling magician.*

"So their father was a magician, which would explain why the money was left to Swedish Magic Circle."

"But he didn't make the money, his wife did. Why wasn't it left to some actors' guild or something?"

"Maybe because she felt bad that her husband never made it big."

JP went back to the Norstrom file and read more documents. "Well, spit in the fire and call the dogs."

"Huh? What did you find?"

"Vanna had problems sleeping, and among other things, was on a medication called Versed, which is the trade name for Midazolam, the same drug they found in Sabre's blood after the magic show."

Just then a young man in his mid-twenties came into DuBois' office. "I ran that plate for you, sir."

"And?"

"It's registered to one Helga Norstrom in Tustin, California, and it's a custom plate, sir."

"I think we need to pay Helga a visit."

Chapter 56

Detective DuBois picked up his office phone and called Helga on the home phone number that was in the file.

When she answered, he said, "This is Detective Vincent DuBois with the San Diego Sheriff's Department. Do you remember me?"

"Yes, sir, of course. It's been a long time."

"We have some new information that might lead us to Vanna. Do you mind if I come by and ask you a few more questions?"

"Of course not. When would you like to come?"

"About an hour, maybe a little more."

"About an hour and a half would be good."

~~~

DuBois and JP arrived in Newport Beach around six-thirty, about twenty minutes ahead of schedule. They pulled up in front of Helga's house. Only a few lights were on, making it difficult to know if anyone was at home.

"We're a little early. Do you think we should wait?"

"Nope," JP said as he exited the car. "I bet she's already gone."

DuBois followed JP to the door and knocked, but no one answered. He tried again. Still nothing. He called out to Helga, identifying himself, but no one responded.

"I think she might be in danger," JP said facetiously.

"Don't go all 'McCloud' on me now. We're not breaking in."

"Have it your way," JP said and started to cross

the street.

"Where are you going?" DuBois asked.

"Anastasia will know if she's home. She doesn't miss much that goes on in this house."

Anastasia answered the door and said, "Well, what a pleasant surprise." She called out, "Ervin, it's that nice cowboy, the one you call McCloud."

"That's too funny," DuBois said, but he was laughing so hard he could barely get it out.

"Come on in," Anastasia said. "Who's your friend?"

"This is Detective DuBois." He was so tempted to say Detective Dumb Bois, but he didn't.

"We don't have a lot of time," JP said. "We just need to know if you've seen Helga tonight?"

"She just left."

"Thank you," JP said, and they turned to leave.

"I think she was going on a trip."

"Why do you say that?"

"Because she left in a cab and the driver loaded her suitcases in the back. It was one of those little minivans or a small SUV or something; I don't know the difference. Earlier her bedroom shade was open and I saw her packing. She seemed to be in a big hurry."

"How long ago was that?" DuBois asked.

"About an hour."

"Do you know what cab company it was?"

"It was the Yellow Cab Company of Greater OC. I know because I recognized the phone number on the side of the car. We use them a lot. And—"

"Let's go," DuBois said.

"And what?" JP asked Anastasia.

"The cab number was 9-1-3."

"You're an angel," JP said.

They darted across the street and hopped in the car.

"She must have spooked when I called," DuBois

said.

"Looks that way, and I think I know why," JP said. "I'm guessing she's headed to the airport, but we don't know which one. It could be Santa Ana, LAX, Ontario, or Pasadena, depending on when she could get a flight to wherever she's going. *If* she's even going to an airport."

"I'm betting on John Wayne Airport," DuBois said and drove in that direction. Then he called his office and asked them to find out where cab #913 was dispatched to. "Let me know as soon as you know something. I'm in pursuit."

They still had another half-hour or so of rush-hour traffic. It was completely stopped in some places on SR-55. Even with DuBois' siren, it was slow going. They were almost to SR 73 when the call came from DuBois' office telling them the destination for cab #913 was San Diego Airport.

"I didn't see that coming," JP said.

"It must have been the earliest flight she could get."

"Or maybe she figured no one would look for her there. After all, you were on your way to Orange County."

DuBois took SR 73 south. It was a toll road in places and a more direct route that dumped into I-5. JP suspected the cab probably took that route as well, and if not, he and DuBois would be at the airport waiting for them when they got there. DuBois didn't need the siren again until they got on Interstate 5. It was congested, but not nearly as bad as if they had gone north toward LAX.

"Who are the detectives on the incident that happened at the Sports Arena?" DuBois asked.

"Eugene Fontenot and Addie Lewis. Do you know them?"

"I know Fontenot. He's a good guy. Knows his stuff. Does his job. Are they investigating your cut brake line too?"

"Yes. Lewis came out and checked out the truck. They believe there's a connection."

"You should call them. If your suspicions are correct, they should be in on this. Besides, they can do some legwork before we get there. Maybe narrow down the airline."

"My guess would be Scandinavia Airlines."

"Does it fly out of San Diego?"

"I don't know, but I bet she's headed to Sweden."

~~~

DuBois and JP were passing through Del Mar, about twenty-five minutes from the San Diego Airport when Detective Fontenot called. DuBois put him on speaker.

"The cab company has agreed to let us know when they arrive, or as soon as the driver dispatches the information. They are not here yet. We do know that they're headed for British Airways, Terminal 2."

"Thanks, Eugene."

The traffic had dispersed and DuBois could maintain seventy-five without the siren so he shut it off. They were passing the Balboa Avenue off-ramp when JP pointed ahead and said, "There they are."

"We could go on ahead and be there waiting for them when they get there."

"But if she spooks again, she could change her mind and go to Tijuana or something. Then we'd never catch her."

DuBois dropped back and stayed behind them until they reached Harbor Drive near the airport. The traffic made it difficult to keep close to the cab. JP texted Detective Addie and read the messages to

DuBois as they came in.

JP: *Just took Terminal 2 exit off Harbor. Taxi is in front.*

Addie: *We're outside British Airways Terminal. No visual yet.*

JP: *I can still see them.*

Addie: *I alerted TSA.*

Addie: *I have a visual now.*

"Tell her to wait for us," DuBois said. "It'll take a few minutes for our friend to pay the driver and get her suitcases."

JP: *Wait for us.*

DuBois parked at the curb, about three cars behind the cab. No one had exited the cab yet. They watched until the driver got out and pulled the woman's suitcases out of the back. Then he opened the door for her. As soon as he closed the door, DuBois and JP got out of the car and approached. The driver was rolling her suitcases and they were walking toward the skycap.

DuBois and JP were about ten feet behind them when JP yelled, "Vanna."

She turned, wide-eyed, looked at JP and DuBois, and then bolted.

"Dammit, McCloud!" DuBois shouted as he took off after her. He'd only gone a few steps when Addie came from her other side and tackled her to the ground. "I'm too old for this," DuBois said when JP reached them.

Addie got up, pulling the perpetrator to her feet, and handcuffed her. She looked at JP. "How did you know I was Vanna?"

"You just told me."

DuBois and JP stepped back as Addie Mirandized Vanna and placed her under arrest.

"How *did* you know she was Vanna, McCloud?"

"Vanna could change her appearance, but she

wasn't likely to change her sexual preference. After that, I just followed the money. Helga had nothing to gain by getting rid of Vanna, but Vanna had everything to gain—her freedom from Helga for starters. She would get control of the trust fund and could live her life in plain sight."

Chapter 57

Harley lived on the side of a hill with a view that extended for miles. His house was large, but not pretentious. The back yard was about a half-acre with half a dozen fruit trees. It had a deck that ran the length of the house, and a walkway that led to a waterfall surrounded by numerous plumeria plants.

The back yard buzzed as everyone became acquainted. Harley's oldest daughter, who Sabre had already met, couldn't attend, but Harley's son Eddie was there with his wife and two little girls. The oldest, Mandy, was four. When they were introduced to JP and Sabre, Mandy said, "I have some cowboy boots too. They're pink."

"I bet they're real pretty," JP said.

"Are you a real cowboy?"

"What's a real cowboy?"

"Real cowboys ride horses."

"Then I guess I'm a real cowboy."

Mandy took JP by the hand. "Come see," she said and started to pull him toward the pond.

"You don't have to go," her father said.

"No, it's fine. I love children."

Sabre and Eddie were discussing the legal profession when a woman around thirty with almond-shaped eyes surrounded by long, dark lashes and a thick head of brown hair that hung a few inches below her shoulders, walked in with a bounce in her step and a smile on her face.

"Let's get this party started," she bellowed.

"Who's that?" Sabre asked.

"That's Chloe, my baby sister. She always knows how to make an entrance."

"She's a beautiful woman."

"She is that. She's a sweet girl too. She has made a few mistakes along the way, but she's back on track and finally finishing school. And she's doing it without help from Dad, which is amazing since she was always the first to have her hand out. I'm very proud of her. We all are."

Sabre walked around the yard watching the interactions. She saw her mother checking on the guests as if she were right at home. Her mother's face seemed to glow with happiness. When Harley walked up and put his arm around her shoulder, she smiled up at him. She seemed so at ease.

"Mom looks happy, doesn't she?" Ron said, as he approached.

"She does. I hope it works out for her, now that we know he's not a killer."

"Well, we don't know that for sure," Ron joked. "We only know he didn't kill Vanna."

Sabre smacked him. "Don't be a goofball. Mom looks happier than I've seen her since..." She stopped and looked at Ron. Her forehead furrowed.

"Since Dad?" Ron said. "I know. It's nice to see."

"Have you met Chloe, yet?"

"No, but I'm about to. She's gorgeous."

As Ron walked away, Sabre watched JP entertain Mandy until Harley walked up and said, "I need to thank you for clearing my name."

"You're welcome, but my motives were very selfish. I was concerned for my mother. I'm sorry I thought you might be a murderer." Sabre smiled.

"I'm glad you cared enough to follow through."

"Actually, the credit goes to JP. He's the one who figured out Vanna was impersonating Helga."

"I'll go thank him, then. Besides, he may need saving from Mandy. She can be relentless. It's easier when her cousins are here so she has other kids to play with. Want to come?"

"Sure."

They reached the pond just in time to hear Mandy explaining about the koi. "That's Billy, and that's Sparkle, and that's Nemo." She stopped and turned. "Hi, Pinpaw."

Harley reached down and picked her up.

"Pinpaw?" Sabre asked.

"Yeah, I don't know why, but my oldest grandchild started calling me that, and it stuck. Now they all call me Pinpaw."

Harley put Mandy down and sent her off to her mother. Then he thanked JP.

"I got lucky," JP said. "The truth is if she hadn't tried to hurt Sabre at the magic show, she probably would've gotten away with everything."

"Beverly never said a word about what happened to Sabre, or I would've known who it was. When Vanna and I were first dating, she told me all about her father being the Great Silent Thunder. She told me how he trained two other people he trusted to fill in and help him during the shows. They were both much younger than him. As long as The Great Silent Thunder didn't talk and wore a mask, all he needed was someone close in size. Vanna loved magic and she learned right along with the others when he trained them, although at the time, she was too small. Later, she would occasionally fill in."

"That's why she had access to tickets and to the show."

"Were the other Silent Thunders in on it?" Harley asked.

"No, they didn't know she was even there until they discovered there was one too many of them."

"There's something I don't understand," Harley said. "Do you know why Vanna was trying to kill

Sabre?"

"She wasn't. She was trying to get rid of *me* because she didn't like that I was investigating her. She was afraid I'd catch on. That's why I was initially supposed to go on stage. She tried some other means to get me out of the picture."

"Like what?"

"For one, she called in a favor from a friend who tried to hire me to go to Alaska and work, which I'm certain would have kept me away for a long time."

"What did they charge her with?"

"Assault on Sabre, attempted murder on me, kidnapping of her sister, Helga, grand theft, and a bunch of related offenses."

"Did they find Helga?"

"Yes, Vanna had her stuffed away in a mental institution in Tucson, Arizona. Your cash lasted Vanna about a year. It would've lasted longer if she hadn't gotten the plastic surgery on her nose to make her look more like Helga."

"You're a good man, JP," Harley said and walked away.

"Yes, you are, JP Torn," Sabre said.

JP and Sabre sat together by the pond. "How's Mary Margaret doing?" JP asked.

"She's doing well. She'll be going home to live with her mother and brothers on Monday. Her mother filed for a divorce and is looking for housing. Once the church has a new pastor, the Fowlers will have to move. If they don't find a house before then, the Cunninghams have agreed to take them in for a while."

"That's good. I'm happy for her."

JP reached out and took Sabre's hand. "We need to spend more time together."

"I know."

"We should try to get away for a while, maybe take

a vacation."

Sabre smiled. "I'd like that."

They sat there watching the family intermingle. Harley started barbequing and Beverly helped him. Eddie put his daughter on the zip line Pinpaw had made for the kids, and her mother retrieved her at the end. Mandy giggled with delight as she flew through the air.

Ron and Chloe sat chatting on the deck.

JP and Sabre walked toward the grill. "Ever think about having kids of your own?" JP asked.

Sabre shuffled back a step, then regained her composure. "Maybe. Possibly," she said, "Someday." She paused. "You?"

"I could take to that like a hog to persimmons."

Dear Reader,

Would you like a FREE copy of a short story about JP when he was young? If so, please go to www.teresaburrell.com and sign up for my mailing list. You will automatically receive a code to retrieve the story.

What did you think of THE ADVOCATE'S ILLUSION? I would love to hear from you. Please email me and let me know at Teresa@teresaburrell.com.

Thank you,

Teresa

ABOUT THE AUTHOR

Teresa Burrell has dedicated her life to helping children and their families. Her first career was spent teaching elementary school in the San Bernardino City School District. As an attorney, Ms. Burrell has spent countless hours working pro bono in the family court system. For twelve years she practiced law in San Diego Superior Court, Juvenile Division. She continues to advocate children's issues and write novels, many of which are inspired by actual legal cases.

Teresa Burrell is available at www.teresaburrell.com.
Like her page on Facebook at
www.facebook.com/theadvocateseries

Made in the USA
San Bernardino, CA
15 February 2018